THE RAILWAY CHILDREN

E. Nesbit

COLLINS
CLASSICS

Harper Press
An imprint of HarperCollins*Publishers*
77–85 Fulham Palace Road
Hammersmith
London W6 8JB

This Harper Press paperback edition published 2011

E. Nesbit asserts the moral right to be identified as the author of this work.

A catalogue record for this book is available from the British Library

ISBN: 978-0-00-790216-3

Printed and bound in Great Britain by Clays Ltd, St Ives plc

MIX
Paper from
responsible sources
FSC® C007454

FSC™ is a non-profit international organisation established to promote
the responsible management of the world's forests. Products carrying the
FSC label are independently certified to assure consumers that they come
from forests that are managed to meet the social, economic and
ecological needs of present and future generations,
and other controlled sources.

Find out more about HarperCollins and the environment at
www.harpercollins.co.uk/green

Life & Times section © Gerard Cheshire
Classic Literature: Words and Phrases adapted from
Collins English Dictionary
Typesetting in Kalix by Palimpsest Book Production Limited,
Falkirk, Stirlingshire

2

History of Collins

In 1819, millworker William Collins from Glasgow, Scotland, set up a company for printing and publishing pamphlets, sermons, hymn books and prayer books. That company was Collins and was to mark the birth of HarperCollins Publishers as we know it today. The long tradition of Collins dictionary publishing can be traced back to the first dictionary William published in 1824, *Greek and English Lexicon*. Indeed, from 1840 onwards, he began to produce illustrated dictionaries and even obtained a licence to print and publish the Bible.

Soon after, William published the first Collins novel, *Ready Reckoner*, however it was the time of the Long Depression, where harvests were poor, prices were high, potato crops had failed and violence was erupting in Europe. As a result, many factories across the country were forced to close down and William chose to retire in 1846, partly due to the hardships he was facing.

Aged 30, William's son, William II took over the business. A keen humanitarian with a warm heart and a generous spirit, William II was truly 'Victorian' in his outlook. He introduced new, up-to-date steam presses and published affordable editions of Shakespeare's works and *Pilgrim's Progress*, making them available to the masses for the first time. A new demand for educational books meant that success came with the publication of travel books, scientific books, encyclopaedias and dictionaries. This demand to be educated led to the later publication of atlases and Collins also held the monopoly on scripture writing at the time.

In the 1860s Collins began to expand and diversify

and the idea of 'books for the millions' was developed. Affordable editions of classical literature were published and in 1903 Collins introduced 10 titles in their Collins Handy Illustrated Pocket Novels. These proved so popular that a few years later this had increased to an output of 50 volumes, selling nearly half a million in their year of publication. In the same year, The Everyman's Library was also instituted, with the idea of publishing an affordable library of the most important classical works, biographies, religious and philosophical treatments, plays, poems, travel and adventure. This series eclipsed all competition at the time and the introduction of paperback books in the 1950s helped to open that market and marked a high point in the industry.

HarperCollins is and has always been a champion of the classics and the current Collins Classics series follows in this tradition – publishing classical literature that is affordable and available to all. Beautifully packaged, highly collectible and intended to be reread and enjoyed at every opportunity.

Life & Times

Nesbit and her Beliefs

Edith Nesbit (1858–1924) was considered something of a Bohemian in Victorian London. As well as her own children, she raised those of her husband's mistress. This libertine approach to life was fashionable amongst writers, artists, actors, musicians and other creatives at the time – it was a cultural reaction to the formalized etiquette of high society and a reaction to conforming to rules of convention.

Nesbit and her husband Hubert Bland were involved with the foundation of the Fabian society, the forerunner to the Labour Party. The Fabianists were socialists who aimed to advance their brand of politics by democratic and gradualist means, as opposed to by revolution, which was the intention of more hard-line socialists at the time. The name Fabian alludes to Roman general Quintus Fabius Maximus Verrucosus who succeeded in wearing down Hannibal's Carthaginian army by a strategy of patience. His nickname was Fabius Cunctator (Fabius Delayer).

As a writer Nesbit was prolific. She wrote fiction and nonfiction, and she also wrote for adults and children, although it is as a children's novelist that she is best known today. Nesbit's first children's novel *The Story of the Treasure Seekers* (1899) is considered significant because it was the first of a new genre of relative realism, taking children's literature away from the world of bizarre fantasy, already so well explored by the likes of Lewis Carroll and Kenneth Grahame. She had already published a number of short stories in the same light, but this novel put Nesbit on the map as a new literary force to be reckoned with. Until Nesbit, child characters had only featured in English novels that were aimed at the adult market – Charles Dickens' books, for example. However, Mark Twain had beaten Nesbit to it in the United States by some 25 years with *The Adventures of Tom Sawyer* (1876).

The areas that Nesbit focused on in her books were human

relationships, sympathy, empathy, loyalty, love, trust, emotions and sensibilities. The plot in her stories tended to be incidental to her exploration of the human condition and the story itself really acted as a vehicle and series of devices for the issues she was preoccupied with. This is what lent her literature the weight it needed for the literati to place it in high regard. In effect, she was writing literature for the thinking child. *The Railway Children* (1906) has become her most famous work largely because it has been dramatized a number of times on television and in film.

Politics

The Railway Children tells the story of a young family who move from London to a house near a railway in the countryside. Their mother has taken them there following the mysterious arrest of their father. The three children, Roberta, Peter and Phyllis see the relocation as something of an adventure, but their mother struggles to make ends meet and to cope with the worry about her missing husband. She writes children's stories to earn a modest living, having previously been sufficiently well-off to live in a villa and employ staff.

It eventually becomes clear that the father was taken for questioning on a charge of treason. The authorities have reason to believe that he has been passing government secrets to the Russians. This relates to the Russo-Japanese War 1904–5, which would lead to the Russian Revolution of 1905. The father is returned to his family at the close of the book, as he has been falsely accused.

In the interim, the three children meet and befriend a number of interesting characters. In this respect their proximity to the railway serves as a vehicle for them to encounter people they otherwise would not. One person they meet happens to be a Russian exile who has travelled to England in search of his family. Naïve to any political agenda, the children react on a human level to the man's plight. The exiled character serves as an allegorical device for Nesbit to express her socialist credentials. In the same year that the book was published the Russian Constitution was established which ended the absolute rule of emperor and gave a certain degree of political say to the masses. By 1917 the monarchy had had its day and the second revolution led to the Communists taking control with dire consequences for the royal family and its sympathizers.

Nesbit's radical political views were very much at the core of her personality. She even lectured on socialism, which was a relatively new concept in the late Victorian era. Robert Owen (1771–1858) was a leading figure in developing the concept as part of his social reform ideas. His interests began to take shape in 1817 in reaction to the effects of the Industrial Revolution on the poor in Britain. Frenchman, Henri de Saint-Simon actually coined the term 'socialism', or rather *socialisme* in French. In the hands of the Germans, Friedrich Engels and Karl Marx, socialism metamorphosed into communism – the *Communist Manifesto* being published in 1848.

As is often the case as people reach middle age, Nesbit began to moderate her views and became less politically active. Her success as a writer also meant that she was much busier and had a public image to consider, so her politics took a back seat. Besides, it became difficult to champion socialist principles when she was becoming famous and wealthy.

Nesbit was a very sociable woman, taking great pleasure from hosting parties. She counted among her friends the writers George Bernard Shaw and H. G. Wells, as well as other leading lights in the Fabian Society. The year 1914 proved a turning point in Nesbit's life. Her first husband died and the First World War began, making it difficult for her to run her large house and grounds as her staff were so depleted in number. She chose to sell Well Hall and build a more modest residence in Kent with her second husband.

Nesbit's Legacy

In addition to the books she wrote, Nesbit held a huge influence over twentieth century and twenty-first century writers. Notable examples who have cited her influence are C. S. Lewis and J. K. Rowling. Both writers have acknowledged Nesbit's naturalistic style of writing while still introducing elements of imagination in many of her children's books. That is to say, the child characters relate to one another in a familiar and everyday way even though they are in stories that involve magic and fantasy. Her style consequently lends her stories beguiling believability even though she often describes supernatural realms. Fundamental to this ability was Nesbit's prowess at 'writing children'. She was able to think and speak as a child in her prose, a rare quality in an author, yet something that is vital for children's literature to succeed. It is also a skill that is much overlooked, even though good children's writing requires an understanding of the psychology of children, which is evidently lost by most people when they attain adulthood.

THE RAILWAY CHILDREN

To my dear Son
PAUL BLAND
behind whose knowledge of railways
my ignorance confidently shelters

CONTENTS

CHAPTER 1

The Beginning of Things

They were not railway children to begin with. I don't suppose they had ever thought about railways except as a means of getting to Maskelyne and Cook's, the Pantomime, Zoological Gardens, and Madame Tussaud's. They were just ordinary suburban children, and they lived with their Father and Mother in an ordinary redbrick-fronted villa, with coloured glass in the front door, a tiled passage that was called a hall, a bathroom with hot and cold water, electric bells, french windows, and a good deal of white paint, and 'every modern convenience', as the house-agents say.

There were three of them. Roberta was the eldest. Of course, Mothers never have favourites, but if their Mother *had* had a favourite, it might have been Roberta. Next came Peter, who wished to be an Engineer when he grew up; and the youngest was Phyllis, who meant extremely well.

Mother did not spend all her time in paying dull calls to dull ladies, and sitting dully at home waiting for dull ladies to pay calls to her. She was almost always there, ready to play with the children, and read to them, and help them to do their home-lessons. Besides this she used to write stories for them while they were at school, and read them aloud after tea, and she always made up funny pieces of poetry for their birthdays and for other great occasions, such as the christening of the new kittens, or the refurnishing of the doll's house, or the time when they were getting over the mumps.

These three lucky children always had everything they needed: pretty clothes, good fires, a lovely nursery with heaps of toys, and a Mother Goose wallpaper. They had a kind and merry nursemaid, and a dog who was called James, and who was their very own. They also had a Father who was just perfect – never cross, never unjust, and always ready for a game – at least, if at any time he was *not* ready, he always had an excellent reason for it, and explained the reason to the children so interestingly and funnily that they felt sure he couldn't help himself.

You will think that they ought to have been very happy. And so they were, but they did not know *how* happy till the pretty life in Edgecombe Villa was over and done with, and they had to live a very different life indeed.

The dreadful change came quite suddenly.

Peter had a birthday – his tenth. Among his other presents was a model engine more perfect than you could ever have dreamed of. The other presents were full of charm, but the Engine was fuller of charm than any of the others were.

Its charm lasted in its full perfection for exactly three days. Then, owing either to Peter's inexperience or Phyllis's good intentions, which had been rather pressing, or to some other cause, the Engine suddenly went off with a bang. James was so frightened that he went out and did not come back all day. All the Noah's Ark people who were in the tender were broken to bits, but nothing else was hurt except the poor little engine and the feelings of Peter. The others said he cried over it – but of course boys of ten do not cry, however terrible the tragedies may be which darken their lot. He said that his eyes were red because he had a cold. This turned out to be true, though Peter did not know it was when he said it, the next day he had to go to bed and stay there. Mother began to be afraid that he might be sickening for measles, when suddenly he sat up in bed and said:

'I hate gruel – I hate barley water – I hate bread and milk. I want to get up and have something *real* to eat.'

'What would you like?' Mother asked.

'A pigeon-pie,' said Peter, eagerly, 'a large pigeon-pie. A very large one.'

So Mother asked the Cook to make a large pigeon-pie. The pie was made. And when the pie was made, it was cooked. And when it was cooked, Peter ate some of it. After that his cold was better. Mother made a piece of poetry to amuse him while the pie was being made. It began by saying what an unfortunate but worthy boy Peter was, then it went on:

> *He had an engine that he loved*
> *With all his heart and soul,*
> *And if he had a wish on earth*
> *It was to keep it whole.*
> *One day – my friends, prepare your minds;*
> *I'm coming to the worst –*

Quite suddenly a screw went mad,
And then the boiler burst!
With gloomy face he picked it up
And took it to his Mother,
Though even he could not suppose
That she could make another;
For those who perished on the line
He did not seem to care,
His engine being more to him
Than all the people there.
And now you see the reason why
Our Peter has been ill:
He soothes his soul with pigeon-pie
His gnawing grief to kill.
He wraps himself in blankets warm
And sleeps in bed till late,
Determined thus to overcome
His miserable fate.
And if his eyes are rather red,
His cold must just excuse it:
Offer him pie; you may be sure
He never will refuse it.

Father had been away in the country for three or four days. All Peter's hopes for the curing of his afflicted Engine were now fixed on his Father, for Father was most wonderfully clever with his fingers. He could mend all sorts of things. He had often acted as veterinary surgeon to the wooden rocking-horse; once he had saved its life when all human aid was despaired of, and the poor creature was given up for lost, and even the carpenter said he didn't see his way to do anything. And it was Father who mended the doll's cradle when no one else could; and with a little glue and some bits of wood and a pen-knife made all the Noah's Ark beasts as strong on their pins as ever they were, if not stronger.

Peter, with heroic unselfishness, did not say anything about his Engine till after Father had had his dinner and his after-dinner cigar. The unselfishness was Mother's idea – but it was Peter who carried it out. And needed a good deal of patience, too.

At last Mother said to Father, 'Now, dear, if you're quite rested, and quite comfy, we want to tell you about the great railway accident, and ask your advice.'

'All right,' said Father, 'fire away!'

So then Peter told the sad tale, and fetched what was left of the Engine.

'Hum,' said Father, when he had looked the Engine over very carefully.

The children held their breaths.

'Is there *no* hope?' said Peter, in a low, unsteady voice.

'Hope? Rather! Tons of it,' said Father, cheerfully; 'but it'll want something besides hope – a bit of brazing, say, or some solder, and a new valve. I think we'd better keep it for a rainy day. In other words, I'll give up Saturday afternoon to it, and you shall all help me.'

'*Can* girls help to mend engines?' Peter asked doubtfully.

'Of course they can. Girls are just as clever as boys, and don't you forget it! How would you like to be an engine-driver, Phil?'

'My face would be always dirty, wouldn't it?' said Phyllis, in unemotional tones, 'and I expect I should break something.'

'I should just love it,' said Roberta – 'do you think I could when I'm grown up, Daddy? Or even a stoker?'

'You mean a fireman,' said Daddy, pulling and twisting at the engine. 'Well, if you still wish it, when you're grown up, we'll see about making you a fire-woman. I remember when I was a boy –'

Just then there was a knock at the front door.

'Who on earth!' said Father. 'An Englishman's house is his castle, of course, but I do wish they built semi-detached villas with moats and drawbridges.'

Ruth – she was the parlour-maid and had red hair – came in and said that two gentlemen wanted to see the master.

'I've shown them into the Library, Sir,' said she.

'I expect it's the subscription to the Vicar's testi-monial,' said Mother, 'or else it's the choir holiday fund. Get rid of them quickly, dear. It does break up an evening so, and it's nearly the children's bed-time.'

But Father did not seem to be able to get rid of the gentlemen at all quickly.

'I wish we *had* got a moat and drawbridge,' said Roberta; 'then, when we didn't want people, we could just pull up the drawbridge and no one else could get in. I expect Father will have forgotten about when he was a boy if they stay much longer.'

Mother tried to make the time pass by telling them a new fairy story about a Princess with green eyes, but it was difficult because they could hear the voices of Father and the gentlemen in the Library, and Father's voice sounded louder and different from the voice he generally used to people who came about testimonials and holiday funds.

Then the Library bell rang, and everyone heaved a breath of relief.

'They're going now,' said Phyllis; 'he's rung to have them shown out.'

But instead of showing anybody out, Ruth showed herself in, and she looked queer, the children thought.

'Please'm,' she said, 'the Master wants you to just step into the Library. He looks like the dead, mum; I think he's had bad news. You'd best prepare yourself for the worst, 'm – p'raps it's a death in the family or a bank busted or –'

'That'll do, Ruth,' said Mother gently; 'you can go.'

Then Mother went into the Library. There was more talking. Then the bell rang again, and Ruth fetched a cab. The children heard boots go out and down the steps. The cab drove away, and the front door shut. Then Mother came in. Her dear face was as white as her lace collar, and her eyes looked very big and shining. Her mouth looked like just a line of pale red – her lips were thin and not their proper shape at all.

'It's bed-time,' she said. 'Ruth will put you to bed.'

'But you promised we should sit up late tonight because Father's come home,' said Phyllis.

'Father's been called away – on business,' said Mother. 'Come, darlings, go at once.'

They kissed her and went. Roberta lingered to give Mother an extra hug and to whisper:

'It wasn't bad news, Mammy, was it? Is anyone dead – or –'

'Nobody's dead – no,' said Mother, and she almost seemed to push Roberta away. 'I can't tell you anything tonight, my pet. Go, dear, go *now*.'

So Roberta went.

Ruth brushed the girls' hair and helped them to undress. (Mother almost always did this herself.)

When she had turned down the gas and left them she found Peter, still dressed, waiting on the stairs.

'I say, Ruth, what's up?' he asked.

'Don't ask me no questions and I won't tell you no lies,' the red-headed Ruth replied. 'You'll know soon enough.'

Late that night Mother came up and kissed all three children as they lay asleep. But Roberta was the only one whom the kiss woke, and she lay mousey-still, and said nothing.

'If Mother doesn't want us to know she's been crying,' she said to herself as she heard through the dark the catching of her Mother's breath, 'we *won't* know it. That's all.'

When they came down to breakfast the next morning, Mother had already gone out.

'To London,' Ruth said, and left them to their breakfast.

'There's something awful the matter,' said Peter, breaking his egg. 'Ruth told me last night we should know soon enough.'

'Did you *ask* her?' said Roberta, with scorn.

'Yes, I did!' said Peter, angrily. 'If you could go to bed without caring whether Mother was worried or not, I couldn't. So there.'

'I don't think we ought to ask the servants things Mother doesn't tell us,' said Roberta.

'That's right, Miss Goody-Goody,' said Peter, 'preach away.'

'*I'm* not goody,' said Phyllis, 'but I think Bobbie's right this time.'

'Of course. She always is. In her own opinion,' said Peter.

'Oh, *don't*!' cried Roberta, putting down her egg-spoon; 'don't let's be horrid to each other. I'm sure some dire calamity is happening. Don't let's make it worse!'

'Who began, I should like to know?' said Peter.

Roberta made an effort, and answered:

'I did, I suppose, but –'

'Well, then,' said Peter, triumphantly. But before he went to school he thumped his sister between the shoulders and told her to cheer up.

The children came home to one o'clock dinner, but Mother was not there. And she was not there at tea-time.

It was nearly seven before she came in, looking so ill and tired that the children felt they could not ask her any questions. She sank into an armchair. Phyllis took the long pins out of her hat, while Roberta took off her gloves, and Peter unfastened her walking-shoes and fetched her soft velvety slippers for her.

When she had had a cup of tea, and Roberta had put eau-de-Cologne on her poor head that ached, Mother said:

'Now, my darlings, I want to tell you something. Those men last night did bring very bad news, and Father will be away for some time. I am very worried about it, and I want you all to help me, and not to make things harder for me.'

'As if we would!' said Roberta, holding Mother's hand against her face.

'You can help me very much,' said Mother, 'by being good and happy and not quarrelling when I'm away' – Roberta and Peter exchanged guilty glances – 'for I shall have to be away a good deal.'

'We won't quarrel. Indeed we won't,' said everybody. And meant it, too.

'Then,' Mother went on, 'I want you not to ask me any questions about this trouble; and not to ask anybody else any questions.'

Peter cringed and shuffled his boots on the carpet.

'You'll promise this, too, won't you?' said Mother.

'I did ask Ruth,' said Peter, suddenly. 'I'm very sorry, but I did.'

'And what did she say?'

'She said I should know soon enough.'

'It isn't necessary for you to know anything about it,' said Mother; 'it's about business, and you never do understand business, do you?'

'No,' said Roberta; 'is it something to do with Government?' For Father was in a Government Office.

'Yes,' said Mother. 'Now it's bed-time, my darlings. And don't *you* worry. It'll all come right in the end.'

'Then don't *you* worry either, Mother,' said Phyllis, 'and we'll all be as good as gold.'

Mother sighed and kissed them.

'We'll begin being good the first thing tomorrow morning,' said Peter, as they went upstairs.

'Why not *now*?' said Roberta.

'There's nothing to be good *about* now, silly,' said Peter.

'We might begin to try to *feel* good,' said Phyllis, 'and not call names.'

'Who's calling names?' said Peter. 'Bobbie knows right enough that when I say "silly", it's just the same as if I said Bobbie.'

'*Well*,' said Roberta.

'No, I don't mean what you mean. I mean it's just a – what is it Father calls it? – a germ of endearment! Good night.'

The girls folded up their clothes with more than usual neatness – which was the only way of being good that they could think of.

'I say,' said Phyllis, smoothing out her pinafore, 'you used to say it was so dull – nothing happening, like in books. Now something *has* happened.'

'I never wanted things to happen to make Mother unhappy,' said Roberta. 'Everything's perfectly horrid.'

Everything continued to be perfectly horrid for some weeks.

Mother was nearly always out. Meals were dull and dirty. The between-maid was sent away, and Aunt Emma came on a visit. Aunt Emma was much older than Mother. She was going abroad to be a governess. She was very busy getting her clothes ready, and they were very ugly, dingy clothes, and she had them always littering about, and the sewing-machine seemed to whirl – on and on all day and most of the night. Aunt Emma believed in keeping children in their proper places. And they more than returned the compliment. Their idea of Aunt Emma's proper place was anywhere where they were not. So they saw very little of her. They preferred the company of the servants, who were more amusing. Cook, if in a good temper, could sing comic songs, and the housemaid, if she happened not to be offended with you, could imitate a hen that has laid an egg, a bottle of champagne being opened, and could mew like two cats fighting. The servants never told the children what the bad news was that the gentlemen had brought to Father. But they kept hinting that they could tell a great deal if they chose – and this was not comfortable.

One day when Peter had made a booby trap over the bathroom door, and it had acted beautifully as

Ruth passed through, that red-haired parlour-maid caught him and boxed his ears.

'You'll come to a bad end,' she said furiously, 'you nasty little limb, you! If you don't mend your ways, you'll go where your precious Father's gone, so I tell you straight!'

Roberta repeated this to her Mother, and next day Ruth was sent away.

Then came the time when Mother came home and went to bed and stayed there two days and the Doctor came, and the children crept wretchedly about the house and wondered if the world was coming to an end.

Mother came down one morning to breakfast, very pale and with lines on her face that used not to be there. And she smiled, as well as she could, and said:

'Now, my pets, everything is settled. We're going to leave this house, and go and live in the country. Such a ducky dear little white house. I know you'll love it.'

A whirling week of packing followed – not just packing clothes, like when you go to the seaside, but packing chairs and tables, covering their tops with sacking and their legs with straw.

All sorts of things were packed that you don't pack when you go to the seaside. Crockery, blankets, candlesticks, carpets, bedsteads, saucepans, and even fenders and fire-irons.

The house was like a furniture warehouse. I think the children enjoyed it very much. Mother was very busy, but not too busy now to talk to them, and read to them, and even to make a bit of poetry for Phyllis to cheer her up when she fell down with a screwdriver and ran it into her hand.

'Aren't you going to pack this, Mother?' Roberta

asked, pointing to the beautiful cabinet inlaid with red turtleshell and brass.

'We can't take everything,' said Mother.

'But we seem to be taking all the ugly things,' said Roberta.

'We're taking the useful ones,' said Mother; 'we've got to play at being Poor for a bit, my chickabiddy.'

When all the ugly useful things had been packed up and taken away in a van by men in green-baize aprons, the two girls and Mother and Aunt Emma slept in the two spare rooms where the furniture was all pretty. All their beds had gone. A bed was made up for Peter on the drawing-room sofa.

'I say, this is larks,' he said, wriggling joyously, as Mother tucked him up. 'I do like moving! I wish we moved once a month.'

Mother laughed.

'I don't!' she said. 'Good night, Peterkin.'

As she turned away Roberta saw her face. She never forgot it.

'Oh, Mother,' she whispered all to herself as she got into bed, 'how brave you are! How I love you! Fancy being brave enough to laugh when you're feeling like *that*!'

Next day boxes were filled, and boxes and more boxes; and then late in the afternoon a cab came to take them to the station.

Aunt Emma saw them off. They felt that *they* were seeing *her* off, and they were glad of it.

'But, oh, those poor little foreign children that she's going to governess!' whispered Phyllis. 'I wouldn't be them for anything!'

At first they enjoyed looking out of the window,

but when it grew dusk they grew sleepier and sleepier, and no one knew how long they had been in the train when they were roused by Mother's shaking them gently and saying:

'Wake up, dears. We're there.'

They woke up, cold and melancholy, and stood shivering on the draughty platform while the baggage was taken out of the train. Then the engine, puffing and blowing, set to work again, and dragged the train away. The children watched the tail-lights of the guard's van disappear into the darkness.

This was the first train the children saw on that railway which was in time to become so very dear to them. They did not guess then how they would grow to love the railway, and how soon it would become the centre of their new life nor what wonders and changes it would bring to them. They only shivered and sneezed and hoped the walk to the new house would not be long. Peter's nose was colder than he ever remembered it to have been before. Roberta's hat was crooked, and the elastic seemed tighter than usual. Phyllis's shoe-laces had come undone.

'Come,' said Mother, 'we've got to walk. There aren't any cabs here.'

The walk was dark and muddy. The children stumbled a little on the rough road, and once Phyllis absently fell into a puddle, and was picked up damp and unhappy. There were no gas-lamps on the road, and the road was uphill. The cart went at a slow pace, and they followed the gritty crunch of its wheels. As their eyes got used to the darkness, they could see the mound of boxes swaying dimly in front of them.

A long gate had to be opened for the cart to pass

through, and after that the road seemed to go across fields – and now it went downhill. Presently a great dark lumpish thing showed over to the right.

'There's the house,' said Mother. 'I wonder why she's shut the shutters.'

'Who's *she?*' asked Roberta.

'The woman I engaged to clean the place, and put the furniture straight and get supper.'

There was a low wall, and trees inside.

'That's the garden,' said Mother.

'It looks more like a dripping-pan full of black cabbages,' said Peter.

The cart went on along by the garden wall, and round to the back of the house, and here it clattered into a cobble-stoned yard and stopped at the back door.

There was no light in any of the windows.

Everyone hammered at the door, but no one came.

The man who drove the cart said he expected Mrs Viney had gone home.

'You see your train was that late,' said he.

'But she's got the key,' said Mother. 'What are we to do?'

'Oh, she'll have left that under the doorstep,' said the cart man; 'folks do hereabouts.' He took the lantern off his cart and stooped.

'Ay, here it is, right enough,' he said.

He unlocked the door and went in and set his lantern on the table.

'Got e'er a candle?' said he.

'I don't know where anything is.' Mother spoke rather less cheerfully than usual.

He struck a match. There was a candle on the table, and he lighted it. By its thin little glimmer the children saw a large bare kitchen with a stone floor. There were no curtains, no hearth-rug. The kitchen table from home stood in the middle of the room. The chairs were in one corner, and the pots, pans, brooms, and crockery in another. There was no fire, and the black grate showed cold, dead ashes.

As the cart man turned to go out after he had brought in the boxes, there was a rustling, scampering sound that seemed to come from inside the walls of the house.

'Oh, what's that?' cried the girls.

'It's only the rats,' said the cart man. And he went away and shut the door, and the sudden draught of it blew out the candle.

'Oh, dear,' said Phyllis, 'I wish we hadn't come!' and she knocked a chair over.

'*Only* the rats!' said Peter, in the dark.

CHAPTER 2

Peter's Coal-Mine

'What fun!' said Mother, in the dark, feeling for the matches on the table. 'How frightened the poor mice were – I don't believe they were rats at all.'

She struck a match and relighted the candle and everyone looked at each other by its winky, blinky light.

'Well,' she said, 'you've often wanted something to happen and now it has. This is quite an adventure, isn't it? I told Mrs Viney to get us some bread and butter and meat and things, and to have supper ready. I suppose she's laid it in the dining-room. So let's go and see.'

The dining-room opened out of the kitchen. It looked much darker than the kitchen when they went in with the one candle. Because the kitchen was whitewashed, but the dining-room was dark wood from floor to ceiling, and across the ceiling there were heavy black beams. There was a muddle maze of dusty furniture – the breakfast-room furniture from the old home where they had lived all their lives. It seemed a very long time ago, and a very long way off.

There was a table certainly, and there were chairs, but there was no supper.

'Let's look in the other rooms,' said Mother; and they looked. And in each room was the same kind of blundering half-arrangement of furniture, and fire-irons and crockery, and all sorts of odd things on the floor, but there was nothing to eat; even in the pantry there were only a rusty cake-tin and a broken plate with whitening mixed in it.

'What a horrid old woman!' said Mother; 'she's just walked off with the money and not got us anything to eat at all.'

'Then shan't we have any supper at all?' asked Phyllis, dismayed, stepping back on to a soap-dish that cracked responsively.

'Oh, yes,' said Mother, 'only it'll mean unpacking one of those big cases that we put in the cellar. Phil, do mind where you're walking to, there's a dear. Peter, hold the light.'

The cellar door opened out of the kitchen. There were five wooden steps leading down. It wasn't a proper cellar at all, the children thought, because its ceiling went up as high as the kitchen's. A bacon-rack hung under its ceiling. There was wood in it, and coal. Also the big cases.

Peter held the candle, all on one side, while Mother tried to open the great packing-case. It was very securely nailed down.

'Where's the hammer?' asked Peter.

'That's just it,' said Mother. 'I'm afraid it's inside the box. But there's a coal-shovel – and there's the kitchen poker.'

And with these she tried to get the case open.

'Let me do it,' said Peter, thinking he could do it better himself. Everyone thinks this when he sees another person stirring a fire, or opening a box, or untying a knot in a bit of string.

'You'll hurt your hands, Mammy,' said Roberta; 'let me.'

'I wish Father was here,' said Phyllis; 'he'd get it open in two shakes. What are you kicking me for, Bobbie?'

'I wasn't,' said Roberta.

Just then the first of the long nails in the packing-case began to come out with a scrunch. Then a lath was raised and then another, till all four stood up with long nails in them shining fiercely like iron teeth in the candle-light.

'Hooray!' said Mother; 'here are some candles – the very first thing! You girls go and light them. You'll find some saucers and things. Just drop a little candle-grease in the saucer and stick the candle upright in it.'

'How many shall we light?'

'As many as ever you like,' said Mother, gaily. 'The great thing is to be cheerful. Nobody can be cheerful in the dark except owls and dormice.'

So the girls lighted candles. The head of the first match flew off and stuck to Phyllis's finger; but, as Roberta said, it was only a little burn, and she might have had to be a Roman martyr and be burned whole if she had happened to live in the days when those things were fashionable.

Then, when the dining-room was lighted by fourteen candles, Roberta fetched coal and wood and lighted a fire.

'It's very cold for May,' she said, feeling what a grown-up thing it was to say.

The fire-light and the candle-light made the dining-room look very different, for now you could see that the dark walls were of wood, carved here and there into little wreaths and loops.

The girls hastily 'tidied' the room, which meant putting the chairs against the wall, and piling all the odds and ends into a corner and partly hiding them with the big leather arm-chair that Father used to sit in after dinner.

'Bravo!' cried Mother, coming in with a tray full of things. 'This is something like! I'll just get a tablecloth and then –'

The tablecloth was in a box with a proper lock that was opened with a key and not with a shovel, and when the cloth was spread on the table, a real feast was laid out on it.

Everyone was very, very tired, but everyone cheered up at the sight of the funny and delightful supper. There were biscuits, the Marie and the plain kind, sardines, preserved ginger, cooking raisins, and candied peel and marmalade.

'What a good thing Aunt Emma packed up all the odds and ends out of the store cupboard,' said Mother. 'Now, Phil, *don't* put the marmalade spoon in among the sardines.'

'No, I won't, Mother,' said Phyllis, and put it down among the Marie biscuits.

'Let's drink Aunt Emma's health,' said Roberta, suddenly; 'what would we have done if she hadn't packed up these things? Here's to Aunt Emma!'

And the toast was drunk in ginger wine and water, out of willow-patterned tea-cups, because the glasses couldn't be found.

They all felt that they had been a little hard on Aunt Emma. She wasn't a nice cuddly person like Mother, but after all it was she who had thought of packing up the odds and ends of things to eat.

It was Aunt Emma, too, who had aired all the sheets ready; and the men who had moved the furniture had put the bedsteads together, so the beds were soon made.

'Good night, chickies,' said Mother. 'I'm sure there aren't any rats. But I'll leave my door open, and then if a mouse comes, you need only scream, and I'll come and tell it exactly what I think of it.'

Then she went to her own room. Roberta woke to hear the little travelling clock chime two. It sounded like a church clock ever so far away, she always thought. And she heard, too, Mother, still moving about in her room.

Next morning Roberta woke Phyllis by pulling her hair gently, but quite enough for her purpose.

'Wassermarrer?' asked Phyllis, still almost wholly asleep.

'Wake up! wake up!' said Roberta. 'We're in the new house – don't you remember? No servants or anything. Let's get up and begin to be useful. We'll just creep down mouse-quietly, and have everything beautiful before Mother gets up. I've woken Peter. He'll be dressed as soon as we are.'

So they dressed quietly and quickly. Of course, there was no water in their room, so when they got down they washed as much as they thought was necessary under the spout of the pump in the yard. One pumped and the other washed. It was splashy but interesting.

'It's much more fun than basin washing,' said Roberta. 'How sparkly the weeds are between the stones, and the moss on the roof – oh, and the flowers!'

The roof of the back kitchen sloped down quite low. It was made of thatch and it had moss on it, and house-leeks and stone-crop and wallflowers, and even a clump of purple flag-flowers, at the far corner.

'This is far, far and away prettier than Edgecombe Villa,' said Phyllis. 'I wonder what the garden's like.'

'We mustn't think of the garden yet,' said Roberta, with earnest energy. 'Let's go in and begin to work.'

They lighted the fire and put the kettle on, and they arranged the crockery for breakfast; they could not find all the right things, but a glass ashtray made an excellent salt-cellar, and a newish baking-tin seemed as if it would do to put bread on if they had any.

When there seemed to be nothing more that they could do, they went out again into the fresh bright morning.

'We'll go into the garden now,' said Peter. But somehow they couldn't find the garden. They went round the house and round the house. The yard occupied the back, and across it were stables and outbuildings. On the other three sides the house stood simply in a field, without a yard of garden to divide it from the short smooth turf. And yet they had certainly seen the garden wall the night before.

It was a hilly country. Down below they could see the line of the railway, and the black yawning mouth of a tunnel. The station was out of sight. There was a great bridge with tall arches running across one end of the valley.

'Never mind the garden,' said Peter; 'let's go down and look at the railway. There might be trains passing.'

'We can see them from here,' said Roberta, slowly; 'let's sit down a bit.'

So they all sat down on a great flat grey stone that had pushed itself up out of the grass; it was one of many that lay about on the hillside, and when Mother came out to look for them at eight o'clock, she found them deeply asleep in a contented, sun-warmed bunch.

They had made an excellent fire, and had set the kettle on it at about half past five. So that by eight the fire had been out for some time, the water had all boiled away, and the bottom was burned out of the kettle. Also they had not thought of washing the crockery before they set the table.

'But it doesn't matter – the cups and saucers, I mean,' said Mother. 'Because I've found another room – I'd quite forgotten there was one. And it's magic! And I've boiled the water for tea in a saucepan.'

The forgotten room opened out of the kitchen. In the agitation and half darkness the night before its door had been mistaken for a cupboard's. It was a little square room, and on its table, all nicely set out, was a joint of cold roast beef, with bread and butter, cheese, and a pie.

'Pie for breakfast!' cried Peter; 'how perfectly ripping!'

'It isn't pigeon-pie,' said Mother; 'it's only apple. Well, this is the supper we ought to have had last night. And there was a note from Mrs Viney. Her son-in-law has broken his arm, and she had to get home early. She's coming this morning at ten.'

That was a wonderful breakfast. It is unusual to begin the day with cold apple pie, but the children all said they would rather have it than meat.

'You see it's more like dinner than breakfast to us,' said Peter, passing his plate for more, 'because we were up so early.'

The day passed in helping Mother to unpack and arrange things. Six small legs quite ached with running about while their owners carried clothes and crockery and all sorts of things to their proper places. It was not till quite late in the afternoon that Mother said:

'There! That'll do for today. I'll lie down for an hour, so as to be as fresh as a lark by suppertime.'

Then they all looked at each other. Each of the three expressive countenances expressed the same thought. That thought was double, and consisted, like the bits of information in the *Child's Guide to Knowledge*, of a question and an answer.

Q. Where shall we go?

A. To the railway.

So to the railway they went, and as soon as they started for the railway they saw where the garden had hidden itself. It was right behind the stables, and it had a high wall all round.

'Oh, never mind about the garden now!' cried Peter. 'Mother told me this morning where it was. It'll keep till tomorrow. Let's get to the railway.'

The way to the railway was all downhill over smooth, short turf with here and there furze bushes and grey and yellow rocks sticking out like candied peel from the top of a cake.

The way ended in a steep run and a wooden fence – and there was the railway with the shining metals and the telegraph wires and posts and signals.

They all climbed on to the top of the fence, and then suddenly there was a rumbling sound that made them look along the line to the right, where the dark mouth of a tunnel opened itself in the face of a rocky cliff; next moment a train had rushed out of the tunnel with a shriek and a snort, and had slid noisily past them. They felt the rush of its passing, and the pebbles on the line jumped and rattled under it as it went by.

'Oh!' said Roberta, drawing a long breath; 'it was like a great dragon tearing by. Did you feel it fan us with its hot wings?'

'I suppose a dragon's lair might look very like that tunnel from the outside,' said Phyllis.

But Peter said:

'I never thought we should ever get so near to a train as this. It's the most ripping sport!'

'Better than toy-engines, isn't it?' said Roberta.

(I am tired of calling Roberta by her name. I don't see why I should. No one else did. Everyone else called her Bobbie, and I don't see why I shouldn't.)

'I don't know; it's different,' said Peter. 'It seems so odd to see *all* of a train. It's awfully tall, isn't it?'

'We've always seen them cut in half by platforms,' said Phyllis.

'I wonder if that train was going to London,' Bobbie said. 'London's where Father is.'

'Let's go down to the station and find out,' said Peter.

So they went.

They walked along the edge of the line, and heard the telegraph wires humming over their heads. When you are in the train, it seems such a little way between post and post, and one after another the posts seem to catch up the wires almost more quickly than you can count them. But when you have to walk, the posts seem few and far between.

But the children got to the station at last.

Never before had any one of them been at a station,

except for the purpose of catching trains – or perhaps waiting for them – and always with grown-ups in attendance, grown-ups who were not themselves interested in stations, except as places from which they wished to get away.

Never before had they passed close enough to a signal-box to be able to notice the wires, and to hear the mysterious 'ping, ping', followed by the strong, firm clicking of machinery.

The very sleepers on which the rails lay were a delightful path to travel by – just far enough apart to serve as the stepping-stones in a game of foaming torrents hastily organized by Bobbie.

Then to arrive at the station, not through the booking office, but in a freebooting sort of way by the sloping end of the platform. This in itself was joy.

Joy, too, it was to peep into the porters' room, where the lamps are, and the Railway almanac on the wall, and one porter half asleep behind a paper.

There were a great many crossing lines at the station; some of them just ran into a yard and stopped short, as though they were tired of business and meant to retire for good. Trucks stood on the rails here, and on one side was a great heap of coal – not a loose heap, such as you see in your coal cellar, but a sort of solid building of coals with large square blocks of coal outside used just as though they were bricks, and built up till the heap looked like the picture of the Cities of the Plain in *Bible Stories for Infants*. There was a line of whitewash near the top of the coaly wall.

When presently the Porter lounged out of his room at the twice-repeated tingling thrill of a gong over the station door, Peter said, 'How do you do?' in his best manner, and hastened to ask what the white mark was on the coal for.

'To mark how much coal there be,' said the Porter, 'so we'll know if anyone nicks it. So don't you go off with none in your pockets, young gentleman!'

This seemed, at the time, but a merry jest, and Peter felt at once that the Porter was a friendly sort with no nonsense about him. But later the words came back to Peter with a new meaning.

Have you ever gone into a farmhouse kitchen on a baking day, and seen the great crock of dough set by the fire to rise? If you have, and if you were at that time still young enough to be interested in everything you saw, you will remember that you found yourself quite unable to resist the temptation to poke your finger into the soft round dough that curved inside the pan like a giant mushroom. And you will remember that your finger made a dent in the dough, and that slowly, but quite surely, the dent disappeared, and the dough looked quite the same as it did before you touched it. Unless, of course, your hand was extra dirty in which case, naturally, there would be a little black mark.

Well, it was just like that with the sorrow the children had felt at Father's going away, and at Mother's being so unhappy. It made a deep impression, but the impression did not last long.

They soon got used to being without Father, though they did not forget him; and they got used to not going to school, and to seeing very little of Mother, who was now almost all day shut up in her upstairs room writing, writing, writing. She used to come down at tea-time and read aloud the stories she had written. They were lovely stories.

The rocks and hills and valleys and trees, the canal, and, above all, the railway, were so new and so perfectly pleasing that the remembrance of the old life in the villa grew to seem almost like a dream.

Mother had told them more than once that they were 'quite poor now,' but this did not seem to be anything but a way of speaking. Grown-up people, even Mothers, often make remarks that don't seem to mean anything in particular, just for the sake of saying something, seemingly. There was always enough to eat, and they wore the same kind of nice clothes they had always worn.

But in June came three wet days; the rain came down, straight as lances, and it was very, very cold. Nobody could go out, and everybody shivered. They all went up to the door of Mother's room and knocked.

'Well, what is it?' asked Mother from inside.

'Mother,' said Bobbie, 'mayn't I light a fire? I do know how.'

And Mother said: 'No, my ducky-love. We mustn't have fires in June – coal is so dear. If you're cold, go and have a good romp in the attic. That'll warm you.'

'But, Mother, it only takes such a very little coal to make a fire.'

'It's more than we can afford, chickeny-love,' said Mother, cheerfully. 'Now run away, there's darlings – I'm madly busy!'

'Mother's always busy now,' said Phyllis, in a whisper to Peter. Peter did not answer. He shrugged his shoulders. He was thinking.

Thought, however, could not long keep itself from the suitable furnishing of a bandit's lair in the attic. Peter was the bandit, of course. Bobbie was his lieutenant, his band of trusty robbers, and, in due course, the parent of Phyllis, who was the captured maiden for whom a magnificent ransom – in horse-beans – was unhesitatingly paid.

They all went down to tea flushed and joyous as any mountain brigands.

But when Phyllis was going to add jam to her bread and butter, Mother said:

'Jam or butter, dear – not jam *and* butter. We can't afford that sort of reckless luxury nowadays.'

Phyllis finished the slice of bread and butter in silence, and followed it up by bread and jam. Peter mingled thought and weak tea.

After tea they went back to the attic and he said to his sisters:

'I have an idea.'

'What's that?' they asked politely.

'I shan't tell you,' was Peter's unexpected rejoinder.

'Oh, very well,' said Bobbie; and Phil said, 'Don't then.'

'Girls,' said Peter, 'are always so hasty tempered.'

'I should like to know what boys are!' said Bobbie, with fine disdain. 'I don't want to know about your silly ideas.'

'You'll know some day,' said Peter, keeping his own temper by what looked exactly like a miracle; 'if you hadn't been so keen on a row, I might have told you about it being only noble-heartedness that made me not tell you my idea. But now I shan't tell you anything at all about it – so there!'

And it was, indeed, some time before he could be induced to say anything, and when he did it wasn't much. He said:

'The only reason why I won't tell you my idea that I'm going to do is because it may be wrong, and I don't want to drag you into it.'

'Don't you do it if it's wrong, Peter,' said Bobbie; 'let me do it.' But Phyllis said:

'*I* should like to do wrong if *you're* going to!'

'No,' said Peter, rather touched by this devotion; 'it's a forlorn hope, and I'm going to lead it. All I ask is that if Mother asks where I am, you won't blab.'

'We haven't got anything *to* blab,' said Bobbie, indignantly.

'Oh, yes, you have!' said Peter, dropping horse-beans through his fingers. 'I've trusted you to the death. You know I'm going to do a lone adventure – and some people might think it wrong – I don't. And if Mother asks where I am, say I'm playing at mines.'

'What sort of mines?'

'You just say mines.'

'You might tell *us*, Pete.'

'Well, then, *coal*-mines. But don't you let the word pass your lips on pain of torture.'

'You needn't threaten,' said Bobbie, 'and I do think you might let us help.'

'If I find a coal-mine, you shall help cart the coal,' Peter condescended to promise.

'Keep your secret if you like,' said Phyllis.

'Keep it if you *can*,' said Bobbie.

'I'll keep it right enough,' said Peter.

Between tea and supper there is an interval even in the most greedily regulated families. At this time Mother was usually writing, and Mrs Viney had gone home.

Two nights after the dawning of Peter's idea he beckoned the girls mysteriously at the twilight hour.

'Come hither with me,' he said, 'and bring the Roman Chariot.'

The Roman Chariot was a very old perambulator that had spent years of retirement in the loft over the coach-house. The children had oiled its works till it glided noiseless as a pneumatic bicycle, and answered to the helm as it had probably done long ago in its best days.

'Follow your dauntless leader,' said Peter, and led the way down the hill towards the station.

Just above the station many rocks had pushed their heads out through the turf as though they, like the children, were interested in the railway.

In a little hollow between three rocks lay a heap of dried brambles and heather.

Peter halted, turned over the brushwood with a well-scarred boot, and said:

'Here's the first coal from the St Peter's Mine. We'll take it home in the chariot. Punctuality and despatch. All orders carefully attended to. Any shaped lump cut to suit regular customers.'

The chariot was packed full of coal. And when it was packed it had to be unpacked again because it was so heavy that it couldn't be got up the hill by the three children, not even when Peter harnessed himself to the handle with his braces, and firmly grasping his waistband in one hand pulled while the girls pushed behind.

Three journeys had to be made before the coal from Peter's mine was added to the heap of Mother's coal in the cellar.

Afterwards Peter went out alone, and came back very black and mysterious.

'I've been to my coal-mine,' he said; 'tomorrow

evening we'll bring home the black diamonds in the chariot.'

It was a week later that Mrs Viney remarked to Mother how well this last lot of coal was holding out.

The children hugged themselves and each other in complicated wriggles of silent laughter as they listened on the stairs. They had all forgotten by now that there had ever been any doubt in Peter's mind as to whether coal-mining was wrong.

But there came a dreadful night when the Station Master put on a pair of old sand shoes that he had worn at the seaside on his summer holiday, and crept out very quietly to the yard where the Sodom and Gomorrah heap of coal was, with the whitewashed line round it. He crept out there, and he waited like a cat by a mouse-hole. On the top of the heap something small and dark was scrabbling and rattling furtively among the coal.

The Station Master concealed himself in the shadow of a brake-van that had a little tin chimney and was labelled:

G.N. & S.R.
34576

Return at once to
White Heather Sidings,

and in this concealment he lurked till the small thing on the top of the heap ceased to scrabble and rattle, came to the edge of the heap, cautiously let itself down, and lifted something after it. Then the arm of the Station Master was raised, the hand of the Station Master fell on a collar, and there was Peter firmly held by the jacket, with an old carpenter's bag full of coal in his trembling clutch.

'So I've caught you at last, have I, you young thief?' said the Station Master.

'I'm not a thief,' said Peter, as firmly as he could. 'I'm a coal-miner.'

'Tell that to the Marines,' said the Station Master.

'It would be just as true whoever I told it to,' said Peter.

'You're right there,' said the man who held him. 'Stow your jaw, you young rip, and come along to the station.'

'Oh, no,' cried in the darkness an agonized voice that was not Peter's.

'Not the *police* station!' said another voice from the darkness.

'Not yet,' said the Station Master. 'The Railway Station first. Why, it's a regular gang. Any more of you?'

'Only us,' said Bobbie and Phyllis, coming out of the shadow of another truck labelled Stavely Colliery, and bearing on it the legend in white chalk: 'Wanted in No. 1 Road.'

'What do you mean by spying on a fellow like this?' said Peter, angrily.

'Time someone did spy on you, *I* think,' said the Station Master. 'Come along to the station.'

'Oh, *don't!*' said Bobbie. 'Can't you decide *now* what you'll do to us? It's our fault just as much as Peter's. We helped to carry the coal away – and we knew where he got it.'

'No, you didn't,' said Peter.

'Yes, we did,' said Bobbie. 'We knew all the time. We only pretended we didn't just to humour you.'

Peter's cup was full. He had mined for coal, he had struck coal, he had been caught, and now he learned that his sisters had 'humoured' him.

'Don't hold me!' he said. 'I won't run away.'

The Station Master loosed Peter's collar, struck a match and looked at them by its flickering light.

'Why,' said he, 'you're the children from the Three Chimneys up yonder. So nicely dressed, too. Tell me now, what made you do such a thing? Haven't you ever been to church or learned your catechism or anything, not to know it's wicked to steal?' He spoke much more gently now, and Peter said:

'I didn't think it was stealing. I was almost sure it wasn't. I thought if I took it from the outside part of the heap, perhaps it would be. But in the middle I thought I could fairly count it only mining. It'll take thousands of years for you to burn up all that coal and get to the middle parts.'

'Not quite. But did you do it for a lark or what?'

'Not much lark carrying that beastly heavy stuff up the hill,' said Peter, indignantly.

'Then why did you?' The Station Master's voice was so much kinder now that Peter replied:

'You know that wet day? Well, Mother said we were too poor to have a fire. We always had fires when it was cold at our other house, and –'

'*Don't!*' interrupted Bobbie, in a whisper.

'Well,' said the Station Master, rubbing his chin thoughtfully, 'I'll tell you what I'll do. I'll look over it this once. But you remember, young gentleman, stealing is stealing, and what's mine isn't yours, whether you call it mining or whether you don't. Run along home.'

'Do you mean you aren't going to do anything to us? Well, you are a brick,' said Peter, with enthusiasm.

'You're a dear,' said Bobbie.

'You're a darling,' said Phyllis.

'That's all right,' said the Station Master.

And on this they parted.

'Don't speak to me,' said Peter, as the three went up the hill. 'You're spies and traitors – that's what you are.'

But the girls were too glad to have Peter between them, safe and free, and on the way to Three Chimneys and not to the Police Station, to mind much what he said.

'We *did* say it was us as much as you,' said Bobbie, gently.

'Well – and it wasn't.'

'It would have come to the same thing in Courts with judges,' said Phyllis. 'Don't be snarky, Peter. It isn't our fault your secrets are so jolly easy to find out.' She took his arm, and he let her.

'There's an awful lot of coal in the cellar, anyhow,' he went on.

'Oh, don't!' said Bobbie. 'I don't think we ought to be glad about *that*.'

'I don't know,' said Peter, plucking up spirit. 'I'm not at all sure, even now, that mining is a crime.'

But the girls were quite sure. And they were also quite sure that he was quite sure, however little he cared to own it.

CHAPTER 3

The Old Gentleman

After the adventure of Peter's coal-mine, it seemed well to the children to keep away from the station – but they did not, they could not, keep away from the railway. They had lived all their lives in a street where cabs and omnibuses rumbled by at all hours, and the carts of butchers and bakers and candlestick makers (I never saw a candlestick maker's cart; did you?) might occur at any moment. Here in the deep silence of the sleeping country the only things that went by were the trains. They seemed to be all that was left to link the children to the old life that had once been theirs. Straight down the hill in front of Three Chimneys the daily passage of their six feet began to mark a path across the crisp, short turf. They began to know the hours when certain trains passed, and they gave names to them. The 9.15 up was called the Green Dragon. The 10.7 down was the Worm of Wantley. The midnight town express, whose shrieking rush they sometimes woke from their dreams to hear, was the Fearsome Fly-by-night. Peter got up once, in chill starshine, and, peeping at it through his curtains, named it on the spot.

It was by the Green Dragon that the old gentleman travelled. He was a very nice-looking old gentleman, and he looked as if he were nice, too, which is not at all the same thing. He had a fresh-coloured, clean-shaven face and white hair, and he wore rather odd-shaped collars and a top-hat that wasn't exactly the same kind as other people's. Of course the children didn't see all this at first. In fact the first thing they noticed about the old gentleman was his hand.

It was one morning as they sat on the fence waiting for the Green Dragon, which was three and a quarter minutes late by Peter's Waterbury watch that he had had given him on his last birthday.

'The Green Dragon's going where Father is,' said Phyllis; 'if it were a really real dragon, we could stop it and ask it to take our love to Father.'

'Dragons don't carry people's love,' said Peter; 'they'd be above it.'

'Yes, they do, if you tame them thoroughly first. They fetch and carry like pet spaniels,' said Phyllis, 'and feed out of your hand. I wonder why Father never writes to us.'

'Mother says he's been too busy,' said Bobbie; 'but he'll write soon, she says.'

'I say,' Phyllis suggested, 'let's all wave to the Green Dragon as it goes by. If it's a magic dragon, it'll understand and take our loves to Father. And if it isn't, three waves aren't much. We shall never miss them.'

So when the Green Dragon tore shrieking out of the mouth of its dark lair, which was the tunnel, all three children stood on the railing and waved their pocket-handkerchiefs without stopping to think whether they were clean handkerchiefs or the reverse. They were, as a matter of fact, very much the reverse.

And out of a first-class carriage a hand waved back. A quite clean hand. It held a newspaper. It was the old gentleman's hand.

After this it became the custom for waves to be exchanged between the children and the 9.15.

And the children, especially the girls, liked to think that perhaps the old gentleman knew Father, and would meet him 'in business', wherever that shady retreat might be, and tell him how his three children stood on a rail far away in the green country and waved their love to him every morning, wet or fine.

For they were now able to go out in all sorts of weather such as they would never have been allowed to go out in when they lived in their villa house. This was Aunt Emma's doing, and the children felt more and more that they had not been quite fair to this unattractive aunt, when they found how useful were the long gaiters and waterproof coats that they had laughed at her for buying for them.

Mother, all this time, was very busy with her writing. She used to send off a good many long blue envelopes with stories in them – and large envelopes of different sizes and colours used to come to her. Sometimes she would sigh when she opened them and say:

'Another story come home to roost. Oh, dear! Oh, dear!' and then the children would be very sorry.

But sometimes she would wave the envelope in the air and say:

'Hooray, hooray. Here's a sensible Editor. He's taken my story and this is the proof of it.'

At first the children thought 'the proof' meant the letter the sensible Editor had written, but they presently got to know that the proof was long slips of paper with the story printed on them.

Whenever an Editor was sensible there were buns for tea.

One day Peter was going down to the village to get buns to celebrate the sensibleness of the Editor of the *Children's Globe*, when he met the Station Master.

Peter felt very uncomfortable, for he had now had time to think over the affair of the coal-mine. He did not like to say 'Good morning' to the Station Master, as you usually do to anyone you meet on a lonely road, because he had a hot feeling, which spread even to his ears, that the Station Master might not care to speak to a person who had stolen coals. 'Stolen' is a nasty word, but Peter felt it was the right one. So he looked down, and said nothing.

It was the Station Master who said 'Good morning' as he passed by. And Peter answered, 'Good morning.' Then he thought:

'Perhaps he doesn't know who I am by daylight, or he wouldn't be so polite.'

And he did not like the feeling which thinking this gave him. And then before he knew what he was going to do he ran after the Station Master, who stopped when he heard Peter's hasty boots crunching the road, and coming up with him very breathless and with his ears now quite magenta-coloured, he said:

'I don't want you to be polite to me if you don't know me when you see me.'

'Eh?' said the Station Master.

'I thought perhaps you didn't know it was me that took the coals,' Peter went on, 'when you said "Good morning". But it was, and I'm sorry. There.'

'Why,' said the Station Master, 'I wasn't thinking anything at all about the precious coals. Let bygones be bygones. And where were you off to in such a hurry?'

'I'm going to buy buns for tea,' said Peter.

'I thought you were all so poor,' said the Station Master.

'So we are,' said Peter, confidentially, 'but we always have three-pennyworth of halfpennies for tea whenever Mother sells a story or a poem or anything.'

'Oh,' said the Station Master, 'so your Mother writes stories, does she?'

'The beautifulest you ever read,' said Peter.

'You ought to be very proud to have such a clever Mother.'

'Yes,' said Peter, 'but she used to play with us more before she had to be so clever.'

'Well,' said the Station Master, 'I must be getting along. You give us a look in at the Station whenever you feel so inclined. And as to coals, it's a word that – well – oh, no, we never mention it, eh?'

'Thank you,' said Peter. 'I'm very glad it's all straightened out between us.' And he went on across the canal bridge to the village to get the buns, feeling more comfortable in his mind than he had felt since the hand of the Station Master had fastened on his collar that night among the coals.

Next day when they had sent the threefold wave of greeting to Father by the Green Dragon, and the old gentleman had waved back as usual, Peter proudly led the way to the station.

'But ought we?' said Bobbie.

'After the coals, she means,' Phyllis explained.

'I met the Station Master yesterday,' said Peter, in an off-hand way, and he pretended not to hear what

Phyllis had said; 'he expressly invited us to go down any time we liked.'

'After the coals?' repeated Phyllis. 'Stop a minute – my bootlace is undone again.'

'It always *is* undone again,' said Peter, 'and the Station Master was more of a gentleman than you'll ever be, Phil – throwing coal at a chap's head like that.'

Phyllis did up her bootlace and went on in silence, but her shoulders shook, and presently a fat tear fell off her nose and splashed on the metal of the railway line. Bobbie saw it.

'Why, what's the matter, darling?' she said, stopping short and putting her arm round the heaving shoulders.

'He called me un – un – ungentlemanly,' sobbed Phyllis. 'I didn't never call him unladylike, not even when he tied my Clorinda to the firewood bundle and burned her at the stake for a martyr.'

Peter had indeed perpetrated this outrage a year or two before.

'Well, you began, you know,' said Bobbie, honestly, 'about coals and all that. Don't you think you'd better both unsay everything since the wave, and let honour be satisfied?'

'I will if Peter will,' said Phyllis, sniffling.

'All right,' said Peter; 'honour is satisfied. Here, use my hankie, Phil, for goodness' sake, if you've lost yours as usual. I wonder what you do with them.'

'You had my last one,' said Phyllis, indignantly, 'to tie up the rabbit-hutch door with. But you're very ungrateful. It's quite right what it says in the poetry-book about sharper than a serpent it is to have a toothless child – but it means ungrateful when its says toothless. Miss Lowe told me so.'

'All right,' said Peter, impatiently, 'I'm sorry, *There!* Now will you come on?'

They reached the station and spent a joyous two hours with the Porter. He was a worthy man and seemed never tired of answering the questions that began with 'Why –' which many people in higher ranks of life often seem weary of.

He told them many things that they had not known before – as, for instance, that the things that hook carriages together are called couplings, and that the pipes like great serpents that hang over the couplings are meant to stop the train with.

'If you could get a holt of one o' them when the train is going and pull 'em apart,' said he, 'she'd stop dead off with a jerk.'

'Who's she?' said Phyllis.

'The train, of course,' said the Porter. After that the train was never again 'It' to the children.

'And you know the thing in the carriages where it says on it, "Five pounds' fine for improper use." If you was to improperly use that, the train 'ud stop.'

'And if you used it properly?' said Roberta.

'It 'ud stop just the same, I suppose,' said he, 'but it isn't proper use unless you're being murdered. There was an old lady once – someone kidded her on it was a refreshment-room bell, and she used it improper, not being in danger of her life, though hungry, and when the train stopped and the guard came along expecting to find someone weltering in their last moments, she says, "Oh, please, Mister, I'll take a glass of stout and a bath bun," she says. And the train was seven minutes behind her time as it was.'

'What did the guard say to the old lady?'

'*I* dunno,' replied the Porter, 'but I lay she didn't forget it in a hurry, whatever it was.'

In such delightful conversation the time went by all too quickly.

The Station Master came out once or twice from that sacred inner temple behind the place where the hole is that they sell you tickets through, and was most jolly with them all.

'Just as if coal had never been discovered,' Phyllis whispered to her sister.

He gave them each an orange, and promised to take them up into the signal-box one of these days, when he wasn't so busy.

Several trains went through the station, and Peter noticed for the first time that engines have numbers on them, like cabs.

'Yes,' said the Porter, 'I knowed a young gent as used to take down the numbers of every single one he seed; in a green leather note-book with silver corners it was, owing to his father being very well-to-do in the wholesale stationery.'

Peter felt that he could take down numbers, too, even if he was not the son of a wholesale stationer. As he did not happen to have a green leather note-book with silver corners, the Porter gave him a yellow envelope and on it he noted:

379

663

and felt that this was the beginning of what would be a most interesting collection.

That night at tea he asked Mother if she had a green

leather note-book with silver corners. She had not; but when she heard what he wanted it for she gave him a little black one.

'It has a few pages torn out,' said she; 'but it will hold quite a lot of numbers, and when it's full I'll give you another. I'm so glad you like the railway. Only, please, you mustn't walk on the line.'

'Not if we face the way the train's coming?' asked Peter, after a gloomy pause, in which glances of despair were exchanged.

'No – really not,' said Mother.

Then Phyllis said, 'Mother, didn't *you* ever walk on the railway lines when you were little?'

Mother was an honest and honourable Mother, so she had to say, 'Yes.'

'Well, then,' said Phyllis.

'But, darlings, you don't know how fond I am of you. What should I do if you got hurt?'

'Are you fonder of us than Granny was of you when you were little?' Phyllis asked. Bobbie made signs to her to stop, but Phyllis never did see signs, no matter how plain they might be.

Mother did not answer for a minute. She got up to put more water in the teapot.

'No one,' she said at last, 'ever loved anyone more than my mother loved me.'

Then she was quiet again, and Bobbie kicked Phyllis hard under the table, because Bobbie understood a little bit the thoughts that were making Mother so quiet – the thoughts of the time when Mother was a little girl and was all the world to *her* mother. It seems so easy and natural to run to Mother when one is in trouble. Bobbie understood a little how people do not leave off running to their mothers when they are in trouble even when they are grown up, and she thought she knew a little what it must be to be sad, and have no mother to run to any more.

So she kicked Phyllis, who said:

'What are you kicking me like that for, Bob?'

And then Mother laughed a little and sighed and said:

'Very well, then. Only let me be sure you do know which way the trains come – and don't walk on the line near the tunnel or near corners.'

'Trains keep to the left like carriages,' said Peter, 'so if we keep to the right, we're bound to see them coming.'

'Very well,' said Mother, and I dare say you think that she ought not to have said it. But she remembered about when she was a little girl herself, and she did say it – and neither her own children nor you nor any other children in the world could ever understand exactly what it cost her to do it. Only some few of you, like Bobbie, may understand a very little bit.

It was the very next day that Mother had to stay in bed because her head ached so. Her hands were burning hot, and she would not eat anything, and her throat was very sore.

'If I was you, Mum,' said Mrs Viney, 'I should take and send for the doctor. There's a lot of catchy complaints a-going about just now. My sister's eldest – she took a chill and it went to her inside, two year ago come Christmas, and she's never been the same gell since.'

Mother wouldn't at first, but in the evening she felt so much worse that Peter was sent to the house in the village that had three laburnum trees by the gate, and on the gate a brass plate with W. W. Forrest, M.D., on it.

W. W. Forrest, M.D., came at once. He talked to Peter on the way back. He seemed a most charming and sensible man, interested in railways, and rabbits, and really important things.

When he had seen Mother, he said it was influenza.

'Now, Lady Grave-airs,' he said in the hall to Bobbie, 'I suppose you'll want to be head-nurse.'

'Of course,' said she.

'Well, then, I'll send down some medicine. Keep up a good fire. Have some strong beef tea made ready to give her as soon as the fever goes down. She can have grapes now, and beef essence – and soda-water and milk, and you'd better get in a bottle of brandy. The best brandy. Cheap brandy is worse than poison.'

She asked him to write it all down, and he did.

When Bobbie showed Mother the list he had written, Mother laughed. It was a laugh, Bobbie decided, though it was rather cold and feeble.

'Nonsense,' said Mother, lying in bed with eyes as bright as beads. 'I can't afford all that rubbish. Tell Mrs Viney to boil two pounds of scrag-end of the neck for your dinners tomorrow, and I can have some of the broth. Yes, I should like some more water now, love. And will you get a basin and sponge my hands?'

Roberta obeyed. When she had done everything she could to make Mother less uncomfortable, she went down to the others. Her cheeks were very red, her lips set tight, and her eyes shone as bright as Mother's.

She told them what the Doctor had said, and what Mother had said.

'And now,' said she, when she had told all, 'there's

no one but us to do anything, and we've got to do it. I've got the shilling for the mutton.'

'We can do without the beastly mutton,' said Peter; 'bread and butter will support life. People have lived on less on desert islands many a time.'

'Of course,' said his sister. And Mrs Viney was sent to the village to get as much brandy and soda-water and beef tea as she could buy for a shilling.

'But even if we never have anything to eat at all,' said Phyllis, 'you can't get all those other things with our dinner money.'

'No,' said Bobbie, frowning, 'we must find out some other way. Now *think*, everybody, just as hard as ever you can.'

They did think. And presently they talked. And later, when Bobbie had gone up to sit with Mother in case she wanted anything, the other two were very busy with scissors and a white sheet, and a paint brush, and the pot of Brunswick black that Mrs Viney used for grates and fenders. They did not manage to do what they wished, exactly, with the first sheet, so they took another out of the linen cupboard. It did not occur to them that they were spoiling good sheets which cost good money. They only knew that they were making a good – but what they were making comes later.

Bobbie's bed had been moved into Mother's room, and several times in the night she got up to mend the fire, and to give her mother milk and soda-water. Mother talked to herself a good deal, but it did not seem to mean anything. And once she woke up suddenly and called out: 'Mamma, mamma!' and Bobbie knew she was calling for Granny, and that she had forgotten that it was no use calling, because Granny was dead.

In the early morning Bobbie heard her name and jumped out of bed and ran to Mother's bedside.

'Oh – ah – yes – I think I was asleep,' said Mother. 'My poor little duck, how tired you'll be – I do hate to give you all this trouble.'

'Trouble!' said Bobbie.

'Ah, don't cry, sweet,' Mother said; 'I shall be all right in a day or two.'

And Bobbie said, 'Yes,' and tried to smile.

When you are used to ten hours of solid sleep, to get up three or four times in your sleep-time makes you feel as though you had been up all night. Bobbie felt quite stupid and her eyes were sore and stiff, but she tidied the room, and arranged everything neatly before the Doctor came.

This was at half past eight.

'Everything going on all right, little Nurse?' he said at the front door. 'Did you get the brandy?'

'I've got the brandy,' said Bobbie, 'in a little flat bottle.'

'I didn't see the grapes or the beef tea, though,' said he.

'No,' said Bobbie, firmly, 'but you will tomorrow. And there's some beef stewing in the oven for beef tea.'

'Who told you to do that?' he asked.

'I noticed what Mother did when Phil had mumps.'

'Right,' said the Doctor. 'Now you get your old woman to sit with your mother, and then you eat a good breakfast, and go straight to bed and sleep till dinner-time. We can't afford to have the head-nurse ill.'

He was really quite a nice doctor.

When the 9.15 came out of the tunnel that morning the old gentleman in the first-class carriage put down his newspaper, and got ready to wave his hand to the three children on the fence. But this morning there were not three. There was only one. And that was Peter.

Peter was not on the railings either, as usual. He was standing in front of them in an attitude like that of a showman showing off the animals in a menagerie, or of the kind clergyman when he points with a wand at the 'Scenes from Palestine,' when there is a magic-lantern and he is explaining it.

Peter was pointing, too. And what he was pointing at was a large white sheet nailed against the fence. On the sheet there were thick black letters more than a foot long.

Some of them had run a little, because of Phyllis having put the Brunswick black on too eagerly, but the words were quite easy to read.

And this was what the old gentleman and several other people in the train read in the large black letters on the white sheet:

> LOOK OUT AT THE STATION

A good many people did look out at the station and were disappointed, for they saw nothing unusual. The old gentleman looked out, too, and at first he too saw nothing more unusual than the gravelled platform and the sunshine and the wall-flowers and forget-me-nots in the station borders. It was only just as the train was beginning to puff and pull itself together to start again that he saw Phyllis. She was quite out of breath with running.

'Oh,' she said, 'I thought I'd missed you. My boot-laces would keep coming down, and I fell over them twice. Here, take it.'

She threw a warm, dampish letter into his hand as the train moved.

He leaned back in his corner and opened the letter. This is what he read:

> *Dear Mr We do not know your name.*
>
> *Mother is ill and the doctor says to give her the things at the end of the letter, but she says she can't afford it and to get mutton for us and she will have the broth. We do not know anybody here but you, because Father is away and we do not know the address. Father will pay you, or if he has lost all his money, or anything, Peter will pay you when he is a man. We promise it on our honer. I.O.U. for all the things Mother wants*
>
> > *sined Peter*
>
> *Will you give the parsel to the Station Master, because of us not knowing what train you come down by? Say it is for Peter that was sorry about the coals and he will know all right.*
> *Roberta*
> *Phyllis*
> *Peter*

Then came the list of things the Doctor had ordered.

The old gentleman read it through once, and his eyebrows went up. He read it twice and smiled a little. When he had read it twice, he put it in his pocket and went on reading *The Times*.

At about six that evening there was a knock at the back door. The three children rushed to open it, and there stood the friendly Porter, who had told them so many interesting things about railways. He dumped down a big hamper on the kitchen flags.

'Old gent,' he said; 'he asked me to fetch it up straight away.'

'Thank you very much,' said Peter, and then, as the Porter lingered, he added:

'I'm most awfully sorry I haven't got twopence to give you like Father does, but –'

'You drop it if you please,' said the Porter, indignantly. 'I wasn't thinking about no tuppences. I only wanted to say I was sorry your Mamma wasn't so well, and to ask how she finds herself this evening – and I've fetched her along a bit of sweetbriar, very sweet to smell it is. Twopence indeed,' said he, and produced a bunch of sweetbriar from his hat, 'just like a conjurer,' as Phyllis remarked afterwards.

'Thank you very much,' said Peter, 'and I beg your pardon about the twopence.'

'No offence,' said the Porter, untruly but politely, and went.

Then the children undid the hamper. First there was straw, and then there were fine shavings, and then came all the things they had asked for, and plenty of them, and then a good many things they had not asked for; among others peaches and port wine and two chickens, a cardboard box of big red roses with long stalks, and a tall thin green bottle of lavender water, and three smaller fatter bottles of eau-de-Cologne. There was a letter, too.

'Dear Roberta and Phyllis and Peter,' it said; 'here

are the things you want. Your mother will want to know where they came from. Tell her they were sent by a friend who heard she was ill. When she is well again you must tell her all about it, of course. And if she says you ought not to have asked for the things, tell her that I say you were quite right, and that I hope she will forgive me for taking the liberty of allowing myself a great pleasure.'

The letter was signed G.P. something that the children couldn't read.

'I think we *were* right,' said Phyllis.

'Right? Of course we were right,' said Bobbie.

'All the same,' said Peter, with his hands in his pockets, 'I don't exactly look forward to telling Mother the whole truth about it.'

'We're not to do it till she's well,' said Bobbie, 'and when she's well we shall be so happy we shan't mind a little fuss like that. Oh, just look at the roses! I must take them up to her.'

'And the sweetbriar,' said Phyllis, sniffing it loudly: 'don't forget the sweetbriar.'

'As if I should!' said Roberta. 'Mother told me the other day there was a thick hedge of it at her mother's house when she was a little girl.'

CHAPTER 4

The Engine-Burglar

What was left of the second sheet and the Brunswick black came in very nicely to make a banner bearing the legend

SHE IS NEARLY WELL, THANK YOU

and this was displayed to the Green Dragon about a fortnight after the arrival of the wonderful hamper. The old gentleman saw it, and waved a cheerful response from the train. And when this had been done the children saw that now was the time when they must tell Mother what they had done when she was ill. And it did not seem nearly so easy as they had thought it would be. But it had to be done. And it was done. Mother was extremely angry. She was seldom angry, and now she was angrier than they had ever known her. This was horrible. But it was much worse when she suddenly began to cry. Crying is catching, I believe, like measles and whooping-cough.

At any rate, everyone at once found itself taking part in a crying-party.

Mother stopped first. She dried her eyes and then she said:

'I'm sorry I was so angry, darlings, because I know you didn't understand.'

'We didn't mean to be naughty, Mammy,' sobbed Bobbie, and Peter and Phyllis sniffed.

'Now, listen,' said Mother; 'it's quite true that we're poor, but we have enough to live on. You mustn't go telling everyone about our affairs – it's not right. And you must never, never, never ask strangers to give you things. Now always remember that – won't you?'

They all hugged her and rubbed their damp cheeks against hers and promised that they would.

'And I'll write a letter to your old gentleman, and I shall tell him that I didn't approve – oh, of course I shall thank him, too, for his kindness. It's *you* I don't approve of, my darlings, not the old gentleman. He was as kind as ever he could be. And you can give the letter to the Station Master to give him – and we won't say any more about it.'

Afterwards, when the children were alone, Bobbie said:

'Isn't Mother splendid? You catch any other grown-up saying they were sorry they had been angry.'

'Yes,' said Peter, 'she *is* splendid; but it's rather awful when she's angry.'

'She's like Avenging and Bright in the song,' said Phyllis. 'I should like to look at her if it wasn't so awful. She looks so beautiful when she's really downright furious.'

They took the letter down to the Station Master.

'I thought you said you hadn't got any friends except in London,' said he.

'We've made him since,' said Peter.

'But he doesn't live hereabouts?'

'No – we just know him on the railway.'

Then the Station Master retired to that sacred inner temple behind the little window where the tickets are sold, and the children went down to the Porter's room and talked to the Porter. They learned several interesting things from him – among others that his name was Perks, that he was married and had three children, that the lamps in front of engines are called head-lights and the ones at the back tail-lights.

'And that just shows,' whispered Phyllis, 'that trains really *are* dragons in disguise, with proper heads and tails.'

It was on this day that the children first noticed that all engines are not alike.

'Alike?' said the Porter whose name was Perks, 'lor, love you, no, Miss. No more alike nor what you an' me are. That little 'un without a tender as went by just now all on her own, that was a tank, that was – she's off to do some shunting t'other side o' Maidbridge. That's as it might be you, Miss. Then there's goods engines, great, strong things with three wheels each side – joined with rods to strengthen 'em as it might be me. Then there's main-line engines as it might be this 'ere young gentleman when he grows up and wins all the races at 'is school – so he will. The main-line engine she's built for speed as well as power. That's one to the 9.15 up.'

'The Green Dragon,' said Phyllis.

'We call her the Snail, Miss, among ourselves,' said the Porter. 'She's oftener be'ind'and nor any train on the line.'

'But the engine's green,' said Phyllis.

'Yes, Miss,' said Perks, 'so's a snail some seasons o' the year.'

The children agreed as they went home to dinner that the Porter was most delightful company.

Next day was Roberta's birthday. In the afternoon she was politely but firmly requested to get out of the way and keep there till tea-time.

'You aren't to see what we're going to do till it's done; it's a glorious surprise,' said Phyllis.

And Roberta went out into the garden all alone. She tried to be grateful, but she felt she would much rather have helped in whatever it was than have to spend her birthday afternoon by herself, no matter how glorious the surprise might be.

Now that she was alone, she had time to think, and one of the things she thought of most was what Mother had said in one of those feverish nights when her hands were so hot and her eyes so bright.

The words were: 'Oh, what a doctor's bill there'll be for this!'

She walked round and round the garden among the rose-bushes that hadn't any roses yet, only buds, and the lilac bushes and syringas and American currants, and the more she thought of the doctor's bill, the less she liked the thought of it.

And presently she made up her mind. She went out through the side door of the garden and climbed up the steep field to where the road runs along by the canal. She walked along until she came to the bridge that crosses the canal and leads to the village, and here she waited. It was very pleasant in the sunshine to lean one's elbow on the warm stone of the bridge and look down at the blue water of the canal. Bobbie had never seen any other canal, except the Regent's Canal, and the water of that is not at all a pretty colour. And she had never seen any river at all except the Thames, which also would be all the better if its face was washed.

Perhaps the children would have loved the canal as much as the railway, but for two things. One was that they had found the railway *first* – on that first, wonderful morning when the house and the country and the moors and rocks and great hills were all new to them. They had not found the canal till some days later. The other reason was that everyone on the railway had been kind to them – the Station Master, the Porter, and the old gentleman who waved. And the people on the canal were anything but kind.

The people on the canal were, of course, the bargees, who steered the slow barges up and down, or walked beside the old horses that trampled up the mud of the towing-path, and strained at the long tow-ropes.

Peter had once asked one of the bargees the time, and had been told to 'get out of that,' in a tone so fierce that he did not stop to say anything about his having just as much right on the towing-path as the man himself. Indeed, he did not even think of saying it till some time later.

Then another day when the children thought they would like to fish in the canal, a boy in a barge threw lumps of coal at them, and one of these hit Phyllis on the back of the neck She was just stooping down to tie up her bootlace – and though the coal hardly hurt at all it made her not care very much about going on fishing.

On the bridge, however, Roberta felt quite safe, because she could look down on the canal, and if any boy showed signs of meaning to throw coal, she could duck behind the parapet.

Presently there was a sound of wheels, which was just what she expected.

The wheels were the wheels of the Doctor's dogcart, and in the cart, of course, was the Doctor.

He pulled up and called out:

'Hullo, head-nurse! Want a lift?'

'I wanted to see you,' said Bobbie.

'Your mother's not worse, I hope?' said the Doctor.

'No – but –'

'Well, step in, then, and we'll go for a drive.'

Roberta climbed in and the brown horse was made to turn round – which it did not like at all, for it was looking forward to its tea – I mean its oats.

'This is jolly,' said Bobbie, as the dogcart flew along the road by the canal.

'We could throw a stone down any one of your three chimneys,' said the Doctor, as they passed the house.

'Yes,' said Bobbie, 'but you'd have to be a jolly good shot.'

'How do you know I'm not?' said the Doctor. 'Now, then, what's the trouble?'

Bobbie fidgeted with the hook of the driving apron.

'Come, out with it,' said the Doctor.

'It's rather hard, you see,' said Bobbie, 'to out with it; because of what Mother said.'

'What *did* Mother say?'

'She said I wasn't to go telling everyone that we're poor. But you aren't everyone, are you?'

'Not at all,' said the Doctor cheerfully. 'Well?'

'Well, I know doctors are very extravagant – I mean expensive, and Mrs Viney told me that her doctoring only cost her twopence a week because she belonged to a Club.'

'Yes?'

'You see she told me what a good doctor you were, and I asked her how she could afford you, because she's much poorer than we are. I've been in her house and I know. And then she told me about the Club, and I thought I'd ask you – and – oh, I don't want Mother to be worried! Can't we be in the Club, too, the same as Mrs Viney?'

The Doctor was silent. He was rather poor himself, and he had been pleased at getting a new family to attend. So I think his feelings at that minute were rather mixed.

'You aren't cross with me, are you?' said Bobbie, in a very small voice.

The Doctor roused himself.

'Cross? How could I be? You're a very sensible little woman. Now look here, don't you worry. I'll make it all right with your Mother, even if I have to make a special brand-new Club all for her. Look here, this is where the Aqueduct begins.'

'What's an Aque – what's its name?' asked Bobbie.

'A water bridge,' said the Doctor. 'Look.'

The road rose to a bridge over the canal. To the left was a steep rocky cliff with trees and shrubs growing in the cracks of the rock. And the canal here left off running along the top of the hill and started to run on a bridge of its own – a great bridge with tall arches that went right across the valley.

Bobbie drew a long breath.

'It *is* grand, isn't it?' she said. 'It's like pictures in the *History of Rome*.'

'Right!' said the Doctor, 'that's just exactly what it

is like. The Romans were dead nuts on aqueducts. It's a splendid piece of engineering.'

'I thought engineering was making engines.'

'Ah, there are different sorts of engineering – making roads and bridges and tunnels is one kind. And making fortifications is another. Well, we must be turning back. And, remember, you aren't to worry about doctor's bills or you'll be ill yourself, and then I'll send you a bill as long as the aqueduct.'

When Bobbie had parted from the Doctor at the top of the field that ran down from the road to Three Chimneys, she could not feel that she had done wrong. She knew that Mother would perhaps think differently. But Bobbie felt that for once she was the one who was right, and she scrambled down the rocky slope with a really happy feeling.

Phyllis and Peter met her at the back door. They were unnaturally clean and neat, and Phyllis had a red bow in her hair. There was only just time for Bobbie to make herself tidy and tie up her hair with a blue bow before a little bell rang.

'There!' said Phyllis, 'that's to show the surprise is ready. Now you wait till the bell rings again and then you may come into the dining-room.'

So Bobbie waited.

'Tinkle, tinkle,' said the little bell, and Bobbie went into the dining-room, feeling rather shy. Directly she opened the door she found herself, as it seemed, in a new world of light and flowers and singing. Mother and Peter and Phyllis were standing in a row at the end of the table. The shutters were shut and there were twelve candles on the table, one for each of Roberta's years. The table was covered with a sort of pattern of flowers, and at Roberta's place was a thick wreath of forget-me-nots and several most interesting little packages. And Mother and Phyllis and Peter were singing – to the first part of the tune of St Patrick's Day. Roberta knew that Mother had written the words on purpose for her birthday. It was a little way of Mother's on birthdays. It had begun on Bobbie's fourth birthday when Phyllis was a baby. Bobbie remembered learning the verses to say to Father 'for a surprise'. She wondered if Mother had remembered, too. The four-year-old verse had been:

> *Daddy dear, I'm only four*
> *And I'd rather not be more.*
> *Four's the nicest age to be,*
> *Two and two and one and three.*
> *What I love is two and two,*
> *Mother, Peter, Phil, and you.*
> *What you love is one and three,*
> *Mother, Peter, Phil and me.*
> *Give your little girl a kiss*
> *Because she learned and told you this.*

The song the others were singing now went like this:

> *Our darling Roberta,*
> *No sorrow shall hurt her*
> *If we can prevent it*
> *Her whole life long.*
> *Her birthday's our fête day,*
> *We'll make it our great day,*
> *And give her our presents*
> *And sing her our song.*
> *May pleasures attend her*

And may the Fates send her
The happiest journey
Along her life's way.
With skies bright above her
And dear ones to love her!
Dear Bob! Many happy
Returns of the day!

When they had finished singing they cried, 'Three cheers for our Bobbie!' and gave them very loudly. Bobbie felt exactly as though she were going to cry – you know that odd feeling in the bridge of your nose and the pricking in your eyelids? But before she had time to begin they were all kissing and hugging her.

'Now,' said Mother, 'look at your presents.'

They were very nice presents. There was a green and red needle-book that Phyllis had made herself in secret moments. There was a darling little silver brooch of Mother's shaped like a buttercup, which Bobbie had known and loved for years, but which she had never, never thought would come to be her very own. There was also a pair of blue glass vases from Mrs Viney. Roberta had seen and admired them in the village shop. And there were three birthday cards with pretty pictures and wishes.

Mother fitted the forget-me-not crown on Bobbie's brown head.

'And now look at the table,' she said.

There was a cake on the table covered with white sugar, with 'Dear Bobbie' on it in pink sweets, and there were buns and jam; but the nicest thing was that the big table was almost covered with flowers – wallflowers were laid all round the tea-tray – there was a ring of forget-me-nots round each plate. The cake had a wreath of white lilac round it, and in the middle was something that looked like a pattern all done with single blooms of lilac or wallflower or laburnum.

'What is it?' asked Roberta.

'It's a map – a map of the railway!' cried Peter. 'Look – those lilac lines are the metals – and there's the station done in brown wallflowers. The laburnum is the train, and there are the signal-boxes, and the road up to here – and those fat red daisies are us three waving to the old gentleman – that's him, the pansy in the laburnum train.'

'And there's "Three Chimneys" done in the purple primroses,' said Phyllis. 'And that little tiny rose-bud is Mother looking for us when we're late for tea. Peter invented it all, and we got all the flowers from the station. We thought you'd like it better.'

'That's my present,' said Peter, suddenly dumping down his adored steam-engine on the table in front of her. Its tender had been lined with fresh white paper, and was full of sweets.

'Oh, Peter!' cried Bobbie, quite overcome by this munificence, 'not your own dear little engine that you're so fond of?'

'Oh, no,' said Peter, very promptly, 'not the engine. Only the sweets.'

Bobbie couldn't help her face changing a little – not so much because she was disappointed at not getting the engine, as because she had thought it so very noble of Peter, and now she felt she had been silly to think it. Also she felt she must have seemed greedy to expect the engine as well as the sweets. So her face changed. Peter saw it. He hesitated a minute; then his face changed, too, and he said: 'I mean not *all* the engine. I'll let you go halves if you like.'

'You're a brick,' cried Bobbie; 'it's a splendid present.' She said no more aloud, but to herself she said:

'That was awfully decent of Peter because I know he didn't mean to. Well, the broken half shall be my half of the engine, and I'll get it mended and give it back to Peter for his birthday.' – 'Yes, Mother dear, I should like to cut the cake,' she added, and tea began.

It was a delightful birthday. After tea Mother played games with them – any game they liked – and of course their first choice was blindman's-buff, in the course of which Bobbie's forget-me-not wreath twisted itself crookedly over one of her ears and stayed there. Then, when it was near bed-time and time to calm down, Mother had a lovely new story to read to them.

'You won't sit up late working, will you, Mother?' Bobbie asked as they said good-night.

And Mother said no, she wouldn't – she would only just write to Father and then go to bed.

But when Bobbie crept down later to bring up her presents – for she felt she really could not be separated from them all night – Mother was not writing, but leaning her head on her arms and her arms on the table. I think it was rather good of Bobbie to slip quietly away, saying over and over, 'She doesn't want me to know she's unhappy, and I won't know; I won't know.' But it made a sad end to the birthday.

~

The very next morning Bobbie began to watch her opportunity to get Peter's engine mended secretly. And the opportunity came the very next afternoon.

Mother went by train to the nearest town to do

shopping. When she went there, she always went to the Post-office. Perhaps to post her letters to Father, for she never gave them to the children or Mrs Viney to post, and she never went to the village herself. Peter and Phyllis went with her. Bobbie wanted an excuse not to go, but try as she would she couldn't think of a good one. And just when she felt that all was lost, her frock caught on a big nail by the kitchen door and there was a great criss-cross tear all along the front of the skirt. I assure you this was really an accident. So the others pitied her and went without her, for there was no time for her to change, because they were rather late already and had to hurry to the station to catch the train.

When they had gone, Bobbie put on her everyday frock, and went down to the railway. She did not go into the station, but she went along the line to the end of the platform where the engine is when the down train is alongside the platform – the place where there are a water tank and a long, limp, leather hose, like an elephant's trunk. She hid behind a bush on the other side of the railway. She had the toy engine done up in brown paper, and she waited patiently with it under her arm.

Then when the next train came in and stopped, Bobbie went across the metals of the up-line and stood beside the engine. She had never been so close to an engine before. It looked much larger and harder than she had expected, and it made her feel very small indeed, and, somehow, very soft – as if she could very, very easily be hurt rather badly.

'I know what silk-worms feel like now,' said Bobbie to herself.

The engine-driver and fireman did not see her. They

were leaning out of the other side, telling the Porter a tale about a dog and a leg of mutton.

'If you please,' said Roberta – but the engine was blowing off steam and no one heard her.

'If you please, Mr Engineer,' she spoke a little louder, but the Engine happened to speak at the same moment, and of course Roberta's soft little voice hadn't a chance.

It seemed to her that the only way would be to climb on to the engine and pull at their coats. The step was high, but she got her knee on it, and clambered into the cab; she stumbled and fell on hands and knees on the base of the great heap of coals that led up to the square opening in the tender. The engine was not above the weaknesses of its fellows; it was making a great deal more noise than there was the slightest need for. And just as Roberta fell on the coals, the engine-driver, who had turned without seeing her, started the engine, and when Bobbie had picked herself up, the train was moving – not fast, but much too fast for her to get off.

All sorts of dreadful thoughts came to her all together in one horrible flash. There were such things as express trains which went on, she supposed, for hundreds of miles without stopping. Suppose this should be one of them? How would she get home again? She had no money to pay for the return journey.

'And I've no business here. I'm an engine-burglar – that's what I am,' she thought. 'I shouldn't wonder if they could lock me up for this.' And the train was going faster and faster.

There was something in her throat that made it impossible for her to speak. She tried twice. The men had their backs to her. They were doing something to things that looked like taps.

Suddenly she put out her hand and caught hold of the nearest sleeve. The man turned with a start, and he and Roberta stood for a minute looking at each other in silence. Then the silence was broken by them both.

The man said, 'Here's a bloomin' go!' and Roberta burst into tears.

The other man said he was blooming well blest – or something like it – but though naturally surprised they were not exactly unkind.

'You're a naughty little girl, that's what you are,' said the fireman, but the engine-driver said:

'Darling little piece, I call her,' but they made her sit down on an iron seat in the cab and told her to stop crying and tell them what she meant by it.

She did stop, as soon as she could. One thing that helped her was the thought that Peter would give almost his ears to be in her place – on a real engine – really going. The children had often wondered whether any engine-driver could be found noble enough to take them for a ride on an engine – and now here she was. She dried her eyes and sniffed earnestly.

'Now, then,' said the fireman, 'out with it. What do you mean by it, eh?'

'Oh, please,' sniffed Bobbie, and stopped.

'Try again,' said the engine-driver, encouragingly.

Bobbie tried again.

'Please, Mr Engineer,' she said, 'I did call out to you from the line, but you didn't hear me – and I just climbed up to touch you on the arm – quite gently I meant to do it – and then I fell into the coals – and I am so sorry if I frightened you. Oh, don't be cross – oh, please don't!' She sniffed again.

'We ain't so much *cross*,' said the fireman, 'as interested like. It ain't every day a little gell tumbles into our coal bunker outer the sky, is it, Bill? What did you *do* it for – eh?'

'That's the point,' agreed the engine-driver; 'what did you do it *for*?'

Bobbie found that she had not quite stopped crying. The engine-driver patted her on the back and said: 'Here, cheer up, Mate. It ain't so bad as all that 'ere, I'll be bound.'

'I wanted,' said Bobbie, much cheered to find herself addressed as 'Mate' – 'I only wanted to ask you if you'd be so kind as to mend this.' She picked up the brown-paper parcel from among the coals and undid the string with hot, red fingers that trembled.

Her feet and legs felt the scorch of the engine fire, but her shoulders felt the wild chill rush of the air. The engine lurched and shook and rattled, and as they shot under a bridge the engine seemed to shout in her ears.

The fireman shovelled on coals.

Bobbie unrolled the brown paper and disclosed the toy engine.

'I thought,' she said wistfully, 'that perhaps you'd mend this for me – because you're an engineer, you know.'

The engine-driver said he was blowed if he wasn't blest.

'I'm blest if I ain't blowed,' remarked the fireman.

But the engine-driver took the little engine and looked at it – and the fireman ceased for an instant to shovel coal, and looked, too.

'It's like your precious cheek,' said the engine-driver – 'whatever made you think we'd be bothered tinkering penny toys?'

'I didn't mean it for precious cheek,' said Bobbie; 'only everybody that has anything to do with railways is so kind and good. I didn't think you'd mind. You don't really – do you?' she added, for she had seen a not unkindly wink pass between the two.

'My trade's driving of a engine, not mending her – especially such a hout-size in engines as this 'ere,' said Bill. 'An' 'ow are we a-goin' to get you back to your sorrowing friends and relations, and all be forgiven and forgotten?'

'If you'll put me down next time you stop,' said Bobbie, firmly, though her heart beat fiercely against her arm as she clasped her hands, 'and lend me the money for a third-class ticket, I'll pay you back – honour bright. I'm not a confidence trick like in the news-papers – really, I'm not.'

'You're a little lady, every inch,' said Bill, relenting suddenly and completely. 'We'll see you get home safe. An' about this engine – Jim – ain't you got ne'er a pal as can use a soldering iron? Seems to me that's about all the little bounder wants doing to it.'

'That's what Father said,' Bobbie explained eagerly. 'What's that for?'

She pointed to a little brass wheel that he had turned as he spoke.

'That's the injector.'

'In – what?'

'Injector to fill up the boiler.'

'Oh,' said Bobbie, mentally registering the fact to tell the others; 'that is interesting.'

'This 'ere's the automatic brake,' Bill went on,

flattered by her enthusiasm. 'You just move this 'ere little handle – do it with one finger, you can – and the train jolly soon stops. That's what they call the Power of Science in the newspapers.'

He showed her two little dials, like clock faces, and told her how one showed how much steam was going, and the other showed if the brake was working properly.

By the time she had seen him shut off steam with a big shining steel handle, Bobbie knew more about the inside working of an engine than she had ever thought there was to know, and Jim had promised that his second cousin's wife's brother should solder the toy engine, or Jim would know the reason why. Besides all the knowledge she had gained Bobbie felt that she and Bill and Jim were now friends for life, and that they had wholly and forever forgiven her for stumbling uninvited among the sacred coals of their tender.

At Stacklepoole Junction she parted from them with warm expressions of mutual regard. They handed her over to the guard of a returning train – a friend of theirs – and she had the joy of knowing what guards do in their secret fastnesses, and understood how when you pull the communication cord in railway carriages, a wheel goes round under the guard's nose and a loud bell rings in his ears. She asked the guard why his van smelt so fishy, and learned that he had to carry a lot of fish every day, and that the wetness in the hollows of the corrugated floor had all drained out of boxes full of plaice and cod and mackerel and soles and smelts.

Bobbie got home in time for tea, and she felt as though her mind would burst with all that had been put into it since she parted from the others. How she blessed the nail that had torn her frock!

'Where have you been?' asked the others.

'To the station, of course,' said Roberta. But she would not tell a word of her adventures till the day appointed, when she mysteriously led them to the station at the hour of 3.19's transit, and proudly introduced them to her friends, Bill and Jim. Jim's second cousin's wife's brother had not been unworthy of the sacred trust imposed in him. The toy engine was, literally, as good as new.

'Good-bye – oh, good-bye,' said Bobbie, just before the engine screamed *its* good-bye. 'I shall always, always love you – and Jim's second cousin's wife's brother as well!'

And as the three children went home up the hill, Peter hugging the engine, now quite its old self again, Bobbie told, with joyous leaps of the heart, the story of how she had been an Engine-burglar.

CHAPTER 5

Prisoners and Captives

It was one day when Mother had gone to Maidbridge. She had gone alone, but the children were to go to the station to meet her. And, loving the station as they did, it was only natural that they should be there a good hour before there was any chance of Mother's train arriving, even if the train were punctual, which was most unlikely. No doubt they would have been just as early, even if it had been a fine day, and the delights of woods and fields and rocks and rivers had been open to them. But it happened to be a very wet day and, for July, very cold. There was a wild wind that drove flocks of dark purple clouds across the sky 'like herds of dream-elephants,' as Phyllis said. And the rain stung sharply, so that the way to the station was finished at a run. Then the rain fell faster and harder, and beat slantwise against the windows of the booking office and of the chill place that had General Waiting Room on its door.

'It's like being in a besieged castle,' Phyllis said; 'look at the arrows of the foe striking against the battlements!'

'It's much more like a great garden-squirt,' said Peter.

They decided to wait on the up side, for the down platform looked very wet indeed, and the rain was driving right into the little black shelter where down-passengers have to wait for their trains.

The hour would be full of incident and of interest, for there would be two up trains and one down to look at before the one that should bring Mother back.

'Perhaps it'll have stopped raining by then,' said Bobbie; 'anyhow, I'm glad I brought Mother's waterproof and umbrella.'

They went into the desert spot labelled General Waiting Room, and the time passed pleasantly enough in a game of advertisements. You know the game, of course. It is something like dumb Crambo. The players take it in turns to go out, and then come back and look as like some advertisement as they can, and the others have to guess what advertisement it is meant to be. Bobbie came in and sat down under Mother's umbrella and made a sharp face, and everyone knew she was the fox who sits under the umbrella in the advertisement. Phyllis tried to make a Magic Carpet of Mother's waterproof, but it would not stand out stiff and raft-like as a Magic Carpet should, and nobody could guess it. Everyone thought Peter was carrying things a little too far when he blacked his face all over with coal-dust and struck a spidery attitude and said he was the blot that advertises somebody's Blue Black Writing Fluid.

It was Phyllis's turn again, and she was trying to look like the Sphinx that advertises What's-his-name's Personally Conducted Tours up the Nile when the sharp ting of the signal announced the up train. The children rushed out to see it pass. On its engine were the particular driver and fireman who were numbered among the children's dearest friends. Courtesies passed between them. Jim asked after the toy engine, and Bobbie pressed on his acceptance a moist, greasy package of toffee that she had made herself.

Charmed by this attention, the engine-driver consented to consider her request that some day he would take Peter for a ride on the engine.

'Stand back, Mates,' cried the engine-driver, suddenly, 'and horf she goes.'

And sure enough, off the train went. The children watched the tail-lights of the train till it disappeared round the curve of the line, and then turned to go back to the dusty freedom of the General Waiting Room and the joys of the advertisement game.

They expected to see just one or two people, the end of the procession of passengers who had given up their tickets and gone away. Instead, the platform round the door of the station had a dark blot round it, and the dark blot was a crowd of people.

'Oh!' cried Peter, with a thrill of joyous excitement, 'something's happened! Come on!'

They ran down the platform. When they got to the crowd, they could, of course, see nothing but the damp backs and elbows of the people on the crowd's outside. Everybody was talking at once. It was evident that something had happened.

'It's my belief he's nothing worse than a natural,' said a farmerish-looking person. Peter saw his red, clean-shaven face as he spoke.

'If you ask me, I should say it was a Police Court case,' said a young man with a black bag.

'Not it; the Infirmary more like –'

Then the voice of the Station Master was heard, firm and official:

'Now then – move along there. I'll attend to this, if *you* please.'

But the crowd did not move. And then came a voice that thrilled the children through and through. For it spoke in a foreign language. And what is more, it was a language that they had never heard. They had heard French spoken and German. Aunt Emma knew German, and tried to sing a song about *bedeuten* and *Zeiten* and *bin* and *Sinn*. Nor was it Latin. Peter had been in Latin for four terms.

It was some comfort, anyhow, to find that none of the crowd understood the foreign language any better than the children did.

'What's that he's saying?' asked the farmer, heavily.

'Sounds like French to me,' said the Station Master, who had once been in Boulogne for the day.

'It isn't French!' cried Peter.

'What is it, then?' asked more than one voice. The crowd fell back a little to see who had spoken, and Peter pressed forward, so that when the crowd closed up again, he was in the front rank.

'I don't know what it is,' said Peter, 'but it isn't French. I know that.' Then he saw what it was the crowd had for its centre. It was a man – the man, Peter did not doubt, who had spoken in that strange tongue. A man with long hair and wild eyes, with shabby clothes of a cut Peter had not seen before – a man whose hands and lips trembled, and who spoke again as his eyes fell on Peter.

'No, it's not French,' said Peter.

'Try him with French if you know so much about it,' said the farmer-man.

'*Parlay voo Frongsay?*' began Peter, boldly, and the next moment the crowd recoiled again, for the man with the wild eyes had left leaning against the wall, and had sprung forward and caught Peter's hands, and began to pour forth a flood of words which, though he could not understand a word of them, Peter knew the sound of.

'There!' said he, and turned, his hands still clasped in the hands of the strange shabby figure, to throw a glance of triumph at the crowd; 'there; *that's* French.'

'What does he say?'

'I don't know.' Peter was obliged to own it.

'Here,' said the Station Master again; 'you move on if you please. *I'll* deal with this case.'

A few of the more timid or less inquisitive travellers moved slowly and reluctantly away. And Phyllis and Bobbie got near to Peter. All three had been *taught* French at school. How deeply they now wished that they had *learned* it! Peter shook his head at the stranger, but he also shook his hands as warmly and looked at him as kindly as he could. A person in the crowd, after some hesitation, said suddenly, 'No comprenny!' and then, blushing deeply, backed out of the press and went away.

'Take him into your room,' whispered Bobbie to the Station Master. 'Mother can talk French. She'll be here by the next train from Maidbridge.'

The Station Master took the arm of the stranger, suddenly but not unkindly. But the man wrenched his arm away, and cowered back coughing and trembling and trying to push the Station Master away.

'Oh, don't!' said Bobbie; 'don't you see how frightened he is? He thinks you're going to shut him up. I know he does – look at his eyes!'

'They're like a fox's eyes when the beast's in a trap,' said the farmer.

'Oh, let me try!' Bobbie went on; 'I do really know one or two French words if I could only think of them.'

Sometimes, in moments of great need, we can do wonderful things – things that in ordinary life we could hardly even dream of doing. Bobbie had never been anywhere near the top of her French class, but she must have learned something without knowing it, for now, looking at those wild, hunted eyes, she actually remembered and, what is more, spoke, some French words. She said:

'*Vous attendre. Ma mère parlez Français. Nous –* what's the French for "being kind"?'

Nobody knew.

'*Bong* is "good",' said Phyllis.

'*Nous être bong pour vous.*'

I do not know whether the man understood her words, but he understood the touch of the hand she thrust into his, and the kindness of the other hand that stroked his shabby sleeve.

She pulled him gently towards the inmost sanctuary of the Station Master. The other children followed, and the Station Master shut the door in the face of the crowd which stood a little while in the booking office talking and looking at the fast-closed yellow door, and then by ones and twos went its way, grumbling.

Inside the Station Master's room Bobbie still held the stranger's hand and stroked his sleeve.

'Here's a go,' said the Station Master; 'no ticket – doesn't even know where he wants to go. I'm not sure now but what I ought to send for the police.'

'Oh, *don't*!' all the children pleaded at once. And suddenly Bobbie got between the others and the stranger, for she had seen that he was crying.

By a most unusual piece of good fortune she had a handkerchief in her pocket. By a still more uncommon accident the handkerchief was moderately clean. Standing in front of the stranger, she got the handkerchief and passed it to him so that the others did not see.

'Wait till Mother comes,' Phyllis was saying: 'she does speak French beautifully. You'd just love to hear her.'

'I'm sure he hasn't done anything like you're sent to prison for,' said Peter.

'Looks like without visible means to me,' said the Station Master. 'Well, I don't mind giving him the benefit of the doubt till your Mamma comes. I *should* like to know what nation's got the credit of *him*, that I should.'

Then Peter had an idea. He pulled an envelope out of his pocket, and showed that it was half full of foreign stamps. 'Look here,' he said, 'let's show him these –'

Bobbie looked and saw that the stranger had dried his eyes with her handkerchief. So she said: 'All right.'

They showed him an Italian stamp, and pointed from him to it and back again, and made signs of questions with their eyebrows. He shook his head. Then they showed him a Norwegian stamp – the common blue kind it was – and again he signed No. Then they showed him a Spanish one, and at that he took the envelope from Peter's hand and searched among the stamps with a hand that trembled. The hand that he reached out at last, with a gesture of one answering a question, contained a *Russian* stamp.

'He's Russian,' cried Peter, 'or else he's like "the man who was" – in Kipling, you know.'

The train from Maidbridge was signalled.

'I'll stay with him till you bring Mother in,' said Bobbie.

'You're not afraid, Missie?'

'Oh, no,' said Bobbie, looking at the stranger, as she might have looked at a strange dog of doubtful temper. 'You wouldn't hurt me, would you?'

She smiled at him, and he smiled back, a queer crooked smile. And then he laughed again. And the heavy rattling swish of the incoming train swept past, and the Station Master and Peter and Phyllis went out to meet it. Bobbie was still holding the stranger's hand when they came back with Mother.

The Russian rose and bowed very ceremoniously.

Then Mother spoke in French, and he replied, haltingly at first, but presently in longer and longer sentences.

The children, watching his face and Mother's, knew that he was telling her things that made her angry and pitying, and sorry and indignant all at once.

'Well, Mum, what's it all about?' The Station Master could not restrain his curiosity any longer.

'Oh,' said Mother, 'it's all right. He's a Russian, and he's lost his ticket. And I'm afraid he's very ill. If you don't mind, I'll take him home with me now. He's really quite worn out. I'll run down and tell you all about him tomorrow.'

'I hope you won't find you're taking home a frozen viper,' said the Station Master, doubtfully.

'Oh, no,' Mother said brightly, and she smiled; 'I'm quite sure I'm not. Why, he's a great man in his own country, writes books – beautiful books – I've read some of them; but I'll tell you all about it tomorrow.'

She spoke again in French to the Russian, and everyone could see the surprise and pleasure and gratitude in his eyes. He got up and politely bowed to the Station Master, and offered his arm most ceremoniously to Mother. She took it, but anybody could have seen that she was helping him along, and not he her.

'You girls run home and light a fire in the sitting-room,' Mother said, 'and Peter had better go for the Doctor.'

But it was Bobbie who went for the Doctor.

'I hate to tell you,' she said breathlessly when she came upon him in his shirt sleeves weeding his pansy-bed, 'but Mother's got a very shabby Russian, and I'm sure he'll have to belong to your Club. I'm certain he hasn't got any money. We found him at the station.'

'Found him! Was he lost, then?' asked the Doctor, reaching for his coat.

'Yes,' said Bobbie, unexpectedly, 'that's just what he was. He's been telling Mother the sad, sweet story of his life in French; and she said would you be kind enough to come directly if you were at home. He has a dreadful cough, and he's been crying.'

The Doctor smiled.

'Oh, don't,' said Bobbie; 'please don't. You wouldn't if you'd seen him. I never saw a man cry before. You don't know what it's like.'

Dr Forrest wished then that he hadn't smiled.

When Bobbie and the Doctor got to Three Chimneys, the Russian was sitting in the armchair that had been Father's, stretching his feet to the blaze of a bright wood fire, and sipping the tea Mother had made him.

'The man seems worn out, mind and body,' was what the Doctor said; 'the cough's bad, but there's nothing that can't be cured. He ought to go straight to bed, though – and let him have a fire at night.'

'I'll make one in my room; it's the only one with a fireplace,' said Mother. She did, and presently the Doctor helped the stranger to bed.

There was a big black trunk in Mother's room that none of the children had ever seen unlocked. Now, when she had lighted the fire, she unlocked it and took some clothes out – men's clothes – and set them to air by the newly lighted fire. Bobbie, coming in with more wood for the fire, saw the mark on the night-shirt, and looked over to the open trunk. All the things she could see were men's clothes. And the name marked on the shirt was Father's name. Then Father hadn't taken his clothes with him. And that night-shirt was one of Father's new ones. Bobbie remembered its being made, just before Peter's birthday. Why hadn't Father taken his clothes? Bobbie slipped from the room. As she went she heard the key turned in the lock of the trunk. Her heart was beating horribly. *Why* hadn't Father taken his clothes? When Mother came out of the room, Bobbie flung tightly clasping arms round her waist, and whispered:

'Mother – Daddy isn't – isn't *dead*, is he?'

'My darling, no! What makes you think of anything so horrible?'

'I – I don't know,' said Bobbie, angry with herself, but still clinging to that resolution of hers, not to see anything that Mother didn't mean her to see.

Mother gave her a hurried hug. 'Daddy was quite, *quite* well when I heard from him last,' she said, 'and he'll come back to us some day. Don't fancy such horrible things, darling!'

Later on, when the Russian stranger had been made comfortable for the night, Mother came into the girls' room. She was to sleep there in Phyllis's bed, and Phyllis was to have a mattress on the floor, a most amusing adventure for Phyllis. Directly Mother came in, two white figures started up, and two eager voices called:

'Now, Mother, tell us all about the Russian gentleman.'

A white shape hopped into the room. It was Peter, dragging his quilt behind him like the tail of a white peacock.

'We have been patient,' he said, 'and I had to bite my tongue not to go to sleep, and I just nearly went to sleep and I bit too hard, and it hurts ever so. *Do* tell us. Make a nice long story of it.'

'I can't make a long story of it tonight,' said Mother; 'I'm very tired.'

Bobbie knew by her voice that Mother had been crying, but the others didn't know.

'Well, make it as long as you can,' said Phil, and Bobbie got her arms round Mother's waist and snuggled close to her.

'Well, it's a story long enough to make a whole book of. He's a writer; he's written wonderful books. In Russia at the time of the Tsar one dared not say anything about the rich people doing wrong, or about the things that ought to be done to make poor people better and happier. If one did one was sent to prison.'

'But they *can't*,' said Peter; 'people only go to prison when they've done wrong.'

'Or when Judges *think* they've done wrong,' said Mother. 'Yes, that's so in England. But in Russia it was different. And he wrote a beautiful book about poor people and how to help them. I've read it. There's nothing in it but goodness and kindness. And they sent him to prison for it. He was three years in a horrible dungeon, with hardly any light, and all damp and dreadful. In prison all alone for three years.'

Mother's voice trembled a little and stopped suddenly.

'But Mother,' said Peter, 'that can't be true *now*. It sounds like something out of a history book – the Inquisition, or something.'

'It *was* true,' said Mother; 'it's all horribly true. Well then they took him out and sent him to Siberia, a convict chained to other convicts – wicked men who'd done all sorts of crimes – a long chain of them, and they walked, and walked, and walked, for days and weeks, till he thought they'd never stop walking. And overseers went behind them with whips – yes, whips – to beat them if they got tired. And some of them went lame, and some fell down, and when they couldn't get up and go on, they beat them, and then left them to die. Oh, it's all too terrible! And at last he got to the mines, and he was condemned to stay there for life – for life, just for writing a good, noble, splendid book.'

'How did he get away?'

'When the war came, some of the Russian prisoners were allowed to volunteer as soldiers. And he volunteered. But he deserted at the first chance he got and –'

'But that's very cowardly, isn't it,' – said Peter – 'to desert? Especially when it's war.'

'Do you think he owed anything to a country that had done *that* to him? If he did, he owed more to his wife and children. He didn't know what had become of them.'

'Oh,' cried Bobbie, 'he had *them* to think about and be miserable about *too*, then, all the time he was in prison?'

'Yes, he had them to think about and be miserable about all the time he was in prison. For anything he knew they might have been sent to prison, too. They did those things in Russia. But while he was in the mines some friends managed to get a message to him that his wife and children had escaped and come to England. So when he deserted he came here to look for them.'

'Had he got their address?' said practical Peter.

'No; just England. He was going to London, and he thought he had to change at our station, and then he found he'd lost his ticket and his purse.'

'Oh, *do* you think he'll find them? – I mean his wife and children, not the ticket and things.'

'I hope so. Oh, I hope and pray that he'll find his wife and children again.'

Even Phyllis now perceived that Mother's voice was very unsteady.

'Why, Mother,' she said, 'how very sorry you seem to be for him!'

Mother didn't answer for a minute. Then she just said, 'Yes,' and then she seemed to be thinking. The children were quiet.

Presently she said, 'Dears, when you say your prayers, I think you might ask God to show His pity upon all prisoners and captives.'

'To show His pity,' Bobbie repeated slowly, 'upon all prisoners and captives. Is that right, Mother?'

'Yes,' said Mother, 'upon all prisoners and captives. All prisoners and captives.'

CHAPTER 6

Saviours of the Train

The Russian gentleman was better the next day, and the day after that better still, and on the third day he was well enough to come into the garden. A basket chair was put for him and he sat there, dressed in clothes of Father's which were too big for him. But when Mother had hemmed up the ends of the sleeves and the trousers, the clothes did well enough. His was a kind face now that it was no longer tired and frightened, and he smiled at the children whenever he saw them. They wished very much that he could speak English. Mother wrote several letters to people she thought might know whereabouts in England a Russian gentleman's wife and family might possibly be; not to the people she used to know before she came to live at Three Chimneys – she never wrote to any of them – but strange people – Members of Parliament and Editors of Papers, and Secretaries of Societies.

And she did not do much of her story-writing, only corrected proofs as she sat in the sun near the Russian, and talked to him every now and then.

The children wanted very much to show how kindly they felt to this man who had been sent to prison and to Siberia just for writing a beautiful book about poor people. They could smile at him, of course; they could and they did. But if you smile too constantly, the smile is apt to get fixed like the smile of the hyena. And then it no longer looks friendly, but simply silly. So they tried other ways, and brought him flowers till the place where he sat was surrounded by little fading bunches of clover and roses and Canterbury bells.

And then Phyllis had an idea. She beckoned mysteriously to the others and drew them into the back yard, and there, in a concealed spot, between the pump and the water-butt, she said:

'You remember Perks promising me the very first strawberries out of his own garden?' Perks, you will recollect, was the Porter. 'Well, I should think they're ripe now. Let's go down and see.'

Mother had been down as she had promised to tell the Station Master the story of the Russian Prisoner. But even the charms of the railway had been unable to tear the children away from the neighbourhood of the interesting stranger. So they had not been to the station for three days.

They went now.

And, to their surprise and distress, were very coldly received by Perks.

''Ighly honoured, I'm sure,' he said when they peeped in at the door of the Porters' Room. And he went on reading his newspaper.

There was an uncomfortable silence.

'Oh, dear,' said Bobbie, with a sigh, 'I do believe you're *cross*.'

'What, me? Not me!' said Perks loftily; 'it ain't nothing to me.'

'*What* ain't nothing to you?' said Peter, too anxious and alarmed to change the form of words.

'Nothing ain't nothing. What 'appens either 'ere or elsewhere,' said Perks; 'if you likes to 'ave your secrets, 'ave 'em and welcome. That's what I say.'

The secret-chamber of each heart was rapidly examined during the pause that followed. Three heads were shaken.

'We haven't got any secrets from *you*,' said Bobbie at last.

'Maybe you 'ave, and maybe you 'aven't,' said Perks; 'it ain't nothing to me. And I wish you all a very good afternoon.' He held up the paper between him and them and went on reading.

'Oh, *don't!*' said Phyllis, in despair; 'this is truly dreadful! Whatever it is, do tell us.'

'We didn't mean to do it whatever it was.'

No answer. The paper was refolded and Perks began on another column.

'Look here,' said Peter, suddenly, 'it's not fair. Even people who do crimes aren't punished without being told what it's for – as once they were in Russia.'

'I don't know nothing about Russia.'

'Oh, yes, you do, when Mother came down on purpose to tell you and Mr Gills all about *our* Russian.'

'Can't you fancy it?' said Perks, indignantly; 'don't you see 'im a-asking of me to step into 'is room and take a chair and listen to what 'er Ladyship 'as to say?'

'Do you mean to say you've not heard?'

'Not so much as a breath. I did go as far as to put a question. And he shuts me up like a rat-trap. "Affairs of State, Perks," says he. But I did think one o' you would 'a' nipped down to tell me – you're here sharp enough when you want to get anything out of old Perks' – Phyllis flushed purple at the thought of the strawberries – 'information about locomotives or signals or the likes,' said Perks.

'We didn't know you didn't know.'

'We thought Mother had told you.'

'We wanted to tell you only we thought it would be stale news.'

The three spoke all at once.

Perks said it was all very well, and still held up the paper. Then Phyllis suddenly snatched it away, and threw her arms round his neck.

'Oh, let's kiss and be friends,' she said; 'we'll say we're sorry first, if you like, but we really didn't know that you didn't know.'

'We are so sorry,' said the others.

And Perks at last consented to accept their apologies.

Then they got him to come out and sit in the sun on the green railway bank, where the grass was quite hot to touch, and there, sometimes speaking one at a time, and sometimes all together, they told the Porter the story of the Russian Prisoner.

'Well, I must say,' said Perks; but he did not say it – whatever it was.

'Yes, it is pretty awful, isn't it?' said Peter, 'and I don't wonder you were curious about who the Russian was.'

'I wasn't curious, not so much as interested,' said the Porter.

'Well, I do think Mr Gills might have told you about it. It was horrid of him.'

'I don't keep no down on 'im for that, Missie,' said the Porter; 'cos why? I see 'is reasons. 'E wouldn't want to give away 'is own side with a tale like that 'ere. It ain't human nature. A man's got to stand up for his own side whatever they does. That's what it means by Party Politics. I should 'a' done the same myself if that long-'aired chap 'ad 'a' been a Jap.'

'But the Japs didn't do cruel, wicked things like that,' said Bobbie.

'P'r'aps not,' said Perks, cautiously; 'still you can't be sure with foreigners. My own belief is they're all tarred with the same brush.'

'Then why were you on the side of the Japs?' Peter asked.

'Well, you see, you must take one side or the other. Same as with Liberals and Conservatives. The great thing is to take your side and then stick to it, whatever happens.'

A signal sounded.

'There's the 3.14 up,' said Perks. 'You lie low till she's through, and then we'll go up along to my place, and see if there's any of them strawberries ripe what I told you about.'

'If there are any ripe, and you *do* give them to me,' said Phyllis, 'you won't mind if I give them to the poor Russian, will you?'

Perks narrowed his eyes and then raised his eyebrows.

'So it was them strawberries you come down for this afternoon, eh?' said he.

This was an awkward moment for Phyllis. To say 'yes' would seem rude and greedy, and unkind to Perks. But she knew if she said 'no', she would not be pleased with herself afterwards. So –

'Yes,' she said, 'it was.'

'Well done!' said the Porter; 'speak the truth and shame the –'

'But we'd have come down the very next day if we'd known you hadn't heard the story,' Phyllis added hastily.

'I believe you, Missie,' said Perks, and sprang across the line six feet in front of the advancing train.

The girls hated to see him do this, but Peter liked it. It was so exciting.

The Russian gentleman was so delighted with the strawberries that the three racked their brains to find some other surprise for him. But all the racking did not bring out any idea more novel than wild cherries. And this idea occurred to them next morning. They had seen the blossom on the trees in the spring, and they knew where to look for wild cherries now that cherry time was here. The trees grew all up and along the rocky face of the cliff out of which the mouth of the tunnel opened. There were all sorts of trees there, birches and beeches and baby oaks and hazels, and among them the cherry blossom had shone like snow and silver.

The mouth of the tunnel was some way from Three Chimneys, so Mother let them take their lunch with them in a basket. And the basket would do to bring the cherries back in if they found any. She also lent them her silver watch so that they should not be late for tea. Peter's Waterbury had taken it into its head not to go since the day when Peter dropped it into the water-butt. And they started. When they got to the top of the cutting, they leaned over the fence and looked down to where the railway lines lay at the bottom of what, as Phyllis said, was exactly like a mountain gorge.

'If it wasn't for the railway at the bottom, it would

be as though the foot of man had never been there, wouldn't it?'

The sides of the cutting were of grey stone, very roughly hewn. Indeed, the top part of the cutting had been a little natural glen that had been cut deeper to bring it down to the level of the tunnel's mouth. Among the rocks, grass and flowers grew, and seeds dropped by birds in the crannies of the stone had taken root and grown into bushes and trees that overhung the cutting. Near the tunnel was a flight of steps leading down to the line – just wooden bars roughly fixed into the earth – a very steep and narrow way, more like a ladder than a stair.

'We'd better get down,' said Peter; 'I'm sure the cherries would be quite easy to get at from the side of the steps. You remember it was there we picked the cherry blossoms that we put on the rabbit's grave.'

So they went along the fence towards the little swing gate that is at the top of these steps. And they were almost at the gate when Bobbie said:

'Hush. Stop! What's that?'

'That' was a very odd noise indeed – a soft noise, but quite plainly to be heard through the sound of the wind in the branches, and the hum and whir of the telegraph wires. It was a sort of rustling, whispering sound. As they listened it stopped and then it began again.

And this time it did not stop, but it grew louder and more rustling and rumbling.

'Look' – cried Peter, suddenly – 'the tree over there!'

The tree he pointed at was one of those that have rough grey leaves and white flowers. The berries, when they come, are bright scarlet, but if you pick them, they disappoint you by turning black before you get them home. And, as Peter pointed, the tree was moving – not just the way trees ought to move when the wind blows through them, but all in one piece, as though it were a live creature and were walking down the side of the cutting.

'It's moving!' cried Bobbie. 'Oh, look! and so are the others. It's like the woods in *Macbeth.*'

'It's magic,' said Phyllis, breathlessly. 'I always knew the railway was enchanted.'

It really did seem a little like magic. For all the trees for about twenty yards of the opposite bank seemed to be slowly walking down towards the railway line, the tree with the grey leaves bringing up the rear like some old shepherd driving a flock of green sheep.

'What is it? Oh, what is it?' said Phyllis; 'it's much too magic for me. I don't like it. Let's go home.'

But Bobbie and Peter clung fast to the rail and watched breathlessly. And Phyllis made no movement towards going home by herself.

The trees moved on and on. Some stones and loose earth fell down and rattled on the railway metals far below.

'It's *all* coming down,' Peter tried to say, but he found there was hardly any voice to say it with. And, indeed, just as he spoke, the great rock, on the top of which the walking trees were, leaned slowly forward. The trees, ceasing to walk, stood still and shivered. Leaning with the rock, they seemed to hesitate a moment, and then rock and trees and grass and bushes, with a rushing sound, slipped right away from the face of the cutting and fell on the line with a blundering crash that could have been heard half a mile off. A cloud of dust rose up.

'Oh,' said Peter, in awestruck tones, 'isn't it exactly like when coals come in? – if there wasn't any roof to the cellar and you could see down.'

'Look what a great mound it's made!' said Bobbie.

'Yes, it's right across the down line,' said Phyllis.

'That'll take some sweeping up,' said Bobbie.

'Yes,' said Peter slowly. He was still leaning on the fence.

'Yes,' he said again, still more slowly.

Then he stood upright.

'The 11.29 down hasn't gone by yet. We must let them know at the station, or there'll be a most frightful accident.'

'Let's run,' said Bobbie, and began.

But Peter cried, 'Come back!' and looked at Mother's watch. He was very prompt and business-like, and his face looked whiter than they had ever seen it.

'No time,' he said; 'it's ten miles away, and it's past eleven.'

'Couldn't we,' suggested Phyllis, breathlessly, 'couldn't we climb up a telegraph post and do something to the wires?'

'We don't know how,' said Peter.

'They do it in war,' said Phyllis; 'I know I've heard of it.'

'They only *cut* them, silly,' said Peter, 'and that doesn't do any good. And we couldn't cut them even if we got up, and we couldn't get up. If we had anything red, we could go down on the line and wave it.'

'But the train wouldn't see us till it got round the corner, and then it could see the mound just as well as us,' said Phyllis; 'better, because it's much bigger than us.'

'If we only had something red,' Peter repeated, 'we could go round the corner and wave to the train.'

'We might wave, anyway.'

'They'd only think it was just *us*, as usual. We've waved so often before. Anyway, let's get down.'

They got down the steep stairs. Bobbie was pale and shivering. Peter's face looked thinner than usual. Phyllis was red-faced and damp with anxiety.

'Oh, how hot I am!' she said; 'and I thought it was going to be cold; I wish we hadn't put on our –' she stopped short, and then ended in quite a different tone – 'our flannel petticoats.'

Bobbie turned at the bottom of the stairs.

'Oh, yes,' she cried, '*they're* red! Let's take them off.'

They did, and with the petticoats rolled up under their arms, ran along the railway, skirting the newly fallen mound of stones and rock and earth, and bent, crushed, twisted trees. They ran at their best pace. Peter led, but the girls were not far behind. They reached the corner that hid the mound from the straight line of railway that ran half a mile without curve or corner.

'Now,' said Peter, taking hold of the largest flannel petticoat.

'You're not' – Phyllis faltered – 'you're not going to *tear* them?'

'Shut up,' said Peter, with brief sternness.

'Oh, yes,' said Bobbie, 'tear them into little bits if you like. Don't you see, Phil, if we can't stop the train, there'll be a real live accident, with people *killed*. Oh, horrible! Here, Peter, you'll never tear it through the band!'

She took the red flannel petticoat from him and tore

it off an inch from the band. Then she tore the other in the same way.

'There!' said Peter, tearing in his turn. He divided each petticoat into three pieces. 'Now, we've got six flags.' He looked at the watch again. 'And we've got seven minutes. We must have flagstaffs.'

The knives given to boys are, for some odd reason, seldom of the kind of steel that keeps sharp. The young saplings had to be broken off. Two came up by the roots. The leaves were stripped from them.

'We must cut holes in the flags, and run the sticks through the holes,' said Peter. And the holes were cut. The knife was sharp enough to cut flannel with. Two of the flags were set up in heaps of loose stones beneath the sleepers of the down line. Then Phyllis and Roberta took each a flag, and stood ready to wave it as soon as the train came in sight.

'I shall have the other two myself,' said Peter, 'because it was my idea to wave something red.'

'They're our petticoats, though,' Phyllis was beginning, but Bobbie interrupted

'Oh, what does it matter who waves what, if we can only save the train?'

Perhaps Peter had not rightly calculated the number of minutes it would take the 11.29 to get from the station to the place where they were, or perhaps the train was late. Anyway, it seemed a very long time that they waited.

Phyllis grew impatient. 'I expect the watch is wrong, and the train's gone by,' said she.

Peter relaxed the heroic attitude he had chosen to show off his two flags. And Bobbie began to feel sick with suspense.

It seemed to her that they had been standing there

for hours and hours, holding those silly little red flannel flags that no one would ever notice. The train wouldn't care. It would go rushing by them and tear round the corner and go crashing into that awful mound. And everyone would be killed. Her hands grew very cold and trembled so that she could hardly hold the flag. And then came the distant rumble and hum of the metals, and a puff of white steam showed far away along the stretch of line.

'Stand firm,' said Peter, 'and wave like mad! When it gets to that big furze bush step back, but go on waving! Don't stand *on* the line, Bobbie!'

The train came rattling along very, very fast.

'They don't see us! They won't see us! It's all no good!' cried Bobbie.

The two little flags on the line swayed as the nearing train shook and loosened the heaps of loose stones that held them up. One of them slowly leaned over and fell on the line. Bobbie jumped forward and caught it up, and waved it; her hands did not tremble now.

It seemed that the train came on as fast as ever. It was very near now.

'Keep off the line, you silly cuckoo!' said Peter, fiercely.

'It's no good,' Bobbie said again.

'Stand back!' cried Peter, suddenly, and he dragged Phyllis back by the arm.

But Bobbie cried, 'Not yet, not yet!' and waved her two flags right over the line. The front of the engine looked black and enormous. Its voice was loud and harsh.

'Oh, stop, stop, stop!' cried Bobbie. No one heard her. At least Peter and Phyllis didn't, for the oncoming rush of the train covered the sound of her voice with a mountain of sound. But afterwards she used to wonder whether the engine itself had not heard her. It seemed almost as though it had – for it slackened swiftly, slackened and stopped, not twenty yards from the place where Bobbie's two flags waved over the line. She saw the great black engine stop dead, but somehow she could not stop waving the flags. And when the driver and the fireman had got off the engine and Peter and Phyllis had gone to meet them and pour out their excited tale of the awful mound just round the corner, Bobbie still waved the flags but more and more feebly and jerkily.

When the others turned towards her she was lying across the line with her hands flung forward and still gripping the sticks of the little red flannel flags.

The engine-driver picked her up, carried her to the train, and laid her on the cushions of a first-class carriage.

'Gone right off in a faint,' he said, 'poor little woman. And no wonder. I'll just 'ave a look at this 'ere mound of yours, and then we'll run you back to the station and get her seen to.'

It was horrible to see Bobbie lying so white and quiet, with her lips blue, and parted.

'I believe that's what people look like when they're dead,' whispered Phyllis.

'*Don't!*' said Peter, sharply.

They sat by Bobbie on the blue cushions and the train ran back. Before it reached their station Bobbie sighed and opened her eyes, and rolled herself over and began to cry. This cheered the others wonderfully. They had seen her cry before, but they had never seen her faint, nor anyone else, for the matter of that. They had not known what to do when she was fainting, but now she was only crying they could thump her on the back and tell her not to, just as they always did. And presently, when she stopped crying, they were able to laugh at her for being such a coward as to faint.

When the station was reached, the three were the heroes of an agitated meeting on the platform.

The praises they got for their 'prompt action', their 'common sense', their 'ingenuity', were enough to have turned anybody's head. Phyllis enjoyed herself thoroughly. She had never been a real heroine before, and the feeling was delicious. Peter's ears got very red. Yet he, too, enjoyed himself. Only Bobbie wished they all wouldn't. She wanted to get away.

'You'll hear from the Company about this, I expect,' said the Station Master.

Bobbie wished she might never hear of it again. She pulled at Peter's jacket.

'Oh, come away, come away! I want to go home,' she said.

So they went. And as they went Station Master and Porter and guards and driver and fireman and passengers sent up a cheer.

'Oh, listen,' cried Phyllis; 'that's for *us*!'

'Yes,' said Peter. 'I say, I am glad I thought about something red and waving it.'

'How lucky we *did* put on our red flannel petticoats!' said Phyllis.

Bobbie said nothing. She was thinking of the horrible mound, and the trustful train rushing towards it.

'And it was *us* that saved them,' said Peter.

'How dreadful if they had all been killed!' said Phyllis; 'wouldn't it, Bobbie?'

'We never got any cherries, after all,' said Bobbie.

The others thought her rather heartless.

CHAPTER 7

For Valour

I hope you don't mind my telling you a good deal about Roberta. The fact is I am growing very fond of her. The more I observe her the more I love her. And I notice all sorts of things about her that I like.

For instance, she was quite oddly anxious to make other people happy. And she could keep a secret, a tolerably rare accomplishment. Also she had the power of silent sympathy. That sounds rather dull, I know, but it's not so dull as it sounds. It just means that a person is able to know that you are unhappy, and to love you extra on that account, without bothering you by telling you all the time how sorry she is for you. That was what Bobbie was like. She knew that Mother was unhappy – and that Mother had not told her the reason. So she just loved Mother more and never said a single word that could let Mother know how earnestly her little girl wondered what Mother was unhappy about. This needs practice. It is not so easy as you might think.

Whatever happened – and all sorts of nice, pleasant ordinary things happened – such as picnics, games, and buns for tea, Bobbie always had these thoughts at the back of her mind. 'Mother's unhappy. Why? I don't know. She doesn't want me to know. I won't try to find out. But she is unhappy. Why? I don't know. She doesn't –' and so on, repeating and repeating like a tune that you don't know the stopping part of.

The Russian gentleman still took up a good deal of everybody's thoughts. All the Editors and Secretaries of Societies and Members of Parliament had answered Mother's letters as politely as they knew how; but none of them could tell where the wife and children of Mr Szczepansky would be likely to be. (Did I tell you that the Russian's very Russian name was that?)

Bobbie had another quality which you will hear differently described by different people. Some of them call it interfering in other people's business – and some call it 'helping lame dogs over stiles', and some call it 'loving-kindness'. It just means trying to help people.

She racked her brains to think of some way of helping the Russian gentleman to find his wife and children. He had learned a few words of English now. He could say 'Good morning' and 'Good night', and 'Please', and 'Thank you', and 'Pretty', when the children brought him flowers, and 'Ver' good', when they asked him how he had slept.

The way he smiled when he 'said his English', was, Bobbie felt, 'just too sweet for anything'. She used to think of his face because she fancied it would help her to some way of helping him. But it did not. Yet his being there cheered her because she saw that it made Mother happier.

'She likes to have someone to be good to, even beside us,' said Bobbie. 'And I know she hated to let him have

Father's clothes. But I suppose it "hurt nice", or she wouldn't have.'

For many and many a night after the day when she and Peter and Phyllis had saved the train from wreck by waving their little red flannel flags, Bobbie used to wake screaming and shivering, seeing again that horrible mound, and the poor, dear trustful engine rushing on towards it – just thinking that it was doing its swift duty, and that everything was clear and safe. And then a warm thrill of pleasure used to run through her at the remembrance of how she and Peter and Phyllis and the red flannel petticoats had really saved everybody.

One morning a letter came. It was addressed to Peter and Bobbie and Phyllis. They opened it with enthusiastic curiosity, for they did not often get letters.

The letter said:

> *Dear Sir, and Ladies – It is proposed to make a small presentation to you, in commemoration of your prompt and courageous action in warning the train on the – inst., and thus averting what must, humanly speaking, have been a terrible accident. The presentation will take place at the – Station at three o'clock on the 30 inst., if this time and place will be convenient to you.*
> *Yours faithfully,*
> *Jabez Inglewood*
> *Secretary, Great Northern and Southern Railway Co.*

There never had been a prouder moment in the lives of the three children. They rushed to Mother with the letter, and she also felt proud and said so, and this made the children happier than ever.

'But if the presentation is money, you must say, "Thank you, but we'd rather not take it,"' said Mother. 'I'll wash your Indian muslins at once,' she added. 'You must look tidy on an occasion like this.'

'Phil and I can wash them,' said Bobbie, 'if you'll iron them, Mother.'

Washing is rather fun. I wonder whether you've ever done it? This particular washing took place in the back kitchen, which had a stone floor and a very big stone sink under its window.

'Let's put the bath on the sink,' said Phyllis; 'then we can pretend we're out-of-doors washer-women like Mother saw in France.'

'But they were washing in the cold river,' said Peter, his hands in his pockets, 'not in hot water.'

'This is a *hot* river, then,' said Phyllis; 'lend a hand with the bath, there's a dear.'

'I should like to see a deer lending a hand,' said Peter, but he lent his.

'Now to rub and scrub and scrub and rub,' said Phyllis, hopping joyously about as Bobbie carefully carried the heavy kettle from the kitchen fire.

'Oh, no!' said Bobbie, greatly shocked; 'you don't rub muslin. You put the boiled soap in the hot water and make it all frothy-lathery – and then you shake the muslin and squeeze it, ever so gently, and all the dirt comes out. It's only clumsy things like tablecloths and sheets that have to be rubbed.'

The lilac and the Gloire de Dijon roses outside the window swayed in the soft breeze.

'It's a nice drying day – that's one thing,' said

Bobbie, feeling very grown up. 'Oh, I do wonder what wonderful feelings we shall have when we *wear* the Indian muslin dresses!'

'Yes, so do I,' said Phyllis, shaking and squeezing the muslin in quite a professional manner.

'*Now* we squeeze out the soapy water. No – we mustn't twist them – and then rinse them. I'll hold them while you and Peter empty the bath and get clean water.'

'A presentation! That means presents,' said Peter, as his sisters, having duly washed the pegs and wiped the line, hung up the dresses to dry. 'Whatever will it be?'

'It might be anything,' said Phyllis; 'what I've always wanted is a baby elephant – but I suppose they wouldn't know that.'

'Suppose it was gold models of steam-engines?' said Bobbie.

'Or a big model of the scene of the prevented accident,' suggested Peter, 'with a little model train, and dolls dressed like us and the engine-driver and fireman and passengers.'

'Do you *like*,' said Bobbie, doubtfully, drying her hands on the rough towel that hung on a roller at the back of the scullery door – 'do you *like* us being rewarded for saving a train?'

'Yes, I do,' said Peter, downrightly; 'and don't you try to come it over us that you don't like it, too. Because I know you do.'

'Yes,' said Bobbie, doubtfully, 'I know I do. But oughtn't we to be satisfied with just having done it, and not ask for anything more?'

'Who did ask for anything more, silly?' said her brother. 'Victoria Cross soldiers don't *ask* for it; but they're glad enough to get it all the same. Perhaps it'll be medals. Then, when I'm very old indeed, I shall show them to my grandchildren and say, "We only did our duty," and they'll be awfully proud of me.'

'You have to be married,' warned Phyllis, 'or you don't have any grandchildren.'

'I suppose I shall *have* to be married some day,' said Peter, 'but it will be an awful bother having her round all the time. I'd like to marry a lady who had trances, and only woke up once or twice a year.'

'Just to say you were the light of her life and then go to sleep again. Yes. That wouldn't be bad,' said Bobbie.

'When *I* get married,' said Phyllis, 'I shall want him to want me to be awake all the time, so that I can hear him say how nice I am.'

'I think it would be nice,' said Bobbie, 'to marry someone very poor, and then you'd do all the work and he'd love you most frightfully, and see the blue wood smoke curling up among the trees from the domestic hearth as he came home from work every night. I say – we've got to answer that letter and say that the time and place *will* be convenient to us. There's the soap, Peter. We're both as clean as clean. That pink book of writing paper you had on your birthday, Phil.'

It took some time to arrange what should be said. Mother had gone back to her writing, and several sheets of pink paper with scalloped gilt edges and green four-leaved shamrocks in the corner were spoiled before the three had decided what to say. Then each made a copy and signed it with its own name.

The threefold letter ran:

> *Dear Mr Jabez Inglewood, – Thank you very*
> *much. We did not want to be rewarded but*
> *only to save the train, but we are glad you*
> *think so and thank you very much. The time*
> *and place you say will be quite convenient to*
> *us. Thank you very much.*
> *Your affecate little friend,*
> *Then came the name, and after it:*
> *P.S. Thank you very much.*

'Washing is much easier than ironing,' said Bobbie, taking the clean dresses off the line. 'I do love to see things come clean. Oh – I don't know how we shall wait till it's time to know what presentation they're going to present!'

When at last – it seemed a very long time after – it was *the* day, the three children went down to the station at the proper time. And everything that happened was so odd that it seemed like a dream. The Station Master came out to meet them – in his best clothes, as Peter noticed at once – and led them into the waiting room where once they had played the advertisement game. It looked quite different now. A carpet had been put down – and there were pots of roses on the mantelpiece and on the window ledges, green branches stuck up, like holly and laurel at Christmas, over the framed advertisements of Cook's Tours and the Beauties of Devon and the Paris-Lyons Railway. There were quite a number of people there besides the Porter – two or three ladies in smart dresses, and quite a crowd of gentlemen in high hats and frock coats – besides everybody who belonged to the station. They recognized several people who had been in the train on the red-flannel-petticoat day. Best of all, their own old gentleman was there, and his coat and hat and collar seemed more than ever different from anyone else's. He shook hands with them and then everybody sat down on chairs, and a gentleman in spectacles – they found afterwards that he was the District Superintendent – began quite a long speech – very clever indeed. I am not going to write the speech down. First, because you would think it dull; and secondly, because it made all the children blush so, and get so hot about the ears that I am quite anxious to get away from this part of the subject; and thirdly, because the gentleman took so many words to say what he had to say that I really haven't time to write them down. He said all sorts of nice things about the children's bravery and presence of mind, and when he had done he sat down, and everyone who was there clapped and said, 'Hear, hear.'

And then the old gentleman got up and said things, too. It was very like a prize-giving. And then he called the children one by one, by their names, and gave each of them a beautiful gold watch and chain. And inside the watches were engraved after the name of the watch's new owner:

'From the Directors of the Northern and Southern Railway in grateful recognition of the courageous and prompt action which averted an accident on – 1905.'

The watches were the most beautiful you can possibly imagine, and each one had a blue leather case to live in when it was at home.

'You must make a speech now and thank everyone for their kindness,' whispered the Station Master in Peter's ear, and pushed him forward. 'Begin "Ladies and Gentlemen",' he added.

Each of the children had already said 'Thank you,' quite properly.

'Oh, dear,' said Peter, but he did not resist the push.

'Ladies and Gentlemen,' he said in a rather husky voice. Then there was a pause, and he heard his heart beating in his throat. 'Ladies and Gentlemen,' he went on with a rush, 'it's most awfully good of you, and we shall treasure the watches all our lives – but really we don't deserve it because what we did wasn't anything, really. At least, I mean it was awfully exciting, and what I mean to say – thank you all very, very much.'

The people clapped Peter more than they had done the District Superintendent, and then everybody shook hands with them, and as soon as politeness would let them, they got away, and tore up the hill to Three Chimneys with their watches in their hands.

It was a wonderful day – the kind of day that very seldom happens to anybody and to most of us not at all.

'I did want to talk to the old gentleman about something else,' said Bobbie, 'but it was so public – like being in church.'

'What did you want to say?' asked Phyllis.

'I'll tell you when I've thought about it more,' said Bobbie.

So when she had thought a little more she wrote a letter.

My dearest old gentleman, [it said] I want most awfully to ask you something. If you could get out of the train and go by the next, it would do. I do not want you to give me anything. Mother says we ought not to. And

besides, we do not want any things. *Only to*
talk to you about a Prisoner and Captive. Your
loving little friend,
Bobbie

She got the Station Master to give the letter to the old
gentleman, and next day she asked Peter and Phyllis to
come down to the station with her at the time when the
train that brought the old gentleman from town would
be passing through.

She explained her idea to them – and they approved
thoroughly.

They had all washed their hands and faces, and
brushed their hair, and were looking as tidy as they knew
how. But Phyllis, always unlucky, had upset a jug of
lemonade down the front of her dress. There was no time
to change – and the wind happening to blow from the
coal yard, her frock was soon powdered with grey, which
stuck to the sticky lemonade stains and made her look,
as Peter said, 'like any little gutter child'.

It was decided that she should keep behind the
others as much as possible.

'Perhaps the old gentleman won't notice,' said
Bobbie. 'The aged are often weak in the eyes.'

There was no sign of weakness, however, in the eyes,
or in any other part of the old gentleman, as he stepped
from the train and looked up and down the platform.

The three children, now that it came to the point,
suddenly felt that rush of deep shyness which makes
your ears red and hot, your hands warm and wet, and
the tip of your nose pink and shiny.

'Oh,' said Phyllis, 'my heart's thumping like a steam-
engine – right under my sash, too.'

'Nonsense,' said Peter, 'people's hearts aren't under their sashes.'

'I don't care – mine is,' said Phyllis.

'If you're going to talk like a poetry-book,' said Peter, 'my heart's in my mouth.'

'My heart's in my boots – if you come to that,' said Bobbie; 'but do come on – he'll think we're idiots.'

'He won't be far wrong,' said Peter, gloomily. And they went forward to meet the old gentleman.

'Hullo,' he said, shaking hands with them all in turn. 'This is a very great pleasure.'

'It *was* good of you to get out,' Bobbie said, perspiring and polite.

He took her arm and drew her into the waiting room where she and the others had played the advertisement game the day they found the Russian. Phyllis and Peter followed. 'Well?' said the old gentleman, giving Bobbie's arm a kind little shake before he let it go. 'Well? What is it?'

'Oh, please!' said Bobbie.

'Yes?' said the old gentleman.

'What I mean to say –' said Bobbie.

'Yes?' said the old gentleman.

'It's all very nice and kind,' said she.

'But?' he said.

'I wish I might say something,' she said.

'Say it,' said he.

'Well, then,' said Bobbie – and out came the story of the Russian who had written the beautiful book about poor people, and had been sent to prison and to Siberia for just that.

'And what we want more than anything in the world is to find his wife and children for him,' said Bobbie, 'but we don't know how. But you must be most horribly clever, or you wouldn't be a Direction of the Railway. And if *you* knew how – and would? We'd rather have that than anything else in the world. We'd go without the watches, even, if you could sell them and find his wife with the money.'

And the others said so, too, though not with so much enthusiasm.

'Hum,' said the old gentleman, pulling down the white waistcoat that had the big gilt buttons on it, 'what did you say the name was – Fryingpansky?'

'No, no,' said Bobbie earnestly. 'I'll write it down for you. It doesn't really look at all like that except when you say it. Have you a bit of pencil and the back of an envelope?' she asked.

The old gentleman got out a gold pencil-case and a beautiful, sweet-smelling green Russian leather notebook and opened it at a new page.

'Here,' he said, 'write here.'

She wrote down, 'Szczepansky,' and said:

'That's how you write it. You *call* it Shepansky.'

The old gentleman took out a pair of gold-rimmed spectacles and fitted them on his nose. When he had read the name, he looked quite different.

'*That* man? Bless my soul!' he said. 'Why, I've read his book! It's translated into every European language. A fine book – a noble book. And so your mother took him in – like the good Samaritan. Well, well. I'll tell you what, youngsters – your mother must be a very good woman.'

'Of course she is,' said Phyllis, in astonishment.

'And you're a very good man,' said Bobbie, very shy, but firmly resolved to be polite.

'You flatter me,' said the old gentleman, taking off

his hat with a flourish. 'And now am I to tell you what I think of you?'

'Oh, please don't,' said Bobbie, hastily.

'Why?' asked the old gentleman.

'I don't exactly know,' said Bobbie. 'Only – if it's horrid, I don't want you to; and if it's nice, I'd rather you didn't.'

The old gentleman laughed.

'Well, then,' he said, 'I'll only just say that I'm very glad you came to me about this – very glad, indeed. And I shouldn't be surprised if I found out something very soon. I know a great many Russians in London, and every Russian knows *his* name. Now tell me all about yourselves.'

He turned to the others, but there were only two others, and those were Peter and Bobbie. Phyllis had disappeared.

'Tell me all about yourselves,' said the old gentleman again. And, quite naturally, they were stricken dumb.

'All right, we'll have an examination,' said the old gentleman; 'you two sit on the table, and I'll sit on the bench and ask questions.'

He did, and out came their names and ages – their Father's name and business – how long they had lived at Three Chimneys and a great deal more.

The questions were beginning to turn on a herring and a half for three-halfpence, and a pound of lead and a pound of feathers, when the door of the waiting room was kicked open by a boot; as the boot entered everyone could see that its lace was coming undone – and in came Phyllis, very slowly and carefully.

In one hand she carried a large tin can, and in the other a thick slice of bread and butter.

'Afternoon tea,' she announced proudly, and held the can and the bread and butter out to the old gentleman, who took them and said:

'Bless my soul!'

'Yes,' said Phyllis.

'It's very thoughtful of you,' said the old gentleman, 'very.'

'But you might have got a cup,' said Bobbie, 'and a plate.'

'Perks always drinks out of the can,' said Phyllis, flushing red. 'I think it was very nice of him to give it me at all – let alone cups and plates,' she added.

'So do I,' said the old gentleman, and he drank some of the tea and tasted the bread and butter.

And then it was time for the next train, and he got into it with many good-byes and kind last words.

'Well,' said Peter, when they were left on the platform, and the tail-lights of the train disappeared round the corner, 'it's my belief that we've lighted a candle today – like Latimer, you know, when he was being burned – and there'll be fireworks for our Russian before long.'

And so there were.

It wasn't ten days after the interview in the waiting room that the three children were sitting on top of the biggest rock in the field below their house watching the 5.15 steam away from the station along the bottom of the valley. They saw, too, the few people who had got out at the station struggling up the road towards the village, and they saw one person leave the road and open the gate that led across the fields to Three Chimneys and to nowhere else.

'Who on earth?' said Peter, scrambling down.

'Let's go and see,' said Phyllis.

So they did. And when they got near enough to see who the person was, they saw it was their old gentleman himself, his brass buttons winking in the afternoon sunshine, and his white waistcoat looking whiter than ever against the green of the field.

'Hullo!' shouted the children, waving their hands.

'Hullo!' shouted the old gentleman, waving his hat.

Then the three started to run – and when they got to him they hardly had breath left to say:

'How do you do?'

'Good news,' said he. 'I've found your Russian friend's wife and child – and I couldn't resist the temptation of giving myself the pleasure of telling him.'

But as he looked at Bobbie's face he felt that he *could* resist the temptation.

'Here,' he said to her, 'you run on and tell him. The other two will show me the way.'

Bobbie ran. But when she had breathlessly panted out the news to the Russian and Mother sitting in the quiet garden – when Mother's face had lighted up so beautifully, and she had said half a dozen quick French words to the Exile – Bobbie wished that she had *not* carried the news. For the Russian sprang up with a cry that made Bobbie's heart leap and then tremble – a cry of love and longing such as she had never heard. Then he took Mother's hand and kissed it gently and reverently – and then he sank down in his chair and covered his face with his hands and sobbed. Bobbie crept away. She did not want to see the others just then.

But she was as gay as anybody when the endless French talking was over, when Peter had torn down to the village for buns and cakes, and the girls had got tea ready and taken it out into the garden.

The old gentleman was most merry and delightful. He seemed to be able to talk in French and English almost at the same moment, and Mother did nearly as well. It was a delightful time. Mother seemed as if she could not make enough fuss about the old gentleman, and she said yes at once when he asked if he might present some 'goodies' to his little friends.

The word was new to the children – but they guessed that it meant sweets, for the three large pink and green boxes, tied with green ribbon, which he took out of his bag, held unheard-of layers of beautiful chocolates.

The Russian's few belongings were packed, and they all saw him off at the station.

Then Mother turned to the old gentleman and said:

'I don't know how to thank you for *everything*. It has been a real pleasure to me to see you. But we live very quietly. I am so sorry that I can't ask you to come and see us again.'

The children thought this very hard. When they *had* made a friend – and such a friend – they would dearly have liked him to come and see them again.

What the old gentleman thought they couldn't tell. He only said:

'I consider myself very fortunate, Madam, to have been received once at your house.'

'Ah,' said Mother, 'I know I must seem very surly and ungrateful – but –'

'You could never seem anything but a most charming and gracious lady,' said the old gentleman, with another of his bows.

And as they turned to go up the hill, Bobbie saw her Mother's face.

'How tired you look, Mammy,' she said; 'lean on me.'

'It's my place to give Mother my arm,' said Peter. 'I'm the head man of the family when Father's away.'

Mother took the arm of each.

'How awfully nice,' said Phyllis, skipping joyfully, 'to think of the dear Russian embracing his long-lost wife. The baby must have grown a lot since he saw her.'

'Yes,' said Mother.

'I wonder whether Father will think *I've* grown,' Phyllis went on, skipping still more gaily. 'I have grown already, haven't I, Mother?'

'Yes,' said Mother, 'oh, yes,' and Bobbie and Peter felt her hands tighten on their arms.

'Poor old Mammy, you *are* tired,' said Peter.

Bobbie said, 'Come on, Phil; I'll race you to the gate.'

And she started the race, though she hated doing it. *You* know why Bobbie did that. Mother only thought that Bobbie was tired of walking slowly. Even Mothers, who love you better than anyone else ever will, don't always understand.

CHAPTER 8

The Amateur Fireman

'That's a likely little brooch you've got on, Miss,' said Perks the Porter; 'I don't know as ever I see a thing more like a buttercup without it *was* a buttercup.'

'Yes,' said Bobbie, glad and flushed by this approval. 'I always thought it was more like a buttercup almost than even a real one – and I *never* thought it would come to be mine, my very own – and then Mother gave it to me for my birthday.'

'Oh, have you had a birthday?' said Perks; and he seemed quite surprised, as though a birthday were a thing only granted to a favoured few.

'Yes,' said Bobbie; 'when's your birthday, Mr Perks?' The children were taking tea with Mr Perks in the Porters' room among the lamps and the railway almanacs. They had brought their own cups and some jam turnovers. Mr Perks made tea in a beer can, as usual, and everyone felt very happy and confidential.

'My birthday?' said Perks, tipping some more dark brown tea out of the can into Peter's cup. 'I give up keeping of my birthday afore you was born.'

'But you must have been born *sometime*, you know,' said Phyllis, thoughtfully, 'even if it was twenty years ago – or thirty or sixty or seventy.'

'Not so long as that, Missie,' Perks grinned as he answered. 'If you really want to know, it was thirty-two years ago, come the fifteenth of this month.'

'Then why don't you keep it?' asked Phyllis.

'I've got something else to keep besides birthdays,' said Perks briefly.

'Oh! What?' asked Phyllis, eagerly. 'Not secrets?'

'No,' said Perks, 'the kids and the Missus.'

It was this talk that set the children thinking, and, presently, talking. Perks was, on the whole, the dearest friend they had made. Not so grand as the Station Master, but more approachable – less powerful than the old gentleman, but more confidential.

'It seems horrid that nobody keeps his birthday,' said Bobbie. 'Couldn't *we* do something?'

'Let's go up to the Canal bridge and talk it over,' said Peter. 'I got a new gut line from the postman this morning. He gave it me for a bunch of roses that I gave him for his sweetheart. She's ill.'

'Then I do think you might have given her the roses for nothing,' said Bobbie, indignantly.

'Nyang, nyang!' said Peter, disagreeably, and put his hands in his pockets.

'He did, of course,' said Phyllis, in haste; 'directly we heard she was ill we got the roses ready and waited by the gate. It was when you were making the brekker-toast. And when he'd said "Thank you" for the roses so many times – much more than he need have – he pulled out the line and gave it to Peter. It wasn't exchange. It was the grateful heart.'

'Oh, I *beg* your pardon, Peter,' said Bobbie, 'I *am* so sorry.'

'Don't mention it,' said Peter, grandly, 'I knew you would be.'

So then they all went up to the Canal bridge. The idea was to fish from the bridge, but the line was not quite long enough.

'Never mind,' said Bobbie. 'Let's just stay here and look at things. Everything's so beautiful.'

It was. The sun was setting in red splendour over the grey and purple hills, and the canal lay smooth and shiny in the shadow – no ripple broke its surface. It was like a grey satin ribbon between the dusky green silk of the meadows that were on each side of its banks.

'It's all right,' said Peter, 'but somehow I can always see how pretty things are much better when I've something to do. Let's get down on the towpath and fish from there.'

Phyllis and Bobbie remembered how the boys on the canal-boats had thrown coal at them, and they said so.

'Oh, nonsense,' said Peter. 'There aren't any boys here now. If there were, I'd fight them.'

Peter's sisters were kind enough not to remind him how he had *not* fought the boys when coal had last been thrown. Instead they said, 'All right, then,' and cautiously climbed down the steep bank to the towing-path. The line was carefully baited, and for half an hour they fished patiently and in vain. Not a single nibble came to nourish hope in their hearts.

All eyes were intent on the sluggish waters that earnestly pretended they had never harboured a single minnow when a loud, rough shout made them start.

'Hi!' said the shout, in most disagreeable tones, 'get out of that, can't you?'

An old white horse coming along the towing-path was within half a dozen yards of them. They sprang to their feet and hastily climbed up the bank.

'We'll slip down again when they've gone by,' said Bobbie.

But, alas, the barge, after the manner of barges, stopped under the bridge.

'She's going to anchor,' said Peter; 'just our luck!'

The barge did not anchor, because an anchor is not part of a canal-boat's furniture, but she was moored with ropes fore and aft – and the ropes were made fast to the palings and to crowbars driven into the ground.

'What you staring at?' growled the Bargee, crossly.

'We weren't staring,' said Bobbie; 'we wouldn't be so rude.'

'Rude be blessed,' said the man; 'get along with you!'

'Get along yourself,' said Peter. He remembered what he had said about fighting boys, and, besides, he felt safe halfway up the bank. 'We've as much right here as anyone else.'

'Oh, *'ave* you, indeed!' said the man. 'We'll soon see about that.' And he came across his deck and began to climb down the side of his barge.

'Oh, come away, Peter, come away!' said Bobbie and Phyllis, in agonized unison.

'Not me,' said Peter, 'but *you'd* better.'

The girls climbed to the top of the bank and stood ready to bolt for home as soon as they saw their brother out of danger. The way home lay all downhill. They knew that they all ran well. The Bargee did not look as if *he* did. He was red-faced, heavy, and beefy.

But as soon as his foot was on the towing-path the children saw that they had misjudged him.

He made one spring up the bank and caught Peter by the leg, dragged him down – set him on his feet with a shake – took him by the ear – and said sternly:

'Now, then, what do you mean by it? Don't you know these 'ere waters is preserved? You ain't no right catching fish 'ere – not to say nothing of your precious cheek.'

Peter was always proud afterwards when he remembered that, with the Bargee's furious fingers tightening on his ear, the Bargee's crimson countenance close to his own, the Bargee's hot breath on his neck, he had the courage to speak the truth.

'I *wasn't* catching fish,' said Peter.

'That's not *your* fault, I'll be bound,' said the man, giving Peter's ear a twist – not a hard one – but still a twist.

Peter could not say that it was. Bobbie and Phyllis had been holding on to the railings above and skipping with anxiety. Now suddenly Bobbie slipped through the railings and rushed down the bank towards Peter, so impetuously that Phyllis, following more temperately, felt certain that her sister's descent would end in the waters of the canal. And so it would have done if the Bargee hadn't let go of Peter's ear – and caught her in his jerseyed arm.

'Who are you a-shoving of?' he said, setting her on her feet.

'Oh,' said Bobbie, breathless, 'I'm not shoving anybody. At least, not on purpose. Please don't be cross with Peter. Of course, it's your canal; we're sorry and we won't fish any more. But we didn't know it was yours.'

'Go along with you,' said the Bargee.

'Yes, we will; indeed we will,' said Bobbie, earnestly; 'but we do beg your pardon – and really we haven't caught a single fish. I'd tell you directly if we had, honour bright I would.'

She held out her hands and Phyllis turned out her little empty pocket to show that really they hadn't any fish concealed about them.

'Well,' said the Bargee, more gently, 'cut along, then, and don't you do it again, that's all.'

The children hurried up the bank.

'Chuck us a coat, M'ria,' shouted the man. And a red-haired woman in a green plaid shawl came out from the cabin door with a baby in her arms and threw a coat to him. He put it on, climbed the bank, and slouched along across the bridge towards the village.

'You'll find me up at the "Rose and Crown" when you've got the kid to sleep,' he called to her from the bridge.

When he was out of sight the children slowly returned. Peter insisted on this.

'The canal may belong to him,' he said, 'though I don't believe it does. But the bridge is everybody's. Doctor Forrest told me it's public property. I'm not going to be bounced off the bridge by him or anyone else, so I tell you.'

Peter's ear was still sore and so were his feelings.

The girls followed him as gallant soldiers might follow the leader of a forlorn hope.

'I do wish you wouldn't,' was all they said.

'Go home if you're afraid,' said Peter; 'leave me alone. *I'm* not afraid.'

The sound of the man's footsteps died away along the quiet road. The peace of the evening was not broken by the notes of the sedge-warblers or by the voice of the woman in the barge, singing her baby to sleep. It was a sad song she sang. Something about Bill Bailey and how she wanted him to come home.

The children stood leaning their arms on the parapet of the bridge; they were glad to be quiet for a few minutes because all three hearts were beating much more quickly.

'I'm not going to be driven away by any old barge-man, I'm not,' said Peter, thickly.

'Of course not,' Phyllis said soothingly; 'you didn't give in to him! So now we might go home, don't you think?'

Nothing more was said till the woman got off the barge, climbed the bank, and came across the bridge.

She hesitated, looking at the three backs of the children, then she said, 'Ahem.'

Peter stayed as he was, but the girls looked round.

'You mustn't take no notice of my Bill,' said the woman; ''is bark's worse'n 'is bite. Some of the kids down Farley way is fair terrors. It was them put 'is back up calling out about who ate the puppy pie under Marlow bridge.'

'Who *did*?' asked Phyllis.

'*I* dunno,' said the woman. 'Nobody don't know! But somehow, and I don't know the why nor the wherefore of it, them words is p'ison to a barge-master. Don't you take no notice. 'E won't be back for two hours good. You might catch a power o' fish afore that. The light's good an' all,' she added.

'Thank you,' said Bobbie. 'You're very kind. Where's your baby?'

'Asleep in the cabin,' said the woman. ''E's all right. Never wakes afore twelve. Reg'lar as a church clock, 'e is.'

'I'm sorry,' said Bobbie; 'I would have liked to see him, close to.'

'And a finer you never did see, Miss, though I says it.' The woman's face brightened as she spoke.

'Aren't you afraid to leave it?' said Peter.

'Lor' love you, no,' said the woman; 'who'd hurt a little thing like 'im? Besides, Spot's there. So long!'

The woman went away.

'Shall we go home?' said Phyllis.

'You can. I'm going to fish,' said Peter briefly.

'I thought we came up here to talk about Perks's birthday,' said Phyllis.

'Perks's birthday'll keep.'

So they got down on the towing-path again and Peter fished. He did not catch anything.

It was almost quite dark, the girls were getting tired, and as Bobbie said, it was past bedtime, when suddenly Phyllis cried, 'What's that?'

And she pointed to the canal boat. Smoke was coming from the chimney of the cabin, had indeed been curling softly into the soft evening air all the time – but now other wreaths of smoke were rising, and these were from the cabin door.

'It's on fire – that's all,' said Peter, calmly. 'Serve him right.'

'Oh – how *can* you?' cried Phyllis. 'Think of the poor dear dog.'

'The *Baby!*' screamed Bobbie.

In an instant all three made for the barge.

Her mooring ropes were slack, and the little breeze, hardly strong enough to be felt, had yet been strong enough to drift her stern against the bank. Bobbie was first – then came Peter, and it was Peter who slipped and fell. He went into the canal up to his neck, and his feet could not feel the bottom, but his arm was on the edge of the barge. Phyllis caught at his hair. It hurt, but it helped him to get out. Next minute he had leaped on to the barge, Phyllis following.

'Not you!' he shouted to Bobbie; '*me*, because I'm wet.'

He caught up with Bobbie at the cabin door, and flung her aside very roughly indeed; if they had been playing, such roughness would have made Bobbie weep with tears of rage and pain. Now, though he flung her on to the edge of the hold, so that her knee and her elbow were grazed and bruised, she only cried:

'No – not you – *me*,' and struggled up again. But not quickly enough.

Peter had already gone down two of the cabin steps into the cloud of thick smoke. He stopped, remembered all he had ever heard of fires, pulled his soaked handkerchief out of his breast pocket and tied it over his mouth. As he pulled it out he said:

'It's all right, hardly any fire at all.'

And this, though he thought it was a lie, was rather good of Peter. It was meant to keep Bobbie from rushing after him into danger. Of course it didn't.

The cabin glowed red. A paraffin lamp was burning calmly in an orange mist.

'Hi,' said Peter, lifting the handkerchief from his mouth for moment. 'Hi, Baby – where are you?' He choked.

'Oh, let *me* go,' cried Bobbie, close behind him. Peter pushed her back more roughly than before and went on.

Now what would have happened if the baby hadn't cried I don't know – but just at that moment it *did* cry. Peter felt his way through the dark smoke, found something small and soft and warm and alive, picked it up and backed out, nearly tumbling over Bobbie, who was close behind. A dog snapped at his leg – tried to bark, choked.

'I've got the kid,' said Peter, tearing off the handkerchief and staggering on to the deck.

Bobbie caught at the place where the bark came from, and her hands met on the fat back of a smooth-haired dog. It turned and fastened its teeth on her hand, but very gently, as much as to say:

'I'm bound to bark and bite if strangers come into my master's cabin, but I know you mean well, so I won't *really* bite.'

Bobbie dropped the dog.

'All right, old man. Good dog,' said she. 'Here – give me the baby, Peter; you're so wet you'll give it cold.'

Peter was only too glad to hand over the strange little bundle that squirmed and whimpered in his arms.

'Now,' said Bobbie, quickly, 'you run straight to the "Rose and Crown" and tell them. Phil and I will stay here with the precious. Hush, then, a dear, a duck, a darling! Go *now*, Peter! Run!'

'I can't run in these things,' said Peter, firmly, 'they're as heavy as lead. I'll walk.'

'Then *I'll* run,' said Bobbie. 'Get on the bank, Phil, and I'll hand you the dear.'

The baby was carefully handed. Phyllis sat down on

the bank and tried to hush the baby. Peter wrung the water from his sleeves and knickerbocker legs as well as he could, and it was Bobbie who ran like the wind across the bridge and up the long white quiet twilight road towards the 'Rose and Crown'.

There is a nice old-fashioned room at the 'Rose and Crown' where Bargees and their wives sit of an evening drinking their supper beer, and toasting their supper cheese at a glowing basketful of coals that sticks out into the room under a great hooded chimney and is warmer and prettier and more comforting than any other fireplace *I* ever saw.

There was a pleasant party of barge people round the fire. You might not have thought it pleasant, but they did; for they were all friends or acquaintances, and they liked the same sort of things, and talked the same sort of talk. This is the real secret of pleasant society. The Bargee Bill, whom the children had found so disagreeable, was considered excellent company by his mates. He was telling a tale of his own wrongs – always a thrilling subject. It was his barge he was speaking about.

'And 'e sent down word "paint her inside hout," not namin' no colour, d'ye see? So I gets a lotter green paint and I paints her stem to stern, and I tell yer she looked A1. Then 'e comes along and 'e says, "Wot yer paint 'er all one colour for?" 'e says. And I says, says I, "Cause I thought she'd look fust-rate," says I, "and I think so still." An' he says, "*Dew* yer? Then ye can just pay for the bloomin' paint yerself," says he. An' I 'ad to, too.' A murmur of sympathy ran round the room. Breaking noisily in on it came Bobbie. She burst open the swing door – crying breathlessly:

'Bill! I want Bill the Bargeman.'

There was a stupefied silence. Pots of beer were held in mid-air, paralysed on their way to thirsty mouths.

'Oh,' said Bobbie, seeing the bargewoman and making for her. 'Your barge cabin's on fire. Go quickly.'

The woman started to her feet, and put a big red hand to her waist on the left side, where your heart seems to be when you are frightened or miserable.

'Reginald Horace!' she cried in a terrible voice; 'my Reginald Horace!'

'All right,' said Bobbie, 'if you mean the baby; got him out safe. Dog, too.' She had no breath for more, except, 'Go on – it's all alight.'

Then she sank on the ale-house bench and tried to get that breath of relief after running which people call the 'second wind'. But she felt as though she would never breathe again.

Bill the Bargee rose slowly and heavily. But his wife was a hundred yards up the road before he had quite understood what was the matter.

Phyllis, shivering by the canal side, had hardly heard the quick approaching feet before the woman had flung herself on the railing, rolled down the bank, and snatched the baby from her.

'Don't,' said Phyllis, reproachfully; 'I'd just got him to sleep.'

～

Bill came up later talking in a language with which the children were wholly unfamiliar. He leaped on to the barge and dipped up pails of water. Peter helped him and they put out the fire. Phyllis, the bargewoman, and the baby – and presently Bobbie, too – cuddled together in a heap on the bank.

'Lord help me, if it was me left anything as could catch alight,' said the woman again and again.

But it wasn't she. It was Bill the Bargeman, who had knocked his pipe out and the red ash had fallen on the hearth-rug and smouldered there and at last broken into flame. Though a stern man he was just. He did not blame his wife for what was his own fault, as many bargemen, and other men, too, would have done.

~

Mother was half wild with anxiety when at last the three children turned up at Three Chimneys, all very wet by now, for Peter seemed to have come off on the others. But when she had disentangled the truth of what had happened from their mixed and incoherent narrative, she owned that they had done quite right, and could not possibly have done otherwise. Nor did she put any obstacles in the way of their accepting the cordial invitation with which the bargeman had parted from them.

'Ye be here at seven tomorrow,' he had said, 'and I'll take you the entire trip to Farley and back, so I will, and not a penny to pay. Nineteen locks!'

They did not know what locks were; but they were at the bridge at seven, with bread and cheese and half a soda cake, and quite a quarter of a leg of mutton in a basket.

It was a glorious day. The old white horse strained at the ropes, the barge glided smoothly and steadily through the still water. The sky was blue overhead. Mr Bill was as nice as anyone could possibly be. No one would have

thought that he could be the same man who had held
Peter by the ear. As for Mrs Bill, she had always been nice,
as Bobbie said, and so had the baby, and even Spot, who
might have bitten them quite badly if he had liked.

'It was simply ripping, Mother,' said Peter, when
they reached home very happy, very tired, and very dirty,
'right over that glorious aqueduct. And locks – you don't
know what they're like. You sink into the ground and
then, when you feel you're never going to stop going
down, two great black gates open slowly, slowly – you
go out, and there you are on the canal just like you were
before.'

'I know,' said Mother, 'there are locks on the
Thames. Father and I used to go on the river at Marlow
before we were married.'

'And the dear, darling, ducky baby,' said Bobbie; 'it
let me nurse it for ages and ages – and it *was* so good.
Mother, I wish we had a baby to play with.'

'And everybody was so nice to us,' said Phyllis,
'everybody we met. And they say we may fish whenever
we like. And Bill is going to show us the way next time
he's in these parts. He says we don't know really.'

'He said *you* didn't know,' said Peter; 'but Mother,
he said he'd tell all the bargees up and down the canal
that we were the real, right sort, and they were to treat
us like good pals, as were we.'

'So then I said,' Phyllis interrupted, 'we'd always
each wear a red ribbon when we went fishing by the
canal, so they'd know it was *Us*, and we were the real,
right sort, and be nice to us!'

'So you've made another lot of friends,' said Mother;
'first the railway and then the canal!'

'Oh, yes,' said Bobbie; 'I think everyone in the world

is friends if you can only get them to see you don't want to be *un*-friends.'

'Perhaps you're right,' said Mother; and she sighed. 'Come, Chicks. It's bedtime.'

'Yes,' said Phyllis. 'Oh, dear – and we went up there to talk about what we'd do for Perks's birthday. And we haven't talked a single thing about it!'

'No more we have,' said Bobbie; 'but Peter's saved Reginald Horace's life. I think that's about good enough for one evening.'

'Bobbie would have saved him if I hadn't knocked her down; twice I did,' said Peter, loyally.

'So would I,' said Phyllis, 'if I'd known what to do.'

'Yes,' said Mother, 'you've saved a little child's life. I do think that's enough for one evening. Oh, my darlings, thank God *you're* all safe!'

CHAPTER 9

The Pride of Perks

It was breakfast-time. Mother's face was very bright as she poured the milk and ladled out the porridge.

'I've sold another story, Chickies,' she said; 'the one about the King of the Mussels, so there'll be buns for tea. You can go and get them as soon as they're baked. About eleven, isn't it?'

Peter, Phyllis, and Bobbie exchanged glances with each other, six glances in all. Then Bobbie said:

'Mother would you mind if we didn't have the buns for tea tonight, but on the fifteenth? That's next Thursday.'

'I don't mind when you have them, dear,' said Mother, 'but why?'

'Because it's Perks's birthday,' said Bobbie; 'he's thirty-two, and he says he doesn't keep his birthday any more, because he's got other things to keep – not rabbits or secrets – but the kids and the missus.'

'You mean his wife and children,' said Mother.

'Yes,' said Phyllis; 'it's the same thing, isn't it?'

'And we thought we'd make a nice birthday for him.

He's been so awfully jolly decent to us, you know, Mother,' said Peter, 'and we agreed that next bun-day we'd ask you if we could.'

'But supposing there hadn't been a bun-day before the fifteenth?' said Mother.

'Oh, then, we meant to ask you to let us anti – antipate it, and go without when the bun-day came.'

'Anticipate,' said Mother. 'I see. Certainly. It would be nice to put his name on the buns with pink sugar, wouldn't it?'

'Perks,' said Peter, 'it's not a pretty name.'

'His other name's Albert,' said Phyllis; 'I asked him once.'

'We might put A.P.,' said Mother; 'I'll show you how when the time comes.'

This was all very well as far as it went. But even fourteen halfpenny buns with A.P. on them in pink sugar do not of themselves make a very grand celebration.

'There are always flowers, of course,' said Bobbie, later, when a really earnest council was being held on the subject in the hay-loft where the broken chaff-cutting machine was, and the row of holes to drop hay through in to the hay-racks over the mangers of the stables below.

'He's got lots of flowers of his own,' said Peter.

'But it's always nice to have them given you,' said Bobbie, 'however many you've got of your own. We can use flowers for trimmings to the birthday. But there must be something to trim besides buns.'

'Let's all be quiet and think,' said Phyllis; 'no one's to speak until it's thought of something.'

So they were all quiet and so very still that a brown rat thought that there was no one in the loft and came out very boldly. When Bobbie sneezed, the rat was quite shocked and hurried away, for he saw that a hay-loft where such things could happen was no place for a respectable middle-aged rat that liked a quiet life.

'Hooray!' cried Peter, suddenly, 'I've got it.' He jumped up and kicked at the loose hay.

'What?' said the others, eagerly.

'Why, Perks is so nice to everybody. There must be lots of people in the village who'd like to help to make him a birthday. Let's go round and ask everybody.'

'Mother said we weren't to ask people for things,' said Bobbie doubtfully.

'For ourselves, she meant, silly, not for other people. I'll ask the old gentleman too. You see if I don't,' said Peter.

'Let's ask Mother first,' said Bobbie.

'Oh, what's the use of bothering Mother about every little thing?' said Peter, 'especially when she's busy. Come on. Let's go down to the village now and begin.'

So they went. The old lady at the Post-office said she didn't see why Perks should have a birthday any more than anyone else.

'No,' said Bobbie. 'I should like everyone to have one. Only we know when his is.'

'Mine's tomorrow,' said the old lady, 'and much notice anyone will take of it. Go along with you.'

So they went.

And some people were kind, and some were crusty. And some would give and some would not. It is rather difficult work asking for things, even for other people, as you have no doubt found if you have ever tried it.

When the children got home and counted up what had been given and what had been promised, they felt that for the first day it was not so bad. Peter wrote down the lists of the things in the little pocket-book where he kept the numbers of his engines. These were the lists:

Given.
A tobacco pipe from the sweet shop.
Half a pound of tea from the grocer's.
A woollen scarf slightly faded from the
   draper's, which was the other side of the
   grocer's.
A stuffed squirrel from the Doctor.

Promised.
A piece of meat from the butcher.
Six fresh eggs from the woman who lived in
   the old turnpike cottage.
A piece of honeycomb and six bootlaces from
   the cobbler, and an iron shovel from the
   blacksmith's.

Very early next morning Bobbie got up and woke Phyllis. This had been agreed on between them. They had not told Peter because they thought he would think it silly. But they told him afterwards, when it had turned out all right.

They cut a big bunch of roses, and put it in a basket with the needle-book that Phyllis had made for Bobbie on her birthday, and a very pretty blue necktie of Phyllis's. Then they wrote on a paper: 'For Mrs Ransome, with our best love, because it is her birthday,' and they put the paper in the basket, and they took it to the Post-office, and went in and put it on the counter and ran away before the old woman at the Post-office had time to get into her shop.

When they got home Peter had grown confidential over helping Mother to get the breakfast and had told her their plans.

'There's no harm in it,' said Mother, 'but it depends *how* you do it. I only hope he won't be offended and think it's *charity*. Poor people are very proud, you know.'

'It isn't because he's poor,' said Phyllis; 'it's because we're fond of him.'

'I'll find some things that Phyllis has outgrown,' said Mother, 'if you're quite sure you can give them to him without his being offended. I should like to do some little thing for him because he's been so kind to you. I can't do much because we're poor ourselves. What are you writing, Bobbie?'

'Nothing particular,' said Bobbie, who had suddenly begun to scribble. 'I'm sure he'd like the things, Mother.'

The morning of the fifteenth was spent very happily in getting the buns and watching Mother make A.P. on them with pink sugar. You know how it's done, of course? You beat up whites of eggs and mix powdered sugar with them, and put in a few drops of cochineal. And then you make a cone of clean white paper with a little hole at the pointed end, and put the pink egg-sugar in at the big end. It runs slowly out at the pointed end, and you write the letters with it just as though it were a great fat pen full of pink sugar-ink.

The buns looked beautiful with A.P. on every one, and, when they were put in a cool oven to set the sugar, the children went up to the village to collect the honey and the shovel and the other promised things.

The old lady at the Post-office was standing on her doorstep. The children said 'Good morning,' politely, as they passed.

'Here, stop a bit,' she said.

So they stopped.

'Those roses,' said she.

'Did you like them?' said Phyllis; 'they were as fresh as fresh. *I* made the needle-book, but it was Bobbie's present.' She skipped joyously as she spoke.

'Here's your basket,' said the Post-office woman. She went in and brought out the basket. It was full of fat, red gooseberries.

'I dare say Perks's children would like them,' said she.

'You *are* an old dear,' said Phyllis, throwing her arms around the old lady's fat waist. 'Perks *will* be pleased.'

'He won't be half so pleased as I was with your needle-book and the tie and the pretty flowers and all,' said the old lady, patting Phyllis's shoulder. 'You're good little souls, that you are. Look here. I've got a pram round the back in the wood-lodge. It was got for my Emmie's first, that didn't live but six months, and she never had but that one. I'd like Mrs Perks to have it. It 'ud be a help to her with that great boy of hers. Will you take it along?'

'*Oh!*' said all the children together.

When Mrs Ransome had got out the perambulator and taken off the careful papers that covered it, and dusted it all over, she said:

'Well, there it is. I don't know but what I'd have given it to her before if I'd thought of it. Only I didn't quite know if she'd accept it from me. You tell her it was my Emmie's little one's pram –'

'Oh, *isn't* it nice to think there is going to be a real live baby in it again!'

'Yes,' said Mrs Ransome, sighing and then laughing;

'here, I'll give you some peppermint cushions for the little ones, and then you must run along before I give you the roof off my head and the clothes off my back.

All the things that had been collected for Perks were packed into the perambulator, and at half past three Peter and Bobbie and Phyllis wheeled it down to the little yellow house where the Perkses lived.

The house was very tidy. On the window ledge was a jug of wild flowers, big daisies, and red sorrel, and feathery, flowery grasses.

There was a sound of splashing from the wash-house, and a partly washed boy put his head round the door.

'Mother's a-changing of herself,' he said.

'Down in a minute,' a voice sounded down the narrow, freshly scrubbed stairs.

The children waited. Next moment the stairs creaked and Mrs Perks came down, buttoning her bodice. Her hair was brushed very smooth and tight, and her face shone with soap and water.

'I'm a bit late changing, Miss,' she said to Bobbie, 'owing to me having had a extry clean-up today, along o' Perks happening to name its being his birthday. I don't know what put it into his head to think of such a thing. We keeps the children's birthdays, of course; but him and me – we're too old for such like, as a general rule.'

'We knew it was his birthday,' said Peter, 'and we've got some presents for him outside in the perambulator.'

As the presents were being unpacked, Mrs Perks gasped. When they were all unpacked, she surprised and horrified the children by sitting suddenly down on a wooden chair and bursting into tears.

'Oh, don't!' said everybody; 'oh, please don't!' And

Peter added, perhaps a little impatiently: 'What on earth is the matter? You don't mean to say you don't like it?'

Mrs Perks only sobbed. The Perks children, now as shiny-faced as anyone could wish, stood at the wash-house door, and scowled at the intruders. There was a silence, an awkward silence.

'*Don't* you like it?' said Peter, again, while his sisters patted Mrs Perks on the back.

She stopped crying as suddenly as she had begun.

'There, there, don't you mind me. *I'm* all right!' she said. 'Like it? Why, it's a birthday such as Perks never 'ad, not even when 'e was a boy and stayed with his uncle, who was a corn-chandler on his own account. He failed afterwards. Like it? Oh –' and then she went on and said all sorts of things that I won't write down, because I am sure that Peter and Bobbie and Phyllis would not like me to. Their ears got hotter and hotter, and their faces redder and redder, at the kind things Mrs Perks said. They felt they had done nothing to deserve all this praise.

At last Peter said: 'Look here, we're glad you're pleased. But if you go on saying things like that, we must go home. And we did want to stay and see if Mr Perks is pleased, too. But we can't stand this.'

'I won't say another single word,' said Mrs Perks, with a beaming face, 'but that needn't stop me thinking, need it? For if ever –'

'Can we have a plate for the buns?' Bobbie asked abruptly. And then Mrs Perks hastily laid the table for tea, and the buns and the honey and the gooseberries were displayed on plates, and the roses were put in two glass jam jars, and the tea-table looked, as Mrs Perks said, 'fit for a Prince'.

'To think!' she said, 'me getting the place tidy early, and the little 'uns getting the wild flowers and all – when never did I think there'd be anything more for him except the ounce of his pet particular that I got o' Saturday and been saving up for 'im ever since. Bless us! 'e *is* early!'

Perks had indeed unlatched the latch of the little front gate.

'Oh,' whispered Bobbie, 'let's hide in the back kitchen, and *you* tell him about it. But give him the tobacco first, because you got it for him. And when you've told him, we'll all come in and shout, "Many happy returns!"'

It was a very nice plan, but it did not quite come off. To begin with, there was only just time for Peter and Bobbie and Phyllis to rush into the wash-house, pushing the young and open-mouthed Perks children in front of them. There was not time to shut the door, so that, without at all meaning it, they had to listen to what went on in the kitchen. The wash-house was a tight fit for the Perks children and the Three Chimneys children, as well as all the wash-house's proper furniture, including the mangle and the copper.

'Hullo, old woman!' they heard Mr Perks's voice say; 'here's a pretty set-out!'

'It's your birthday tea, Bert,' said Mrs Perks, 'and here's a ounce of your extry particular. I got it o' Saturday along o' your happening to remember it was your birthday today.'

'Good old girl!' said Mr Perks, and there was a sound of a kiss.

'But what's that pram doing here? And what's all these bundles? And where did you get the sweetstuff, and –'

The children did not hear what Mrs Perks replied, because just then Bobbie gave a start, put her hand in her pocket, and all her body grew stiff with horror.

'Oh!' she whispered to the others, 'whatever shall we do? I forgot to put the labels on any of the things! He won't know what's from who. He'll think it's all *us*, and that we're trying to be grand or charitable or something horrid.'

'Hush!' said Peter.

And then they heard the voice of Mr Perks, loud and rather angry.

'I don't care,' he said; 'I won't stand it, and so I tell you straight.'

'But,' said Mrs Perks, 'it's them children you make such a fuss about – the children from the Three Chimneys.'

'I don't care,' said Perks, firmly, 'not if it was a angel from Heaven. We've got on all right all these years and no favours asked. I'm not going to begin these sort of charity goings-on at my time of life, so don't you think it, Nell.'

'Oh, hush!' said poor Mrs Perks; 'Bert, shut your silly tongue, for goodness' sake. The all three of 'em's in the wash-house a-listening to every word you speaks.'

'Then I'll give them something to listen to,' said the angry Perks; 'I've spoke my mind to them afore now, and I'll do it again,' he added, and he took two strides to the wash-house door, and flung it wide open – as wide, that is, as it would go, with the tightly packed children behind it.

'Come out,' said Perks, 'come out and tell me what you mean by it. 'Ave I ever complained to you of being short as you comes this charity lay over me?'

'*Oh!*' said Phyllis, 'I thought you'd be so pleased; I'll never try to be kind to anyone else as long as I live. No, I won't, not never.'

She burst into tears.

'We didn't mean any harm,' said Peter.

'It ain't what you means so much as what you does,' said Perks.

'Oh, *don't!*' cried Bobbie, trying hard to be braver than Phyllis, and to find more words than Peter had done for explaining it. 'We thought you'd love it. We always have things on our birthdays.'

'Oh, yes,' said Perks, 'your own relations; that's different.'

'Oh, no,' Bobbie answered. '*Not* our own relations. All the servants always gave us things at home, and us to them when it was their birthdays. And when it was mine, and Mother gave me the brooch like a buttercup, Mrs Viney gave me two lovely glass pots, and nobody thought she was coming the charity lay over us.'

'If it had been glass pots here,' said Perks, 'I wouldn't ha' said so much. It's there being all this heap and heaps of things I can't stand. No – nor won't neither.'

'But they're not all from us –' said Peter, 'only we forgot to put the labels on. They're from all sorts of people in the village.'

'Who put 'em up to it, I'd like to know?' asked Perks.

'Why, we did,' said Phyllis.

Perks sat down heavily in the elbow-chair and looked at them with what Bobbie afterwards described as withering glances of gloomy despair.

'So you've been round telling the neighbours we can't make both ends meet? Well, now you've disgraced us as deep as you can in the neighbourhood, you can just take the whole bag of tricks back where it came from. Very much obliged, I'm sure. I don't doubt but what you meant it kind, but I'd rather not be acquainted with you any longer if it's all the same to you.' He deliberately turned the chair round so that his back was turned to the children. The legs of the chair grated on the brick floor, and that was the only sound that broke the silence.

Then suddenly Bobbie spoke.

'Look here,' she said, 'this is most awful.'

'That's what I says,' said Perks, not turning round.

'Look here,' said Bobbie, desperately, 'we'll go if you like – and you needn't be friends with us any more if you don't want, but –'

'*We* shall always be friends with *you*, however nasty you are to us,' sniffed Phyllis, wildly.

'Be quiet,' said Peter, in a fierce aside.

'But before we go,' Bobbie went on desperately, 'do let us show you the labels we wrote to put on the things.'

'I don't want to see no labels,' said Perks, 'except proper luggage ones in my own walk of life. Do you think I've kept respectable and outer debt on what I gets, and her having to take in washing, to be give away for a laughing-stock to all the neighbours?'

'Laughing?' said Peter; 'you don't know.'

'You're a very hasty gentleman,' whined Phyllis; 'you know you were wrong once before, about us not telling you the secrets about the Russian. Do let Bobbie tell you about the labels!'

'Well. Go ahead!' said Perks, grudgingly.

'Well, then,' said Bobbie, fumbling miserably, yet not without hope, in her tightly-stuffed pocket, 'we wrote down all the things everybody said when they gave us the things, with the people's names, because Mother said we ought to be careful – because – but I wrote down what she said – and you'll see.'

But Bobbie could not read the labels just at once. She had to swallow once or twice before she could begin.

Mrs Perks had been crying steadily ever since her husband had opened the wash-house door. Now she caught her breath, choked, and said:

'Don't you upset yourself, Missy. *I* know you meant it kind if he doesn't.'

'May I read the labels?' said Bobbie, crying on to the slips as she tried to sort them. 'Mother's first. It says:

'"Little Clothes for Mrs Perks's children." Mother said, "I'll find some of Phyllis's things that she's grown out of if you're quite sure Mr Perks wouldn't be offended and think it's meant for charity. I'd like to do some little thing for him, because he's so kind to you. I can't do much because we're poor ourselves."'

Bobbie paused.

'That's all right,' said Perks, 'your Ma's a born lady. We'll keep the little frocks, and what-not, Nell.'

'Then there's the perambulator and the gooseberries, and the sweets,' said Bobbie, 'they're from Mrs Ransome. She said: "I dare say Mr Perks's children would like the sweets. And the perambulator was got for my Emmie's first – it didn't live but six months, and she's never had but that one. I'd like Mrs Perks to have it. It would be a help with her fine boy. I'd have given it before if I'd been sure she'd accept of it from me." She told me to tell you,' Bobbie added, 'that it was her Emmie's little one's pram.'

'I can't send the pram back, Bert,' said Mrs Perks, firmly, 'and I won't. So don't you ask me –'

'I'm not a-asking anything,' said Perks, gruffly.

'Then the shovel,' said Bobbie. 'Mr James made it for you himself. And he said – where is it? Oh, yes, here! He said, "You tell Mr Perks it's a pleasure to make a little trifle for a man as is so much respected," and then he said he wished he could shoe your children and his own children, like they do the horses, because, well, he knew what shoe leather was.'

'James is a good enough chap,' said Perks.

'Then the honey,' said Bobbie, in haste, 'and the bootlaces. *He* said he respected a man that paid his way – and the butcher said the same. And the old turnpike woman said many was the time you'd lent her a hand with her garden when you were a lad – and things like that came home to roost – I don't know what she meant. And everybody who gave anything said they liked you, and it was a very good idea of ours; and nobody said anything about charity or anything horrid like that. And the old gentleman gave Peter a gold pound for you, and said you were a man who knew your work. And I thought you'd *love* to know how fond people are of you, and I never was so unhappy in my life. Good-bye. I hope you'll forgive us some day –'

She could say no more, and she turned to go.

'Stop,' said Perks, still with his back to them; 'I take back every word I've said contrary to what you'd wish. Nell, set on the kettle.'

'We'll take the things away if you're unhappy about them,' said Peter; 'but I think everybody'll be most awfully disappointed as well as us.'

'I'm not unhappy about them,' said Perks; 'I don't know,' he added, suddenly wheeling the chair round and showing a very odd-looking screwed-up face, 'I don't know as ever I was better pleased. Not so much with the presents – though they're an A1 collection – but the kind respect of our neighbours. That's worth having, eh, Nell?'

'I think it's all worth having,' said Mrs Perks, 'and you've made a most ridiculous fuss about nothing, Bert, if you ask me.'

'No, I ain't,' said Perks, firmly; 'if a man didn't respect hisself, no one wouldn't do it for him.'

'But everyone respects you,' said Bobbie; 'they all said so.'

'I knew you'd like it when you really understood,' said Phyllis, brightly.

'Humph! You'll stay to tea?' said Mr Perks.

Later on Peter proposed Mr Perks's health. And Mr Perks proposed a toast, also honoured in tea, and the toast was, 'May the garland of friendship be ever green,' which was much more poetical than anyone had expected from him.

～

'Jolly good little kids, those,' said Mr Perks to his wife as they went to bed.

'Oh, they're all right, bless their heart,' said his wife; 'it's you that's the aggravatingest old thing that ever was. I was ashamed of you – I tell you –'

'You didn't need to be, old gal. I climbed down handsome soon as I understood it wasn't charity. But charity's what I never did abide, and won't neither.'

～

All sorts of people were made happy by that birthday party. Mr Perks and Mrs Perks and the little Perkses by all the nice things and by the kind thoughts of their neighbours; the Three Chimneys children by the success, undoubted though unexpectedly delayed, of their plan; and Mrs Ransome every time she saw the fat Perks baby in the perambulator. Mrs Perks made quite a round of visits to thank people for their kind birthday presents, and after each visit felt that she had a better friend than she had thought.

'Yes,' said Perks reflectively, 'it's not so much what you does as what you means; that's what I say. Now if it had been charity.'

'Oh, drat charity,' said Mrs Perks; 'nobody won't offer you charity, Bert, however much you was to want it, I lay. That was just friendliness, that was.'

When the clergyman called on Mrs Perks, she told him all about it. 'It *was* friendliness, wasn't it, Sir?' said she.

'I think,' said the clergyman, 'it was what is sometimes called loving-kindness.'

So you see it was all right in the end. But if one does that sort of thing, one has to be careful to do it in the right way. For, as Mr Perks said, when he had time to think it over, it's not so much what you do, as what you mean.

CHAPTER 10

The Terrible Secret

When they first went to live at Three Chimneys, the children had talked a great deal about their Father, and had asked a great many questions about him, and what he was doing and where he was and when he would come home. Mother always answered their questions as well as she could. But as the time went on they grew to speak less of him. Bobbie had felt almost from the first that for some strange miserable reason these questions hurt Mother and made her sad. And little by little the others came to have this feeling, too, though they could not have put it into words.

One day, when Mother was working so hard that she could not leave off even for ten minutes, Bobbie carried up her tea to the big bare room that they called Mother's workshop. It had hardly any furniture. Just a table and chair and a rug. But always big pots of flowers on the window-sills and on the mantelpiece. The children saw to that. And from the three long uncurtained windows the beautiful stretch of meadow and moorland, the far violet of the hills, and the unchanging change-fulness of cloud and sky.

'Here's your tea, Mother-love,' said Bobbie; 'do drink it while it's hot.'

Mother laid down her pen among the pages that were scattered all over the table, pages covered with her writing, which was almost as plain as print, and much prettier. She ran her hands into her hair, as if she were going to pull it out by handfuls.

'Poor dear head,' said Bobbie, 'does it ache?'

'No – yes – not much,' said Mother. 'Bobbie, do you think Peter and Phil are *forgetting* Father?'

'*No*,' said Bobbie, indignantly. 'Why?'

'You none of you ever speak of him now.'

Bobbie stood first on one leg and then on the other.

'We often talk about him when we're by ourselves,' she said.

'But not to me,' said Mother. 'Why?'

Bobbie did not find it easy to say why.

'I – you –' she said and stopped. She went over to the window and looked out.

'Bobbie, come here,' said her Mother, and Bobbie came.

'Now,' said Mother, putting her arm round Bobbie and laying her ruffled head against Bobbie's shoulder, 'try to tell me, dear.'

Bobbie fidgeted.

'Tell Mother.'

'Well, then,' said Bobbie, 'I thought you were so unhappy about Daddy not being here, it made you worse when I talked about him. So I stopped doing it.'

'And the others?'

'I don't know about the others,' said Bobbie. 'I never said anything about *that* to them. But I expect they felt the same about it as me.'

'Bobbie dear,' said Mother, still leaning her head against her, 'I'll tell you. Besides parting from Father, he and I have had a great sorrow – oh, terrible – worse than anything you can think of, and at first it did hurt to hear you all talking of him as if everything were just the same. But it would be much more terrible if you were to forget him. That would be worse than anything.'

'The trouble,' said Bobbie, in a very little voice – 'I promised I would never ask you any questions, and I never have, have I? But – the trouble – it won't last always?'

'No,' said Mother, 'the worst will be over when Father comes home to us.'

'I wish I could comfort you,' said Bobbie.

'Oh, my dear, do you suppose you don't? What should I do without you – you and the others? Do you think I haven't noticed how good you've all been, not quarrelling nearly as much as you used to – and all the little kind things you do for me – the flowers, and cleaning my shoes, and tearing up to make my bed before I get time to do it myself?'

Bobbie *had* sometimes wondered whether Mother noticed these things.

'That's nothing,' she said, 'to what –'

'I *must* get on with my work,' said Mother, giving Bobbie one last squeeze. 'Don't say anything to the others.'

That evening in the hour before bedtime instead of reading to the children Mother told them stories of the games she and Father used to have when they were children and lived near each other in the country – tales of the adventures of Father with Mother's brothers when they were all boys together. Very funny stories they were, and the children laughed as they listened.

'Uncle Edward died before he was grown up, didn't he?' said Phyllis, as Mother lighted the bedroom candles.

'Yes, dear,' said Mother, 'you would have loved him. He was such a brave boy, and so adventurous. Always in mischief, and yet friends with everybody in spite of it. And your Uncle Reggie's in Ceylon – yes, and Father's away, too. But I think they'd all like to think we'd enjoyed talking about the things they used to do. Don't you think so?'

'Not Uncle Edward,' said Phyllis, in a shocked tone; 'he's in Heaven.'

'You don't suppose he's forgotten us and all the old times, because God has taken him, any more than I forget him. Oh, no, he remembers. He's only away for a little time. We shall see him some day.'

'And Uncle Reggie – and Father, too?' said Peter.

'Yes,' said Mother. 'Uncle Reggie and Father, too. Good night, my darlings.'

'Good night,' said everyone. Bobbie hugged her mother more closely even than usual, and whispered in her ear. 'Oh, I do love you so, Mummy – I do – I do –'

When Bobbie came to think it all over, she tried not to wonder what the great trouble was. But she could not always help it. Father was not dead – like poor Uncle Edward – Mother had said so. And he was not ill, or Mother would have been with him. Being poor wasn't the trouble. Bobbie knew it was something nearer the heart than money could be.

'I mustn't try to think what it is,' she told herself; 'no, I mustn't. I *am* glad Mother noticed about us not quarrelling so much. We'll keep that up.'

And alas, that very afternoon she and Peter had what Peter called a first-class shindy.

They had not been a week at Three Chimneys before they had asked Mother to let them have a piece of garden each for their very own, and she had agreed, and the south border under the peach trees had been divided into three pieces and they were allowed to plant whatever they liked there.

Phyllis had planted mignonette and nasturtium and Virginia stock in hers. The seeds came up, and though they looked just like weeds, Phyllis believed that they would bear flowers some day. The Virginia stock justified her faith quite soon, and her garden was gay with a band of bright little flowers, pink and white and red and mauve.

'I can't weed for fear I pull up the wrong things,' she used to say comfortably; 'it saves such a lot of work.'

Peter sowed vegetable seeds in his – carrots and onions and turnips. The seed was given to him by the farmer who lived in the nice black-and-white, wood-and-plaster house just beyond the bridge. He kept turkeys and guinea fowls, and was a most amiable man. But Peter's vegetables never had much of a chance, because he liked to use the earth of his garden for digging canals, and making forts and earthworks for his toy soldiers, and the seeds of vegetables rarely come to much in a soil that is constantly disturbed for the purposes of war and irrigation.

Bobbie planted rose-bushes in her garden, but all the little new leaves of the rose-bushes shrivelled and withered, perhaps because she moved them from the other part of the garden in May, which is not at all the right time of the year for moving roses. But she would not own that they were dead, and hoped on against hope, until the day when Perks came up to see the garden, and told her quite plainly that all her roses were as dead as door nails.

'Only good for bonfires, Miss,' he said. 'You just dig 'em up and burn 'em, and I'll give you some nice fresh roots outer my garden; pansies and stocks, and sweet willies, and forget-me-nots. I'll bring 'em along tomorrow if you get the ground ready.'

So next day she set to work, and that happened to be the day when Mother had praised her and the others about not quarrelling. She moved the rose-bushes and carried them to the other end of the garden, where the rubbish heap was that they meant to make a bonfire of when Guy Fawkes' Day came.

Meanwhile Peter had decided to flatten out all his forts and earthworks, with a view to making a model of the railway-tunnel, cutting, embankment, canal, aqueduct, bridges and all.

So when Bobbie came back from her last thorny journey with the dead rose-bushes, he had got the rake and was using it busily.

'*I* was using the rake,' said Bobbie.

'Well, I'm using it now,' said Peter.

'But I had it first,' said Bobbie.

'Then it's my turn now,' said Peter. And that was how the quarrel began.

'You're always being disagreeable about nothing,' said Peter, after some heated argument.

'I had the rake first,' said Bobbie, flushed and defiant, holding on to its handle.

'Didn't I tell you this morning I meant to have it? Didn't I, Phil?'

Phyllis said she didn't want to be mixed up in their rows. And instantly, of course, she was.

'If you remember, you ought to say.'

'Of course, she doesn't remember – but she might say so.'

'I wish I'd had a brother instead of two whiny little kiddy sisters,' said Peter. This was always recognized as indicating the high-water mark of Peter's rage.

Bobbie made the reply she always made to it.

'I can't think why little boys were ever invented,' and just as she said it she looked up, and saw the three long windows of Mother's workshop flashing in the red rays of the sun. The sight brought back those words of praise:

'You don't quarrel like you used to do.'

'*Oh!*' cried Bobbie, just as if she had been hit, or had caught her finger in a door, or had felt the hideous sharp beginning of toothache.

'What's the matter?' said Phyllis.

Bobbie wanted to say: 'Don't let's quarrel, Mother hates it so,' but though she tried hard, she couldn't. Peter was looking too disagreeable and insulting.

'Take the horrid rake, then,' was the best she could manage. And she suddenly let go her hold on the handle. Peter had been holding on to it too, firmly and pullingly, and now that the pull the other way was suddenly stopped, he staggered and fell over backwards, the teeth of the rake between his feet.

'Serve you right,' said Bobbie, before she could stop herself.

Peter lay still for half a moment – long enough to frighten Bobbie a little. Then he frightened her a little more, for he sat up – screamed once – turned rather pale, and then lay back and began to shriek, faintly but steadily. It sounded exactly like a pig being killed a quarter of a mile off.

Mother put her head out of the window, and it wasn't half a minute after that she was in the garden kneeling by the side of Peter, who never for an instant ceased to squeal.

'What happened, Bobbie?' Mother asked.

'It was the rake,' said Phyllis. 'Peter was pulling at it, so was Bobbie, and she let go and he went over.'

'Stop that noise, Peter,' said Mother. 'Come. Stop at once.'

Peter used up what breath he had left in a last squeal and stopped.

'Now,' said Mother, 'are you hurt?'

'If he was really hurt, he wouldn't make such a fuss,' said Bobbie, still trembling with fury; 'he's not a coward!'

'I think my foot's broken off, that's all,' said Peter huffily, and sat up. Then he turned quite white. Mother put her arm round him.

'He *is* hurt,' she said; 'he's fainted. Here, Bobbie, sit down and take his head on your lap.'

Then Mother undid Peter's boots. As she took the right one off, something dripped from his foot on to the ground. It was red blood. And when the stocking came off there were three red wounds in Peter's foot and ankle, where the teeth of the rake had bitten him, and his foot was covered with red smears.

'Run for water – a basinful,' said Mother, and Phyllis ran. She upset most of the water out of the basin in her haste, and had to fetch more in a jug.

Peter did not open his eyes again till Mother had tied her handkerchief round his foot, and she and Bobbie had carried him in and laid him on the brown wooden settle in the dining-room. By this time Phyllis was halfway to the Doctor's.

Mother sat by Peter and bathed his foot and talked to him, and Bobbie went out and got tea ready, and put on the kettle.

'It's all I can do,' she told herself. 'Oh, suppose Peter should die, or be a helpless cripple for life, or have to walk with crutches, or wear a boot with a sole like a log of wood!'

She stood by the back door reflecting on these gloomy possibilities, her eyes fixed on the water-butt.

'I wish I'd never been born,' she said, and she said it out loud.

'Why, lawk a mercy, what's that for?' asked a voice, and Perks stood before her with a wooden trug basket full of green-leaved things and soft, loose earth.

'Oh, it's you,' she said. 'Peter's hurt his foot with a rake – three great gaping wounds, like soldiers get. And it was partly my fault.'

'That it wasn't I'll go bail,' said Perks. 'Doctor seen him?'

'Phyllis has gone for the Doctor.'

'He'll be all right; you see if he isn't,' said Perks. 'Why, my father's second cousin had a hay-fork run into him, right into his inside, and he was right as ever in a few weeks, all except his being a bit weak in the head afterwards, and they did say that it was along of his getting a touch of the sun in the hay-field, and not the fork at all. I remember him well. A kind-'earted chap, but soft, as you might say.'

Bobbie tried to let herself be cheered by this heartening reminiscence.

'Well,' said Perks, 'you won't want to be bothered with gardening just this minute, I daresay. You show me where your garden is, and I'll pop the bits of stuff in for you. And I'll hang about, if I may make so free, to see the Doctor as he comes out and hear what he says. You cheer up, Missie. I lay a pound he ain't hurt, not to speak of.'

But he was. The Doctor came and looked at the foot and bandaged it beautifully, and said that Peter must not put it to the ground for at least a week.

'He won't be lame, or have to wear crutches or a lump on his foot, will he?' whispered Bobbie, breathlessly, at the door.

'My aunt! No!' said Dr Forrest; 'he'll be as nimble as ever on his pins in a fortnight. Don't you worry, little Mother Goose.'

It was when Mother had gone to the gate with the Doctor to take his last instructions and Phyllis was filling the kettle for tea, that Peter and Bobbie found themselves alone.

'He says you won't be lame or anything,' said Bobbie.

'Oh, course I shan't, silly,' said Peter, very much relieved all the same.

'Oh, Peter, I *am* so sorry,' said Bobbie, after a pause.

'That's all right,' said Peter, gruffly.

'It was *all* my fault,' said Bobbie.

'Rot,' said Peter.

'If we hadn't quarrelled, it wouldn't have happened. I knew it was wrong to quarrel. I wanted to say so, but somehow I couldn't.'

'Don't drivel,' said Peter. 'I shouldn't have stopped if you *had* said it. Not likely. And besides, us rowing hadn't anything to do with it. I might have caught my

E. NESBIT

foot in the hoe, or taken off my fingers in the chaff-cutting machine or blown my nose off with fireworks. It would have been hurt just the same whether we'd been rowing or not.'

'But I knew it was wrong to quarrel,' said Bobbie, in tears, 'and now you're hurt and –'

'Now look here,' said Peter, firmly, 'you just dry up. If you're not careful you'll turn into a beastly little Sunday-school prig, so I tell you.'

'I don't mean to be a prig. But it's so hard not to be when you're really trying to be good.'

(The Gentle Reader may perhaps have suffered from this difficulty.)

'Not it,' said Peter; 'it's a jolly good thing it wasn't you was hurt. I'm glad it was *me*. There! If it had been you, you'd have been lying on the sofa looking like a suffering angel and being the light of the anxious household and all that. And I couldn't have stood it.'

'No, I shouldn't,' said Bobbie.

'Yes, you would,' said Peter.

'I tell you I shouldn't.'

'I tell you you would.'

'Oh, children,' said Mother's voice at the door. 'Quarrelling again? Already?'

'We aren't quarrelling – not really,' said Peter. 'I wish you wouldn't think it's rows every time we don't agree!' When Mother had gone out again, Bobbie broke out:

'Peter, I *am* sorry you're hurt. But you *are* a beast to say I'm a prig.'

'Well,' said Peter unexpectedly, 'perhaps I am. You did say I wasn't a coward, even when you were in such a wax. The only thing is – don't you be a prig, that's all.

You keep your eyes open and if you feel priggishness coming on just stop in time. See?'

'Yes,' said Bobbie, 'I see.'

'Then let's call it Pax,' said Peter magnanimously: 'bury the hatchet in the fathoms of the past. Shake hands on it. I say, Bobbie, old chap, I am tired.'

He was tired for many days after that, and the settle seemed hard and uncomfortable in spite of all the pillows and bolsters and soft folded rugs. It was terrible not to be able to go out. They moved the settle to the window, and from there Peter could see the smoke of the trains winding along the valley. But he could not see the trains.

At first Bobbie found it quite hard to be as nice to him as she wanted to be, for fear he should think her priggish. But that soon wore off, and both she and Phyllis were, as he observed, jolly good sorts. Mother sat with him when the sisters were out. And the words, 'he's not a coward,' made Peter determined not to make any fuss about the pain in his foot, though it was rather bad, especially at night.

Praise helps people very much sometimes.

There were visitors, too. Mrs Perks came up to ask how he was, and so did the Station Master, and several of the village people. But the time went slowly, slowly.

'I do wish there was something to read,' said Peter, 'I've read all our books about fifty times over.'

'I'll go to the Doctor's,' said Phyllis; 'he's sure to have some.'

'Only about how to be ill, and about people's nasty insides, I expect,' said Peter.

'Perks has a whole heap of Magazines that come out of trains when people are tired of them,' said Bobbie. 'I'll run down and ask him.'

So the girls went their two ways.

Bobbie found Perks busy cleaning lamps.

'And how's the young gent?' said he.

'Better, thanks,' said Bobbie, 'but he's most frightfully bored. I came to ask if you'd got any Magazines you could lend him.'

'There, now,' said Perks, regretfully, rubbing his ear with a black and oily lump of cotton waste, 'why didn't I think of that, now? I was trying to think of something as 'ud amuse him only this morning, and I couldn't think of anything better than a guinea-pig. And a young chap I know's going to fetch that over for him this tea-time.'

'How lovely! A real live guinea-pig! He will be pleased. But he'd like the Magazines as well.'

'That's just it,' said Perks. 'I've just sent the pick of 'em to Snigson's boy – him what's just getting over the pewmonia. But I've lots of illustrated papers left.'

He turned to the pile of papers in the corner and took up a heap six inches thick.

'There!' he said. 'I'll just slip a bit of string and a bit of paper round 'em.'

He pulled an old newspaper from the pile and spread it on the table, and made a neat parcel of it.

'There,' said he, 'there's lots of pictures, and if he likes to mess 'em about with his paint-box or coloured chalks or what not, why let him. *I* don't want 'em.'

'You're a dear,' said Bobbie, took the parcel, and started. The papers were heavy, and when she had to wait at the level-crossing while a train went by, she rested the parcel on the top of the gate. And idly she looked at the printing on the paper that the parcel was wrapped in.

Suddenly she clutched the parcel tighter and bent

her head over it. It seemed like some horrible dream. She read on – the bottom of the column was torn off – she could read no farther.

She never remembered how she got home. But she went on tiptoe to her room and locked the door. Then she undid the parcel and read that printed column again, sitting on the edge of her bed, her hands and feet icy cold and her face burning. When she had read all there was, she drew a long, uneven breath.

'So now I know,' she said.

What she had read was headed, 'End of the Trial. Verdict. Sentence'.

The name of the man who had been tried was the name of her father. The verdict was 'Guilty'. And the sentence was 'Five years' Penal Servitude'.

'Oh, Daddy,' she whispered, crushing the paper hard, 'it's not true – I don't believe it. You never did it! Never, never, never!'

There was a hammering at the door.

'What is it?' said Bobbie.

'It's me,' said the voice of Phyllis; 'tea's ready, and a boy's brought Peter a guinea-pig. Come along down.'

And Bobbie had to.

CHAPTER 11

The Hound in the Red Jersey

Bobbie knew the secret now. A sheet of old newspaper wrapped round a parcel – just a little chance like that – had given the secret to her. And she had to go down to tea and pretend that there was nothing the matter. The pretence was bravely made, but it wasn't very successful.

For when she came in, everybody looked up from tea and saw her pink-lidded eyes and her pale face with red tear-blotches on it.

'My darling,' cried Mother, jumping up from the tea-tray, 'whatever *is* the matter?'

'My head aches, rather,' said Bobbie. And indeed it did.

'Has anything gone wrong?' Mother asked.

'I'm all right, really,' said Bobbie, and she telegraphed her Mother from her swollen eyes this brief, imploring message – '*Not* before the others!'

Tea was not a cheerful meal. Peter was so distressed by the obvious fact that something horrid had happened to Bobbie that he limited his speech to repeating, 'More bread and butter, please,' at startlingly short intervals.

Phyllis stroked her sister's hand under the table to express sympathy, and knocked her cup over as she did it. Fetching a cloth and wiping up the spilt milk helped Bobbie a little. But she thought that tea would never end. Yet at last it did end, as all things do at last, and when Mother took out the tray, Bobbie followed her.

'She's gone to own up,' said Phyllis to Peter; 'I wonder what she's done.'

'Broken something, I suppose,' said Peter, 'but she needn't be so silly over it. Mother never rows for accidents. Listen! Yes, they're going upstairs. She's taking Mother up to show her – the water-jug with storks on it, I expect it is.'

Bobbie, in the kitchen, had caught hold of Mother's hand as she set down the tea-things.

'What is it?' Mother asked.

But Bobbie only said, 'Come upstairs, come up where nobody can hear us.'

When she had got Mother alone in her room she locked the door and then stood quite still, and quite without words.

All through tea she had been thinking of what to say; she had decided that 'I know all', or 'All is known to me', or 'The terrible secret is a secret no longer', would be the proper thing. But now that she and her Mother and that awful sheet of newspaper were alone in the room together, she found that she could say nothing.

Suddenly she went to Mother and put her arms round her and began to cry again. And still she could find no words, only 'Oh, Mammy, oh, Mammy, oh, Mammy!' over and over again.

Mother held her close and waited.

Suddenly Bobbie broke away from her and went to

her bed. From under her mattress she pulled out the paper she had hidden there, and held it out, pointing to her Father's name with a finger that shook.

'Oh, Bobbie,' Mother cried, when one little quick look had shown her what it was, 'you don't *believe* it? You don't believe Daddy did it?'

'*No,*' Bobbie almost shouted. She had stopped crying.

'That's all right,' said Mother. 'It's not true. And they've shut him up in prison, but he's done nothing wrong. He's good and noble and honourable, and he belongs to us. We have to think of that, and be proud of him and wait.'

Again Bobbie clung to her Mother, and again only one word came to her, but now that word was 'Daddy,' and 'Oh, Daddy, oh, Daddy, oh, Daddy!' again and again.

'Why didn't you tell me, Mammy?' she asked presently.

'Are you going to tell the others?' Mother asked.

'No.'

'Why?'

'Because –'

'Exactly,' said Mother; 'so you understand why I didn't tell you. We two must help each other to be brave.'

'Yes,' said Bobbie. 'Mother, will it make you more unhappy if you tell me all about it? I want to understand.'

So then, sitting cuddled up close to her Mother, Bobbie heard 'all about it'. She heard how those men, who had asked to see Father on that remembered last night when the Engine was being mended, had come to arrest him, charging him with selling State secrets to the Russians – with being, in fact, a spy and a traitor. She heard about the trial, and about the evidence – letters, found in Father's desk at the office, letters that convinced the jury that Father was guilty.

'Oh, how could they look at him and believe it!' cried Bobbie; 'and how could *any*one do such a thing!'

'*Someone* did it,' said Mother, 'and all the evidence was against Father. Those letters –'

'Yes. How did the letters get into his desk?'

'Someone put them there. And the person who put them there was the person who was really guilty.'

'*He* must be feeling pretty awful all this time,' said Bobbie, thoughtfully.

'I don't believe he had any feelings,' Mother said hotly; 'he couldn't have done a thing like that if he had.'

'Perhaps he just shoved the letters into the desk to hide them when he thought he was going to be found out. Why don't you tell the lawyers, or someone, that it must have been that person? There wasn't anyone that would have hurt Father on purpose, was there?'

'I don't know – I don't know. The man under him who got Daddy's place when he – when the awful thing happened – he was always jealous of your Father because Daddy was so clever and everyone thought such a lot of him. And Daddy never quite trusted that man.'

'Couldn't we explain all that to someone?'

'Nobody will listen,' said Mother, very bitterly, 'nobody at all. Do you suppose I've not tried everything? no, my dearest, there's nothing to be done. All we can do, you and I and Daddy, is to be brave, and patient, and' – she spoke very softly – 'to pray, Bobbie, dear.'

'Mother, you've got very thin,' said Bobbie, abruptly.

'A little perhaps.'

'And oh,' said Bobbie, 'I do think you're the bravest person in the world as well as the nicest!'

'We won't talk of all this any more, will we, dear?' said Mother; 'we must bear it and be brave. And darling, try not to think of it. It's much easier for me if you can be a little bit happy and enjoy things. Wash your poor little round face, and let's go out into the garden for a bit.'

The other two were very gentle and kind to Bobbie. And they did not ask her what was the matter. This was Peter's idea, and he had drilled Phyllis, who would have asked a hundred questions if she had been left to herself.

A week later Bobbie managed to get away alone and once more she wrote a letter. And once more it was to the old gentleman.

> *My dear friend, [she said] you see what is in*
> *this paper. It is not true. Father never did it.*
> *Mother says someone put the papers in Father's*
> *desk, and she says the man under him that got*
> *Father's place afterwards was jealous of*
> *Father, and Father suspected him a long time.*
> *But nobody listens to a word she says, but you*
> *are so good and clever, and you found out*
> *about the Russian gentleman's wife directly.*
> *Can't you find out who did the treason because*
> *he wasn't Father upon my honour; he is an*
> *Englishman and uncapable to do such things,*
> *and then they would let Father out of prison. It*
> *is dreadful, and Mother is getting so thin. She*
> *told us once to pray for all prisoners and*
> *captives. I see now. Oh, do help me – there is*
> *only just Mother and me know, and we can't*
> *do anything. Peter and Phil don't know. I'll*

pray for you twice every day as long as I live if
you'll only try – just try to find out. Think if it
was your *Daddy, what you would feel. Oh, do,*
do, *help me. With love*
I remain Your affectionately little friend
Roberta

P.S. Mother would send her kind regards if she
knew I am writing – but it is no use telling her I
am, in case you can't do anything. But I know
you will. Bobbie, with best love.

She cut the account of her Father's trial out of the newspaper with Mother's big cutting-out scissors, and put it
in the envelope with her letter.

Then she took it down to the station, going out the
back way and round by the road, so that the others should
not see her and offer to come with her, and she gave the
letter to the Station Master to give to the old gentleman
next morning.

'Where *have* you been?' shouted Peter, from the top
of the yard wall where he and Phyllis were.

'To the station, of course,' said Bobbie; 'give us a
hand, Pete.'

She set her foot on the lock of the yard door. Peter
reached down a hand.

'What on earth?' she asked as she reached the wall-
top – for Phyllis and Peter were very muddy. A lump of
wet clay lay between them on the wall, they had each a
slip of slate in a very dirty hand, and behind Peter, out
of the reach of accidents, were several strange rounded
objects rather like very fat sausages, hollow, but closed
up at one end.

'It's nests,' said Peter, 'swallows' nests. We're going to dry them in the oven and hang them up with string under the eaves of the coach-house.'

'Yes,' said Phyllis; 'and then we're going to save up all the wool and hair we can get, and in the spring we'll line them, and then how pleased the swallows will be!'

'I've often thought people don't do nearly enough for dumb animals,' said Peter with an air of virtue. 'I do think people might have thought of making nests for poor little swallows before this.'

'Oh,' said Bobbie, vaguely, 'if everybody thought of everything, there'd be nothing left for anybody else to think about.'

'Look at the nests – aren't they pretty?' said Phyllis, reaching across Peter to grasp a nest.

'Look out, Phil, you goat,' said her brother. But it was too late; her strong little fingers had crushed the nest.

'There now,' said Peter.

'Never mind,' said Bobbie.

'It *is* one of my own,' said Phyllis, 'so you needn't jaw, Pete. Yes, we've put our initial names on the ones we've done, so that the swallows will know who they've got to be so grateful to and fond of.'

'Swallows can't read, silly,' said Peter.

'Silly yourself,' retorted Phyllis: 'how do you know?'

'Who thought of making the nests, anyhow?' shouted Peter.

'I did,' screamed Phyllis.

'Nya,' rejoined Peter, 'you only thought of making hay ones and sticking them in the ivy for the sparrows, and they'd have been sopping *long* before egg-laying time. It was me said clay and swallows.'

'I don't care what you said.'

'Look,' said Bobbie, 'I've made the nest all right again. Give me the bit of stick to mark your initial name on it. But how can you? Your letter and Peter's are the same. P. for Peter, P. for Phyllis.'

'I put F. for Phyllis,' said the child of that name. 'That's how it sounds. The swallows wouldn't spell Phyllis with a P., I'm certain-sure.'

'They can't spell at all,' Peter was still insisting.

'Then why do you see them always on Christmas cards and valentines with letters round their necks? How would they know where to go if they couldn't read?'

'That's only in pictures. You never saw one really with letters round its neck.'

'Well, I have a pigeon, then; at least Daddy told me they did. Only it was under their wings and not round their necks, but it comes to the same thing, and –'

'I say,' interrupted Bobbie, 'there's to be a paper-chase tomorrow.'

'Who?' Peter asked.

'Grammar School. Perks thinks the hare will go along by the line at first. We might go along the cutting. You can see a long way from there.'

The paper-chase was found to be a more amusing subject of conversation than the reading powers of swallows. Bobbie had hoped it might be. And next morning Mother let them take their lunch and go out for the day to see the paper-chase.

'If we go to the cutting,' said Peter, 'we shall see the workmen, even if we miss the paper-chase.'

Of course it had taken some time to get the line clear from the rocks and earth and trees that had fallen on it when the great landslip happened. That was the occasion, you will remember, when the three children saved the train from being wrecked by waving six little red-flannel-petticoat flags. It is always interesting to watch people working, especially when they work with such interesting things as spades and picks and shovels and planks and barrows, when they have cindery red fires in iron pots with round holes in them, and red lamps hanging near the works at night. Of course the children were never out at nights; but once, at dusk, when Peter had got out of his bedroom skylight on to the roof, he had seen the red lamp shining far away at the edge of the cutting. The children had often been down to watch the work, and this day the interest of picks and spades, and barrows wheeled along planks, completely put the paper-chase out of their heads, so that they quite jumped when a voice just behind them panted, 'Let me pass, please.' It was the hare – a big-boned, loose-limbed boy, with dark hair lying flat on a very damp forehead. The bag of torn paper under his arm was fastened across one shoulder by a strap. The children stood back. The hare ran along the line, and the workmen leaned on their picks to watch him. He ran on steadily and disappeared into the mouth of the tunnel.

'That's against the by-laws,' said the foreman.

'Why worry?' said the oldest workman; 'live and let live's what I always say. Ain't you never been young yourself, Mr Bates?'

'I ought to report him,' said the foreman.

'Why spoil sport's what I always say.'

'Passengers are forbidden to cross the line on any pretence,' murmured the foreman, doubtfully.

'He ain't no passenger,' said one of the workmen.

'Nor 'e ain't crossed the line, not where we could see 'em do it,' said another.

'Nor yet 'e ain't made no pretences,' said a third.

'And,' said the oldest workman, ''e's outer sight now. What the eye don't see the 'art needn't take no notice of's what I always say.'

And now, following the track of the hare by the little white blots of scattered paper, came the hounds. There were thirty of them, and they all came down the steep, ladder-like steps by ones and twos and threes and sixes and sevens. Bobbie and Phyllis and Peter counted them as they passed. The foremost ones hesitated a moment at the foot of the ladder, then their eyes caught the gleam of scattered whiteness along the line and they turned towards the tunnel, and, by ones and twos and threes and sixes and sevens, disappeared in the dark mouth of it. The last one, in a red jersey, seemed to be extinguished by the darkness like a candle that is blown out.

'They don't know what they're in for,' said the foreman; 'it isn't so easy running in the dark. The tunnel takes two or three turns.'

'They'll take a long time to get through, you think?' Peter asked.

'An hour or more, I shouldn't wonder.'

'Then let's cut across the top and see them come out at the other end,' said Peter; 'we shall get there long before they do.' The counsel seemed good, and they went.

They climbed the steep steps from which they had picked the wild cherry blossom for the grave of the little wild rabbit, and reaching the top of the cutting, set their faces towards the hill through which the tunnel was cut. It was stiff work.

'It's like Alps,' said Bobbie, breathlessly.

'Or Andes,' said Peter.

'It's like Himmy what's its names?' gasped Phyllis. 'Mount Everlasting. Do let's stop.'

'Stick to it,' panted Peter; 'you'll get your second wind in a minute.'

Phyllis consented to stick to it – and on they went running when the turf was smooth and the slope easy, climbing over stones, helping themselves up rocks by the branches of trees, creeping through narrow openings between tree trunks and rocks, and so on and on, up and up, till at last they stood on the very top of the hill where they had so often wished to be.

'Halt!' cried Peter, and threw himself flat on the grass. For the very top of the hill was a smooth, turfed table-land, dotted with mossy rocks and little mountain-ash trees.

The girls also threw themselves down flat.

'Plenty of time,' Peter panted; 'the rest's all downhill.'

When they were rested enough to sit up and look round them, Bobbie cried:

'Oh, look!'

'What at?' said Phyllis.

'The view,' said Bobbie.

'I hate views,' said Phyllis, 'don't you, Peter?'

'Let's get on,' said Peter.

'But this isn't like a view they take you to in carriages when you're at the seaside, all sea and sand and bare hills. It's like the "coloured counties" in one of Mother's poetry books.'

'It's not so dusty,' said Peter: 'look at the aqueduct straddling slap across the valley like a giant centipede, and then the town's church spires sticking up out of the trees like pens out of an inkstand. *I* think it's more like

> *'There could we see the banners*
> *Of twelve fair cities shine.'*

'I love it,' said Bobbie; 'it's worth the climb.'

'The paper-chase is worth the climb,' said Phyllis, 'if we don't lose it. Let's get on. It's all downhill now.'

'*I* said that ten minutes ago,' said Peter.

'Well, *I've* said it now,' said Phyllis; 'come on.'

'Loads of time,' said Peter. And there was. For when they had got down to a level with the top of the tunnel's mouth – they were a couple of hundred yards out of their reckoning and had to creep along the face of the hill – there was no sign of the hare or the hounds.

'They've gone long ago, of course,' said Phyllis, as they leaned on the brick parapet above the tunnel.

'I don't think so,' said Bobbie, 'but even if they had, it's ripping here, and we shall see the trains come out of the tunnel like dragons out of lairs. We've never seen that from the top side before.'

'No more we have,' said Phyllis, partially appeased.

It was really a most exciting place to be in. The top of the tunnel seemed ever so much farther from the line than they had expected, and it was like being on a bridge, but a bridge overgrown with bushes and creepers and grass and wild flowers.

'I *know* the paper-chase has gone long ago,' said Phyllis every two minutes, and she hardly knew whether she was pleased or disappointed when Peter, leaning over the parapet, suddenly cried:

'Look out. Here he comes!'

They all leaned over the sun-warmed brick wall in time to see the hare, going very slowly, come out from the shadow of the tunnel.

'There now,' said Peter, 'what did I tell you? Now for the hounds!'

Very soon came the hounds – by ones and twos and threes and sixes and sevens – and they also were going slowly and seemed very tired. Two or three who lagged far behind came out long after the others.

'There,' said Bobbie, 'that's all – now what shall we do?'

'Go along into the tulgy wood over there and have lunch,' said Phyllis; 'we can see them for miles from up there.'

'Not yet,' said Peter. 'That's not the last. There's the one in the red jersey to come yet. Let's see the last of them come out.'

But though they waited and waited and waited, the boy in the red jersey did not appear.

'Oh, let's have lunch,' said Phyllis; 'I've got a pain in my front with being so hungry. You must have missed seeing the red-jerseyed one when he came out with the others –'

But Bobbie and Peter agreed that he had not come out with the others.

'Let's go down to the tunnel mouth,' said Peter: 'then perhaps we shall see him coming along from the inside. I expect he felt spun-chuck, and rested in one of the manholes. You stay up here and watch, Bob, and when I signal from below, you come down. We might miss seeing him on the way down, with all these trees.'

So the others climbed down and Bobbie waited till they signalled to her from the line below. And then she, too, scrambled down the roundabout slippery path among roots and moss till she stepped out between two dogwood trees and joined the others on the line. And still there was no sign of the hound with the red jersey.

'Oh, do, do let's have something to eat,' wailed Phyllis. 'I shall die if you don't and then you'll be sorry.'

'Give her the sandwiches, for goodness' sake, and stop her silly mouth,' said Peter, not quite unkindly. 'Look here,' he added, turning to Bobbie, 'perhaps we'd better have one each, too. We may need all our strength. Not more than one, though. There's no time.'

'What for?' asked Bobbie, her mouth already full, for she was just as hungry as Phyllis.

'Don't you see,' replied Peter, impressively, 'that red-jerseyed hound has had an accident – that's what it is. Perhaps even as we speak he's lying with his head on the metals, an unresisting prey to any passing express –'

'Oh, don't try to talk like a book,' cried Bobbie, bolting what was left of her sandwich; 'come on, Phil, keep close behind me. If a train comes, stand flat against the tunnel wall and hold your petticoats close to you.'

'Give me one more sandwich,' pleaded Phyllis, 'and I will.' 'I'm going first,' said Peter; 'it was my idea,' and he went.

Of course you know what going into a tunnel is like? The engine gives a scream and then suddenly the noise of the running, rattling train changes and grows different and much louder. Grown-up people pull up the windows and hold them by the strap. The railway carriage suddenly grows like night – with lamps, of course, unless you are in a slow local train, in which case lamps are not always provided. Then by and by the darkness outside the carriage window is touched by puffs of cloudy whiteness, then you see a blue light on the walls of the tunnel, then the sound of the moving train changes once more, and you are out in the good open air again, and grown-ups let the straps go. The windows, all dim with the yellow breath of the tunnel, rattle down into their places, and you see once more the dip and catch of the telegraph wires besides the line, and the straight-cut hawthorn hedges with the tiny baby trees growing up out of them every thirty yards.

All this, of course, is what a tunnel means when you are in a train. But everything is quite different when you walk into a tunnel on your own feet, and tread on shifting, sliding stones and gravel on a path that curves downwards from the shining metals to the wall. Then you see slimy, oozy trickles of water running down the inside of the tunnel, and you notice that the bricks are not red or brown, as they are at the tunnel's mouth, but dull, sticky, sickly green. Your voice, when you speak, is quite changed from what it was out in the sunshine, and it is a long time before the tunnel is quite dark.

It was not yet quite dark in the tunnel when Phyllis caught at Bobbie's skirt, ripping out half a yard of gathers, but no one noticed this at the time.

'I want to go back,' she said, 'I don't like it. It'll be pitch dark in a minute. I *won't* go on in the dark. I don't care what you say, I *won't*.'

'Don't be a silly cuckoo,' said Peter; 'I've got a candle end and matches, and what's that?'

'That' was a low, humming sound on the railway line, a trembling of the wires beside it, a buzzing humming sound that grew louder and louder as they listened.

'It's a train,' said Bobbie.

'Which line?'

'Let me go back,' cried Phyllis, struggling to get away from the hand by which Bobbie held her.

'Don't be a coward,' said Bobbie; 'it's quite safe. Stand back.'

'Come on,' shouted Peter, who was a few yards ahead. 'Quick! Manhole!'

The roar of the advancing train was now louder than the noise you hear when your head is under water in the bath and both taps are running, and you are kicking with your heels against the bath's tin sides. But Peter had shouted for all he was worth, and Bobbie heard him. She dragged Phyllis along to the manhole. Phyllis, of course, stumbled over the wires and grazed both her legs. But they dragged her in, and all three stood in the dark, damp, arch recess while the train roared louder and louder. It seemed as if it would deafen them. And, in the distance, they could see its eyes of fire growing bigger and brighter every instant.

'It *is* a dragon – I always knew it was – it takes its own shape in here, in the dark,' shouted Phyllis. But nobody heard her. You see the train was shouting, too, and its voice was bigger than hers.

And now, with a rush and a roar and a rattle and a long dazzling flash of lighted carriage windows, a smell of smoke, and blast of hot air, the train hurtled by, clanging and jangling and echoing in the vaulted roof of the tunnel. Phyllis and Bobbie clung to each other. Even Peter caught hold of Bobbie's arm, 'in case she should be frightened,' as he explained afterwards.

And now, slowly and gradually, the tail-lights grew smaller and smaller, and so did the noise, till with one last *whiz* the train got itself out of the tunnel, and silence settled again on its damp walls and dripping roof.

'Oh!' said the children, all together in a whisper.

Peter was lighting the candle end with a hand that trembled.

'Come on,' he said; but he had to clear his throat before he could speak in his natural voice.

'Oh,' said Phyllis, 'if the red-jerseyed one was in the way of the train!'

'We've got to go and see,' said Peter.

'Couldn't we go and send someone from the station?' said Phyllis.

'Would you rather wait here for us?' asked Bobbie, severely, and of course, that settled the question.

So the three went on into the deeper darkness of the tunnel. Peter led, holding his candle end high to light the way. The grease ran down his fingers, and some of it right up his sleeve. He found a long streak from wrist to elbow when he went to bed that night.

It was not more than a hundred and fifty yards from the spot where they had stood while the train went by that Peter stood still, shouted 'Hullo' and then went on much quicker than before. When the others caught him up, he stopped. And he stopped within a yard of what they had come into the tunnel to look for. Phyllis saw a gleam of red, and shut her eyes tight. There, by the curved, pebbly down line, was the red-jerseyed hound. His back was against the wall, his arms hung limply by his sides, and his eyes were shut.

'Was the red, blood? Is he all killed?' asked Phyllis, screwing her eyelids more tightly together.

'Killed? Nonsense!' said Peter. 'There's nothing red about him except his jersey. He's only fainted. What on earth are we to do?'

'Can we move him?' asked Bobbie.

'I don't know; he's a big chap.'

'Suppose we bathe his forehead with water. No, I know we haven't any, but milk's just as well. There's a whole bottle.'

'Yes,' said Peter, 'and they rub people's hands, I believe.'

'They burn feathers, I know,' said Phyllis.

'What's the use of saying that when we haven't any feathers!'

'As it happens,' said Phyllis, in a tone of exasperated triumph, 'I've got a shuttlecock in my pocket. So there!'

And now Peter rubbed the hands of the red-jerseyed one. Bobbie burned the feathers of the shuttlecock one by one under his nose, Phyllis splashed warmish milk on his forehead, and all three kept on saying as fast and as earnest as they could:

'Oh, look up, speak to me! For my sake, speak!'

CHAPTER 12

What Bobbie Brought Home

'Oh, look up! Speak to me! For *my* sake, speak!' The children said the words over and over again to the unconscious hound in a red jersey, who sat with closed eyes and pale face against the side of the tunnel.

'Wet his ears with milk,' said Bobbie. 'I know they do it to people that faint – with eau-de-Cologne. But I expect milk's just as good.'

So they wetted his ears, and some of the milk ran down his neck under the red jersey. It was very dark in the tunnel. The candle end Peter had carried, and which now burned on a flat stone, gave hardly any light at all.

'Oh, *do* look up,' said Phyllis. 'For *my* sake! I believe he's dead.'

'For *my* sake,' repeated Bobbie. 'No, he isn't.'

'For *any* sake,' said Peter; 'come out of it.' And he shook the sufferer by the arm.

And then the boy in the red jersey sighed, and opened his eyes, and shut them again and said in a very small voice, 'Chuck it.'

'Oh, he's *not* dead,' said Phyllis. 'I *knew* he wasn't,' and she began to cry.

'What's up? I'm all right,' said the boy.

'Drink this,' said Peter, firmly, thrusting the nose of the milk bottle into the boy's mouth. The boy struggled, and some of the milk was upset before he could get his mouth free to say:

'What is it?'

'It's milk,' said Peter. 'Fear not, you are in the hands of friends. Phil, you stop bleating this minute.'

'Do drink it,' said Bobbie gently; 'it'll do you good.'

So he drank. And the three stood by without speaking to him.

'Let him be a minute,' Peter whispered; 'he'll be all right as soon as the milk begins to run like fire through his veins.'

He was.

'I'm better now,' he announced. 'I remember all about it.' He tried to move, but the movement ended in a groan. 'Bother! I believe I've broken my leg,' he said.

'Did you tumble down?' asked Phyllis, sniffing.

'Of course not – I'm not a kiddie,' said the boy, indignantly; 'it was one of those beastly wires tripped me up, and when I tried to get up again I couldn't stand, so I sat down. Gee whillikins! It does hurt though. How did *you* get here?'

'We saw you all go into the tunnel and then we went across the hill to see you all come out. And the others did – all but you, and you didn't. So we are a rescue party,' said Peter, with pride.

'You've got some pluck, I will say,' remarked the boy.

'Oh, that's nothing,' said Peter with modesty. 'Do you think you could walk if we helped you?'

'I could try,' said the boy.

He did try. But he could only stand on one foot; the other dragged in a very nasty way.

'Here, let me sit down. I feel like dying,' said the boy.

'Let go of me – let go, quick –' He lay down and closed his eyes. The others looked at each other by the dim light of the little candle.

'What on earth!' said Peter.

'Look here,' said Bobbie quickly, 'you must go and get help. Go to the nearest house.'

'Yes, that's the only thing,' said Peter. 'Come on.'

'If you take his feet and Phil and I take his head, we could carry him to the manhole.'

They did it. It was perhaps as well for the sufferer that he had fainted again.

'Now,' said Bobbie, 'I'll stay with him. You take the longest bit of candle, and, oh – be quick, for this bit won't burn long.'

'I don't think Mother would like me leaving you,' said Peter, doubtfully. 'Let me stay, and you and Phil go.'

'No, no,' said Bobbie, 'you and Phil go – and lend me your knife. I'll try to get his boot off before he wakes up again.'

'I hope it's all right what we're doing,' said Peter.

'Of course it's right,' said Bobbie, impatiently. 'What else *would* you do? Leave him here all alone because it's dark? Nonsense. Hurry up, that's all.'

So they hurried up.

Bobbie watched their dark figures and the little light of the little candle with an odd feeling of having come to the end of everything. She knew now, she thought, what nuns who were bricked up alive in convent walls felt like. Suddenly she gave herself a little shake.

'Don't be a silly little girl,' she said. She was always very angry when anyone else called her a little girl, even if the adjective that went first was not 'silly' but 'nice' or 'good' or 'clever'. And it was only when she was very angry with herself that she allowed Roberta to use that expression to Bobbie.

She fixed the little candle end on a broken brick near the red-jerseyed boy's foot. Then she opened Peter's knife. It was always hard to manage – a halfpenny was generally needed to get it open at all. This time Bobbie somehow got it open with her thumbnail. She broke the nail, and it hurt horribly. Then she cut the boy's boot-lace, and got the boot off. She tried to pull off his stocking, but his leg was dreadfully swollen, and it did not seem to be the proper shape. So she cut the stocking down, very slowly and carefully. It was a brown knitted stocking, and she wondered who had knitted it, and whether it was the boy's mother, and whether she was feeling anxious about him, and how she would feel when he was brought home with his leg broken. When Bobbie got the stocking off and saw the poor leg, she felt as though the tunnel was growing darker, and the ground felt unsteady, and nothing seemed quite real.

'*Silly* little girl!' said Roberta to Bobbie, and felt better.

'The poor leg,' she told herself; 'it ought to have a cushion – ah!'

She remembered the day when she and Phyllis had torn up their red flannel petticoats to make danger signals to stop the train and prevent an accident. Her flannel petticoat today was white, but it would be quite as soft as a red one. She took it off.

'Oh, what useful things flannel petticoats are!' she said; 'the man who invented them ought to have a statue directed to him.' And she said it aloud, because it seemed that any voice, even her own, would be comfort in that darkness.

'*What* ought to be directed? Who to?' asked the boy, suddenly and very feebly.

'Oh,' said Bobbie, 'now you're better! Hold your teeth and don't let it hurt too much. Now!'

She had folded the petticoat, and lifting his leg laid it on the cushion of folded flannel.

'Don't faint again, *please* don't,' said Bobbie, as he groaned. She hastily wetted her handkerchief with milk and spread it over the poor leg.

'Oh, that hurts,' cried the boy, shrinking. 'Oh – no, it doesn't – it's nice, really.'

'What's your name?' said Bobbie.

'Jim.'

'Mine's Bobbie.'

'But you're a girl, ain't you?'

'Yes, my long name's Roberta.'

'I say – Bobbie.'

'Yes?'

'Wasn't there some more of you just now?'

'Yes, Peter and Phil – that's my brother and sister. They've gone to get someone to carry you out.'

'What rum names. All boys.'

'Yes – I wish I was a boy, don't you?'

'I think you're all right as you are.'

'I didn't mean that – I meant don't you wish *you* were a boy, but of course you are without wishing.'

'You're just as brave as a boy. Why didn't you go with the others?'

'Somebody had to stay with you,' said Bobbie.

'Tell you what, Bobbie,' said Jim, 'you're a brick. Shake.' He reached out a red-jerseyed arm and Bobbie squeezed his hand.

'I won't shake it,' she explained, 'because it would shake *you*, and that would shake your poor leg, and that would hurt. Have you got a hanky?'

'I don't expect I have.' He felt in his pocket. 'Yes, I have. What for?'

She took it and wetted it with milk and put it on his forehead.

'That's jolly,' he said; 'what is it?'

'Milk,' said Bobbie. 'We haven't any water –'

'You're a jolly good little nurse,' said Jim.

'I do it for Mother sometimes,' said Bobbie – 'not milk, of course, but scent, or vinegar and water. I say, I must put the candle out now, because there mayn't be enough of the other one to get you out by.'

'By George,' said he, 'you think of everything.'

Bobbie blew. Out went the candle. You have no idea how black-velvety the darkness was.

'I say, Bobbie,' said a voice through the blackness, 'aren't you afraid of the dark?'

'Not – not – very, that is –'

'Let's hold hands,' said the boy, and it was really rather good of him, because he was like most boys of his age and hated all material tokens of affection, such as kissing, and holding of hands. He called all such things 'pawing', and detested them.

The darkness was more bearable to Bobbie now that her hand was held in the large rough hand of the red-jerseyed sufferer; and he, holding her little smooth hot paw, was surprised to find that he did not mind it so much as he expected. She tried to talk, to amuse him, and 'take his mind off' his sufferings, but it is very difficult to go on talking in the dark, and presently they found themselves in a silence, only broken now and then by a –

'You all right, Bobbie?'

Or an –

'I'm afraid it's hurting you most awfully, Jim. I *am* so sorry.'

And it was very cold.

~

Peter and Phyllis tramped down the long way of the tunnel towards daylight, the candle-grease dripping over Peter's fingers. There were no accidents unless you count Phyllis's catching her frock on a wire, and tearing a long, jagged slit in it, and tripping over her bootlace when it came undone, or going down on her hands and knees, all four of which were grazed.

'There's no end to this tunnel,' said Phyllis – and indeed it did seem very, very long.

'Stick to it,' said Peter; 'everything has an end, and you get to it if you only keep on.'

Which is quite true, if you come to think of it, and a useful thing to remember in seasons of trouble – such as measles, arithmetic, impositions, and those times when you are in disgrace, and feel as though no one would ever love you again, and you could never – never again – love anybody.

'Hurray,' said Peter, suddenly, 'there's the end of

the tunnel – looks just like a pin-hole in a bit of black paper, doesn't it?'

The pin-hole got larger – blue lights lay along the sides of the tunnel. The children could see the gravel way that lay in front of them; the air grew warmer and sweeter. Another twenty steps and they were out in the good glad sunshine with the green trees on both sides.

Phyllis drew a long breath.

'I'll never go into a tunnel again, as long as ever I live,' said she, 'not if there are twenty hundred thousand million hounds inside with red jerseys and their legs broken.'

'Don't be a silly cuckoo,' said Peter, as usual. 'You'd *have* to.'

'I think it was very brave and good of me,' said Phyllis.

'Not it,' said Peter; 'you didn't go because you were brave, but because Bobbie and I aren't skunks. Now where's the nearest house, I wonder? You can't see anything here for the trees.'

'There's a roof over there,' said Phyllis, pointing down the line.

'That's the signal-box,' said Peter, 'and you know you're not allowed to speak to signalmen on duty. It's wrong.'

'I'm not near so afraid of doing wrong as I was of going into that tunnel,' said Phyllis. 'Come on,' and she started to run along the line. So Peter ran, too.

It was very hot in the sunshine, and both children were hot and breathless by the time they stopped, and bending their heads back to look up at the open windows of the signal-box, shouted 'Hi!' as loud as their breathless state allowed. But no one answered. The signal-box stood quiet as an empty nursery, and the handrail of its steps was hot to the hands of the children as they climbed softly up. They peeped in at the open door. The signalman was sitting on a chair tilted back against the wall. His head leaned sideways, and his mouth was open. He was fast asleep.

'My hat!' cried Peter; 'wake up!' And he cried it in a terrible voice, for he knew that if a signalman sleeps on duty, he risks losing his situation, let alone all the other dreadful risks to trains which expect him to tell them when it is safe for them to go their ways.

The signalman never moved. Then Peter sprang to him and shook him. And slowly, yawning and stretching, the man awoke. But the moment he *was* awake he leapt to his feet, put his hands to his head 'like a mad maniac,' as Phyllis said afterwards, and shouted:

'Oh, my heavens – what's o'clock?'

'Twelve thirteen,' said Peter, and indeed it was by the white-faced, round-faced clock on the wall of the signal-box.

The man looked at the clock, sprang to the levers, and wrenched them this way and that. An electric bell tingled – the wires and cranks creaked, and the man threw himself into a chair. He was very pale, and the sweat stood on his forehead 'like large dewdrops on a white cabbage,' as Phyllis remarked later. He was trembling, too; the children could see his big hairy hands shake from side to side, 'with quite extra-sized trembles,' to use the subsequent words of Peter. He drew long breaths. Then suddenly he cried, 'Thank God, thank God you come in when you did – oh, thank God!' and his shoulders began to heave and his face grew red again, and he hid it in those large hairy hands of his.

'Oh, don't cry – don't,' said Phyllis, 'it's all right now,' and she patted him on one big, broad shoulder, while Peter conscientiously thumped the other.

But the signalman seemed quite broken down, and the children had to pat him and thump him for quite a long time before he found his handkerchief – a red one with mauve and white horseshoes on it – and mopped his face and spoke. During this patting and thumping interval a train thundered by.

'I'm downright shamed, that I am,' were the words of the big signalman when he had stopped crying; 'snivelling like a kid.' Then suddenly he seemed to get cross. 'And what was you doing up here, anyway?' he said; 'you know it ain't allowed.'

'Yes,' said Phyllis, 'we knew it was wrong – but I wasn't afraid of doing wrong, and it so turned out right. You aren't sorry we came.'

'Lor' love you – if you hadn't 'a' come –' he stopped and then went on. 'It's a disgrace, so it is, sleeping on duty. If it was to come to be known – even as it is, when no harm's come of it.'

'It won't come to be known,' said Peter; 'we aren't sneaks. All the same, you oughtn't to sleep on duty – it's dangerous.'

'Tell me something I don't know,' said the man, 'but I can't help it. I know'd well enough just how it 'ud be. But I couldn't get off. They couldn't get no one to take on my duty. I tell you I ain't had ten minutes' sleep this last five days. My little chap's ill – pewmonia, the Doctor says – and there's no one but me and 'is little sister to do for him. That's where it is. The gell must 'ave her sleep. Dangerous? Yes, I believe you. Now go and split on me if you like.'

'Of course we won't,' said Peter, indignantly, but Phyllis ignored the whole of the signalman's speech, except the first six words.

'You asked us,' she said, 'to tell you something you don't know. Well, I will. There's a boy in the tunnel over there with a red jersey and his leg broken.'

'What did he want to go into the blooming tunnel for, then?' said the man.

'Don't be so cross,' said Phyllis, kindly. '*We* haven't done anything wrong except coming and waking you up and that was right, as it happens.'

Then Peter told how the boy came to be in the tunnel.

'Well,' said the man, 'I don't see as I can do anything. I can't leave the box.'

'You might tell us where to go after someone who isn't in a box, though,' said Phyllis.

'There's Brigden's farm over yonder – where you see the smoke a-coming up through the trees,' said the man, more and more grumpy, as Phyllis noticed.

'Well, good-bye then,' said Peter.

But the man said, 'Wait a minute.' He put his hand in his pocket and brought out some money – a lot of pennies and one or two shillings and sixpence and half a crown. He picked out two shillings and held them out.

'Here,' he said. 'I'll give you this to hold your tongues about what's taken place today.'

There was a short, unpleasant pause. Then:

'You *are* a nasty man, though, aren't you?' said Phyllis.

Peter took a step forward and knocked the man's hand up, so that the shillings leapt out of it and rolled on the floor.

'If anything *could* make me sneak, *that* would!' he said. 'Come, Phil,' and marched out of the signal-box with flaming cheeks.

Phyllis hesitated. Then she took the hand, still held out stupidly, that the shillings had been in.

'I forgive you,' she said, 'even if Peter doesn't. You're not in your proper senses, or you'd never have done that. I know want of sleep sends people mad. Mother told me. I hope your little boy will soon be better, and –'

'Come on, Phil,' cried Peter, eagerly.

'I'll give you my sacred honour-word we'll never tell anyone. Kiss and be friends,' said Phyllis, feeling how noble it was of her to try to make up a quarrel in which she was not to blame.

The signalman stooped and kissed her.

'I do believe I'm a bit off my head, Missie,' he said. 'Now run along home to Mother. I didn't mean to put you about – there.'

So Phil left the hot signal-box and followed Peter across the fields to the farm.

When the farm men, led by Peter and Phyllis and carrying a hurdle covered with horse-cloths, reached the manhole in the tunnel, Bobbie was fast asleep and so was Jim. Worn out with the pain, the Doctor said afterwards.

'Where does he live?' the bailiff from the farm asked, when Jim had been lifted on to a hurdle.

'In Northumberland,' answered Bobbie.

'I'm at school at Maidbridge,' said Jim. 'I suppose I've got to get back there, somehow.'

'Seems to me the Doctor ought to have a look in first,' said the bailiff.

'Oh, bring him up to our house,' said Bobbie. 'It's

only a little way by the road. I'm sure Mother would say we ought to.'

'Will your Ma like you bringing home strangers with broken legs?'

'She took the poor Russian home herself,' said Bobbie. 'I know she'd say we ought.'

'All right,' said the bailiff, 'you ought to know what your Ma 'ud like. I wouldn't take it upon me to fetch him up to our place without I asked the Missus first, and they call me the Master, too.'

'Are you sure your Mother won't mind?' whispered Jim.

'Certainly,' said Bobbie.

'Then we're to take him up to Three Chimneys?' said the bailiff.

'Of course,' said Peter.

'Then my lad shall nip up to the Doctor's on his bike, and tell him to come down there. Now, lads, lift him quiet and steady. One, two, three!'

~

Thus it happened that Mother, writing away for dear life at a story about a Duchess, a designing villain, a secret passage, and a missing will, dropped her pen as her work-room door burst open, and turned to see Bobbie hatless and red with running.

'Oh, Mother,' she cried, 'do come down. We found a hound in a red jersey in the tunnel, and he's broken his leg and they're bringing him home.'

'They ought to take him to the vet,' said Mother, with a worried frown; 'I really *can't* have a lame dog here.'

'He's not a dog, really – he's a boy,' said Bobbie, between laughing and choking.

'Then he ought to be taken home to his mother.'

'His mother's dead,' said Bobbie, 'and his father's in Northumberland. Oh, Mother, you will be nice to him? I told him I was sure you'd want us to bring him home. You always want to help everybody.'

Mother smiled, but she sighed, too. It is nice that your children should believe you willing to open house and heart to any and every one who needs help. But it is rather embarrassing sometimes, too, when they act on their belief.

'Oh, well,' said Mother, 'we must make the best of it.'

When Jim was carried in, dreadfully white and with set lips whose red had faded to a horrid bluey violet colour, Mother said:

'I am glad you brought him here. Now, Jim, let's get you comfortable in bed before the Doctor comes!'

And Jim, looking at her kind eyes, felt a little, warm, comforting flush of new courage.

'It'll hurt rather, won't it?' he said. 'I don't mean to be a coward. You won't think I'm a coward if I faint again, will you? I really and truly don't do it on purpose. And I do hate to give you all this trouble.'

'Don't you worry,' said Mother; 'it's you that have the trouble, you poor dear – not us.'

And she kissed him just as if he had been Peter. 'We love to have you here – don't we, Bobbie?'

'Yes,' said Bobbie – and she saw by her Mother's face how right she had been to bring home the wounded hound in the red jersey.

CHAPTER 13

The Hound's Grandfather

Mother did not get back to her writing all that day, for the red-jerseyed hound whom the children had brought to Three Chimneys had to be put to bed. And then the Doctor came, and hurt him most horribly. Mother was with him all through it, and that made it a little better than it would have been, but 'bad was the best,' as Mrs Viney said.

The children sat in the parlour downstairs and heard the sound of the Doctor's boots going backwards and forwards over the bedroom floor. And once or twice there was a groan.

'It's horrible,' said Bobbie. 'Oh, I wish Dr Forrest would make haste. Oh, poor Jim!'

'It *is* horrible,' said Peter, 'but it's very exciting. I wish Doctors weren't so stuck-up about who they'll have in the room when they're doing things. I should most awfully like to see a leg set. I believe the bones crunch like anything.'

'Don't!' said the two girls at once.

'Rubbish!' said Peter. 'How are you going to be

Red Cross Nurses, like you were talking of coming home, if you can't even stand hearing me say about bones crunching? You'd have to *hear* them crunch on the field of battle – and be steeped in gore up to the elbows as like as not, and –'

'Stop it!' cried Bobbie, with a white face; 'you don't know how funny you're making me feel.'

'Me, too,' said Phyllis, whose face was pink.

'Cowards!' said Peter.

'I'm not,' said Bobbie. 'I helped Mother with your rake-wounded foot, and so did Phil – you know we did.'

'Well, then!' said Peter. 'Now look here. It would be a jolly good thing for you if I were to talk to you every day for half an hour about broken bones and people's insides, so as to get you used to it.'

A chair was moved above.

'Listen,' said Peter, 'that's the bone crunching.'

'I do wish you wouldn't,' said Phyllis. 'Bobbie doesn't like it.'

'I'll tell you what they do,' said Peter. I can't think what made him so horrid. Perhaps it was because he had been so very nice and kind all the earlier part of the day, and now he had to have a change. This is called reaction. One notices it now and then in oneself. Sometimes when one has been extra good for a longer time than usual, one is suddenly attacked by a violent fit of not being good at all. 'I'll tell you what they do,' said Peter; 'they strap the broken man down so that he can't resist or interfere with their doctorish designs, and then someone holds his head, and someone holds his leg – the broken one, and pulls it till the bones fit in – with a crunch, mind you! Then they strap it up and – let's play at bone-setting!'

'Oh, no!' said Phyllis.

But Bobbie said suddenly: 'All right – *let's!* I'll be the doctor, and Phil can be the nurse. You can be the broken boner; we can get at your legs more easily, because you don't wear petticoats.'

'I'll get the splints and bandages,' said Peter; 'you get the couch of suffering ready.'

The ropes that had tied up the boxes that had come from home were all in a wooden packing-case in the cellar. When Peter brought in a trailing tangle of them, and two boards for splints, Phyllis was excitedly giggling.

'Now, then,' he said, and lay down on the settle, groaning most grievously.

'Not so loud!' said Bobbie, beginning to wind the rope round him and the settle. 'You pull, Phil.'

'Not so tight,' moaned Peter. 'You'll break my other leg.'

Bobbie worked on in silence, winding more and more rope round him.

'That's enough,' said Peter. 'I can't move at all. Oh, my poor leg!' He groaned again.

'*Sure* you can't move?' asked Bobbie, in a rather strange tone.

'Quite sure,' replied Peter. 'Shall we play it's bleeding freely or not?' he asked cheerfully.

'*You* can play what you like,' said Bobbie, sternly, folding her arms and looking down at him where he lay all wound round and round with cord. 'Phil and I are going away. And we shan't untie you till you promise never, never to talk to us about blood and wounds unless we say you may. Come, Phil!'

'You beast!' said Peter, writhing. 'I'll never promise, never. I'll yell, and Mother will come.'

'Do,' said Bobbie, 'and tell her why we tied you up! Come on, Phil. No, I'm not a beast, Peter. But you wouldn't stop when we asked you and –'

'Yah,' said Peter, 'it wasn't even your own idea. You got it out of Stalky!'

Bobbie and Phil, retiring in silent dignity, were met at the door by the Doctor. He came in rubbing his hands and looking pleased with himself.

'Well,' he said, '*that* job's done. It's a nice clean fracture, and it'll go on all right, I've no doubt. Plucky young chap, too – hullo! What's all this?'

His eye had fallen on Peter who lay mousey-still in his bonds on the settle.

'Playing at prisoners, eh?' he said; but his eyebrows had gone up a little. Somehow he had not thought that Bobbie would be playing while in the room above someone was having a broken bone set.

'Oh, no!' said Bobbie, 'not at *prisoners*. We were playing at setting bones. Peter's the broken boner, and I was the doctor.'

'I was the nurse,' put in Phyllis cheerfully.

The Doctor frowned.

'Then I must say,' he said, and he said it rather sternly, 'that it's a very heartless game. Haven't you enough imagination even to faintly picture what's been going on upstairs? That poor chap, with drops of sweat on his forehead, and biting his lips so as not to cry out, and every touch on his leg agony and –'

'*You* ought to be tied up,' said Phyllis; 'you're as bad as –'

'Hush,' said Bobbie; 'I'm sorry, but we weren't heartless, really.'

'I was, I suppose,' said Peter, crossly. 'All right,

Bobbie, don't you go on being noble and screening me, because I jolly well won't have it. It was only that I kept on talking about blood and wounds. I wanted to train them for Red Cross Nurses. And I wouldn't stop when they asked me.'

'Well?' said Dr Forrest, sitting down.

'Well – then I said, "Let's play at setting bones." It was all rot. I knew Bobbie wouldn't. I only said it to tease her. And then when she said "yes", of course I had to go through with it. And they tied me up. They got it out of Stalky. And I think it's a beastly shame.'

He managed to writhe over and hide his face against the wooden back of the settle.

'I didn't think that anyone would know but us,' said Bobbie, indignantly answering Peter's unspoken reproach. 'I never thought of your coming in. And hearing about blood and wounds does really make me feel most awfully funny. It was only a joke our tying him up. Let me untie you, Peter.'

'I don't care if you never untie me,' said Peter; 'and if that's your idea of a joke –'

'If I were you,' said the Doctor, though really he did not quite know what to say, 'I should be untied before your Mother comes down. You don't want to worry her just now, do you?'

'I don't promise anything about not saying about wounds, mind,' said Peter, in very surly tones, as Bobbie and Phyllis began to untie the knots.

'I'm very sorry, Pete,' Bobbie whispered, leaning close to him as she fumbled with the big knot under the settle; 'but if you only knew how sick you made me feel.'

'You've made *me* feel pretty sick, I can tell you,'

Peter rejoined. Then he shook off the loose cords, and stood up.

'I looked in,' said Dr Forrest, 'to see if one of you would come along to the surgery. There are some things that your Mother will want at once, and I've given my man a day off to go and see the circus; will you come, Peter?'

Peter went without a word or a look to his sisters.

The two walked in silence up to the gate that led from the Three Chimneys field to the road. Then Peter said:

'Let me carry your bag. I say, it is heavy – what's in it?'

'Oh, knives and lancets and different instruments for hurting people. And the ether bottle. I had to give him ether, you know – the agony was so intense.'

Peter was silent.

'Tell me all about how you found that chap,' said Dr Forrest.

Peter told. And then Dr Forrest told him stories of brave rescues; he was a most interesting man to talk to, as Peter had often remarked.

Then in the surgery Peter had a better chance than he had ever had of examining the Doctor's balance, and his microscope, and his scales and measuring glasses. When all the things were ready that Peter was to take back, the Doctor said suddenly:

'You'll excuse my shoving my oar in, won't you? But I should like to say something to you.'

'Now for a rowing,' thought Peter, who had been wondering how it was that he had escaped one.

'Something scientific,' added the Doctor.

'Yes,' said Peter, fiddling with the fossil ammonite that the Doctor used for a paper-weight.

'Well,' said the Doctor, 'you know men have to do the work of the world and not be afraid of anything – so they have to be hardy and brave. But women have to take care of their babies and cuddle them and nurse them and be very patient and gentle.'

'Yes,' said Peter, wondering what was coming next.

'Well then, you see. Boys and girls are only little men and women. And *we* are much harder and hardier than they are' – (Peter liked the 'we'. Perhaps the Doctor had known he would.) – 'and much stronger, and things that hurt *them* don't hurt *us*. You know you mustn't hit a girl –'

'I should think not, indeed,' muttered Peter, indignantly.

'Not even if she's your own sister. That's because girls are so much softer and weaker than we are; they have to be, you know,' he added, 'because if they weren't, it wouldn't be nice for the babies. And that's why all the animals are so good to the mother animals. They never fight them, you know.'

'I know,' said Peter, interested; 'two buck rabbits will fight all day if you let them, but they won't hurt a doe.'

'No; and quite wild beasts – lions and elephants – they're immensely gentle with the female beasts. And we've got to be, too.'

'I see,' said Peter.

'And their hearts are soft, too,' the Doctor went on, 'and things that we shouldn't think anything of hurt them dreadfully. So that a man has to be very careful, not only of his fists, but of his words. They're awfully brave, you know,' he went on. 'Think of Bobbie waiting alone in the tunnel with that poor chap. It's an odd thing – the softer and more easily hurt a woman is the better she can screw herself up to do what *has* to be done. I've seen some brave women – your Mother's one,' he ended abruptly.

'Yes,' said Peter.

'Well, that's all; excuse my mentioning it. But nobody knows everything without being told. And you see what I mean, don't you?'

'Yes,' said Peter. 'I'm sorry. There!'

'Of course you are! People always are – directly they understand. Everyone ought to be taught these scientific facts. So long!'

They shook hands heartily. When Peter came home, his sisters looked at him doubtfully.

'It's Pax,' said Peter, dumping down the basket on the table. 'Dr Forrest has been talking scientific to me. No, it's no use my telling you what he said; you wouldn't understand. But it all comes to you girls being poor, soft, weak, frightened things like rabbits, so us men have just got to put up with them. He said you were female beasts. Shall I take this up to Mother, or will you?'

'I know what *boys* are,' said Phyllis, with flaming cheeks; 'they're just the nastiest, rudest –'

'They're very brave,' said Bobbie, 'sometimes.'

'Ah, you mean the chap upstairs? I see. Go ahead, Phil – I shall put up with you whatever you say because you're a poor, weak, frightened, soft –'

'Not if I pull your hair you won't,' said Phyllis, springing at him.

'He said "Pax",' said Bobbie, pulling her away. 'Don't you see,' she whispered as Peter picked up the basket and stalked out with it, 'he's sorry, really, only he won't say so? Let's say we're sorry.'

'It's so goody-goody,' said Phyllis, doubtfully; 'he said we were female beasts, and soft and frightened –'

'Then let's show him we're not frightened of him thinking us goody-goody,' said Bobby; 'and we're not any more beasts than he is.'

And when Peter came back, still with his chin in the air, Bobbie said:

'We're sorry we tied you up, Pete.'

'I thought you would be,' said Peter, very stiff and superior.

This was hard to bear. But –

'Well, so we are,' said Bobbie. 'Now let honour be satisfied on both sides.'

'I did call it Pax,' said Peter, in an injured tone.

'Then let it *be* Pax,' said Bobbie. 'Come on, Phil, let's get the tea. Peter, you might lay the cloth.'

'I say,' said Phyllis, when peace was really restored, which was not till they were washing up the cups after tea, 'Dr Forrest didn't really say we were female beasts, did he?'

'Yes,' said Peter, firmly, 'but I think he meant we men were wild beasts, too.'

'How funny of him!' said Phyllis, breaking a cup.

~

'May I come in, Mother?' Peter was at the door of Mother's writing-room, where Mother sat at her table with two candles in front of her. Their flames looked orange and violet against the clear grey blue of the sky where already a few stars were twinkling.

'Yes, dear,' said Mother, absently, 'anything wrong?' She wrote a few more words and then laid down her pen and began to fold up what she had written. 'I was just writing to Jim's grandfather. He lives near here, you know.'

'Yes, you said so at tea. That's what I want to say. Must you write to him, Mother? Couldn't we keep Jim, and not say anything to his people till he's well? It would be such a surprise for them.'

'Well, yes,' said Mother, laughing, 'I think it would.'

'You see,' Peter went on, 'of course the girls are all right and all that – I'm not saying anything against *them*. But I should like it if I had another chap to talk to sometimes.'

'Yes,' said Mother, 'I know it's dull for you, dear. But I can't help it. Next year perhaps I can send you to school – you'd like that, wouldn't you?'

'I do miss the other chaps, rather,' Peter confessed; 'but if Jim could stay after his leg was well, we could have awful larks.'

'I've no doubt of it,' said Mother. 'Well – perhaps he could, but you know, dear, we're not rich. I can't afford to get him everything he'll want. And he must have a nurse.'

'Can't you nurse him, Mother? You do nurse people so beautifully.'

'That's a pretty compliment, Pete – but I can't do nursing and my writing as well. That's the worst of it.'

'Then you *must* send the letter to his grandfather?'

'Of course – and to his schoolmaster, too. We telegraphed to them both, but I must write as well. They'll be most dreadfully anxious.'

'I say, Mother, why can't his grandfather pay for a nurse?' Peter suggested. 'That would be ripping. I expect the old boy's rolling in money. Grandfathers in books always are.'

'Well, this one isn't in a book,' said Mother, 'so we mustn't expect him to roll much.'

'I say,' said Peter, musingly, 'wouldn't it be jolly if we all *were* in a book and you were writing it? Then you could make all sorts of jolly things happen, and make Jim's leg get well at once and be all right tomorrow, and Father come home soon and –'

'Do you miss your Father very much?' Mother asked, rather coldly, Peter thought.

'Awfully,' said Peter, briefly.

Mother was enveloping and addressing the second letter.

'You see,' Peter went on slowly, 'you see, it's not only him *being* Father, but now he's away there's no other man in the house but me – that's why I want Jim to stay so frightfully much. Wouldn't you like to be writing that book with us all in it, Mother, and make Daddy come home soon?'

Peter's mother put her arm round him suddenly, and hugged him in silence for a minute. Then she said:

'Don't you think it's rather nice to think that we're in a book that God's writing? If I were writing a book, I might make mistakes. But God knows how to make the story end just right – in the way that's best for us.'

'Do you really believe that, Mother?' Peter asked quietly.

'Yes,' she said, 'I do believe it – almost always – except when I'm so sad that I can't believe anything. But even when I can't believe it, I know it's true – and I try to believe it. You don't know how I try, Peter. Now take the letters to the post and don't let's be sad any more.

Courage, courage! That's the finest of all the virtues! I dare say Jim will be here for two or three weeks yet.'

For what was left of the evening Peter was so angelic that Bobbie feared he was going to be ill. She was quite relieved in the morning to find him plaiting Phyllis's hair on the back of her chair in quite his old manner.

It was soon after breakfast that a knock came at the door. The children were hard at work cleaning the brass candlesticks in honour of Jim's visit.

'That'll be the Doctor,' said Mother. 'I'll go. Shut the kitchen door – you're not fit to be seen.'

But it wasn't the Doctor. They knew that by the voice and by the sound of the boots that went upstairs. They did not recognize the sound of the boots, but everyone was certain that they had heard the voice before.

There was a longish interval. The boots and the voice did not come down again.

'Who can it possibly be?' they kept on asking themselves and each other.

'Perhaps,' said Peter at last, 'Dr Forrest has been attacked by highwaymen and left for dead, and this is the man he's telegraphed for to take his place. Mrs Viney said he had a local tenant to do his work when he went for a holiday, didn't you, Mrs Viney?'

'I did so, my dear,' said Mrs Viney from the back kitchen.

'He's fallen down in a fit, more likely,' said Phyllis, 'all human aid despaired of. And this is his man come to break the news to Mother.'

'Nonsense!' said Peter, briskly. 'Mother wouldn't have taken the man up into Jim's bedroom. Why should she? Listen – the door's opening. Now they'll come down. I'll open the door a crack.'

He did.

'It's not listening,' he replied indignantly to Bobbie's scandalized remarks; 'nobody in their senses would talk secrets on the stairs. And Mother can't have secrets to talk with Dr Forrest's stable-man – and you said it was him.'

'Bobbie,' called Mother's voice.

They opened the kitchen door, and Mother leaned over the stair railing.

'Jim's grandfather has come,' she said; 'wash your hands and faces and then you can see him. He wants to see you!' The bedroom door shut again.

'There now!' said Peter; 'fancy us not even thinking of that! Let's have some hot water, Mrs Viney. I'm as black as your hat.'

The three were indeed dirty, for the stuff you clean brass candlesticks with is very far from cleaning to the cleaner.

They were still busy with soap and flannel when they heard the boots and the voice come down the stairs and go into the dining-room. And when they were clean, though still damp – because it takes such a long time to dry your hands properly, and they were very impatient to see the grandfather – they filed into the dining-room.

Mother was sitting in the window-seat, and in the leather-covered arm-chair that Father always used to sit in at the other house sat –

THEIR OWN OLD GENTLEMAN!

'Well, I never did,' said Peter, even before he said, 'How do you do?' He was, as he explained afterwards, too surprised even to remember that there was such a thing as politeness – much less to practise it.

'It's our own old gentleman!' said Phyllis.

'Oh, it's you!' said Bobbie. And then they remembered themselves and their manners and said, 'How do you do?' very nicely.

'This is Jim's grandfather, Mr –' said Mother, naming the old gentleman's name.

'How splendid!' said Peter; 'that's just exactly like a book, isn't it, Mother?'

'It is, rather,' said Mother, smiling; 'things do happen in real life that are rather like books, sometimes.'

'I am so awfully glad it *is* you,' said Phyllis; 'when you think of the lots of old gentlemen there are in the world – it might have been almost anyone.'

'I say, though,' said Peter, 'you're not going to take Jim away, though, are you?'

'Not at present,' said the old gentleman. 'Your Mother has most kindly consented to let him stay here. I thought of sending a nurse, but your Mother is good enough to say that she will nurse him herself.'

'But what about her writing?' said Peter, before anyone could stop him. 'There won't be anything for him to eat if Mother doesn't write.'

'That's all right,' said Mother hastily.

The old gentleman looked very kindly at Mother.

'I see,' he said, 'you trust your children, and confide in them.'

'Of course,' said Mother.

'Then I may tell them our little arrangement,' he said. 'Your Mother, my dears, has consented to give up writing for a little while and to become a Matron of my Hospital.'

'Oh!' said Phyllis, blankly; 'and shall we have to

go away from Three Chimneys and the Railway and everything?'

'No, no, darling,' said Mother, hurriedly.

'The Hospital is called Three Chimneys Hospital,' said the old gentleman, 'and my unlucky Jim's the only patient, and I hope he'll continue to be so. Your Mother will be Matron, and there'll be a hospital staff of a house-maid and a cook – till Jim's well.'

'And then will Mother go on writing again?' asked Peter.

'We shall see,' said the old gentleman, with a swift, slight glance at Bobbie; 'perhaps something nice may happen and she won't have to.'

'I love my writing,' said Mother, very quickly.

'I know,' said the old gentleman; 'don't be afraid that I'm going to try to interfere. But one never knows. Very wonderful and beautiful things do happen, don't they? And we live most of our lives in the hope of them. I may come again to see the boy?'

'Surely,' said Mother, 'and I don't know how to thank you for making it possible for me to nurse him. Dear boy!'

'He kept calling Mother, Mother, in the night,' said Phyllis. 'I woke up twice and heard him.'

'He didn't mean me,' said Mother, in a low voice to the old gentleman; 'that's why I wanted so much to keep him.'

The old gentleman rose.

'I'm so glad,' said Peter, 'that you're going to keep him, Mother.'

'Take care of your Mother, my dears,' said the old gentleman. 'She's a woman in a million.'

'Yes, isn't she?' whispered Bobbie.

'God bless her,' said the old gentleman, taking both Mother's hands, 'God bless her! Ay, and she shall be blessed. Dear me, where's my hat? Will Bobbie come with me to the gate?'

At the gate he stopped and said:

'You're a good child, my dear – I got your letter. But it wasn't needed. When I read about your Father's case in the papers at the time, I had my doubts. And ever since I've known who you were, I've been trying to find out things. I haven't done very much yet. But I have hopes, my dear – I have hopes.'

'Oh!' said Bobbie, choking a little.

'Yes – I may say great hopes. But keep your secret a little longer. Wouldn't do to upset your Mother with a false hope, would it?'

'Oh, but it isn't false!' said Bobbie; 'I *know* you can do it. I knew you could when I wrote. It isn't a false hope, is it?'

'No,' he said, 'I don't think it's a false hope, or I wouldn't have told you. And I think you deserve to be told that there *is* a hope.'

'And you don't think Father did it, do you? Oh, say you don't think he did.'

'My dear,' he said, 'I'm perfectly *certain* he didn't.'

If it was a false hope, it was none the less a very radiant one that lay warm at Bobbie's heart, and through the days that followed lighted her little face as a Japanese lantern is lighted by the candle within.

CHAPTER 14

The End

Life at Three Chimneys was never quite the same again after the old gentleman came to see his grandson. Although they now knew his name, the children never spoke of him by it – at any rate, when they were by themselves. To them he was always the old gentleman, and I think he had better be the old gentleman to us, too. It wouldn't make him seem any more real to you, would it, if I were to tell you that his name was Snooks or Jenkins (which it wasn't)? – and, after all, I must be allowed to keep one secret. It's the only one; I have told you everything else, except what I am going to tell you in this chapter, which is the last. At least, of course, I haven't told you *everything*. If I were to do that, the book would never come to an end, and that would be a pity, wouldn't it?

Well, as I was saying, life at Three Chimneys was never quite the same again. The cook and the house-maid were very nice (I don't mind telling you their names – they were Clara and Ethelwyn), but they told Mother they did not seem to want Mrs Viney, and that she was an old muddler. So Mrs Viney came only two days a week to do washing and ironing. Then Clara and Ethelwyn said they could do the work all right if they weren't interfered with, and that meant that the children no longer got the tea and cleared it away and washed up the tea-things and dusted the rooms.

This would have left quite a blank in their lives, although they had often pretended to themselves and to each other that they hated housework. But now that Mother had no writing and no housework to do, she had time for lessons. And lessons the children had to do. However nice the person who is teaching you may be, lessons are lessons all the world over, and at their best are worse fun than peeling potatoes or lighting a fire.

On the other hand, if Mother now had time for lessons, she also had time for play, and to make up little rhymes for the children as she used to do. She had not had much time for rhymes since she came to Three Chimneys.

There was one very odd thing about these lessons. Whatever the children were doing, they always wanted to be doing something else. When Peter was doing his Latin, he thought it would be nice to be learning History like Bobbie. Bobbie would have preferred Arithmetic, which was what Phyllis happened to be doing, and Phyllis of course thought Latin much the most interesting kind of lesson. And so on.

So, one day, when they sat down to lessons, each of them found a little rhyme at its place. I put the rhymes in to show you that their Mother really did understand a little how children feel about things, and also the kind of words they use, which is the case with very few grown-up people. I suppose most grown-ups have very bad memories, and have forgotten how they felt when they were little. Of course, the verses are supposed to be spoken by the children.

Peter

I once thought Caesar easy pap –
How very soft I must have been!
When they start Caesar with a chap
He little knows what that will mean.
Oh, verbs are silly stupid things.
I'd rather learn the dates of kings!

Bobbie

The worst of all my lesson things
Is learning who succeeded who
In all the rows of queens and kings,
With dates to everything they do;
With dates enough to make you sick; –
I wish it was Arithmetic!

Phyllis

Such pounds and pounds of apples fill
My slate – what is the price you'd spend!
You scratch the figures out until
You cry upon the dividend.
I'd break the slate and scream for joy
If I did Latin like a boy!

This kind of thing, of course, made lessons much jollier. It is something to know that the person who is teaching you sees that it is not all plain sailing for you, and does not think that it is just your stupidness that makes you not know your lessons till you've learned them!

Then as Jim's leg got better it was very pleasant to go up and sit with him and hear tales about his school life and the other boys. There was one boy, named Parr, of whom Jim seemed to have formed the lowest possible opinion, and another boy named Wigsby Minor, for whose views Jim had a great respect. Also there were three brothers named Paley, and the youngest was called Paley Terts, and was much given to fighting.

Peter drank in all this with deep joy, and Mother seemed to have listened with some interest, for one day she gave Jim a sheet of paper on which she had written a rhyme about Parr, bringing in Paley and Wigsby by name in a most wonderful way, as well as all the reasons Jim had for not liking Parr, and Wigsby's wise opinion on the matter. Jim was immensely pleased. He had never had a rhyme written expressly for him before. He read it till he knew it by heart and then he sent it to Wigsby, who liked it almost as much as Jim did. Perhaps you may like it, too.

The New Boy

His name is Parr; he says that he
Is given bread and milk for tea.
He says his father killed a bear.
He says his mother cuts his hair.

He wears goloshes when it's wet.
I've heard his people call him 'Pet'!
He has no proper sense of shame;
He told the chaps his Christian name.

He cannot wicket-keep at all,
He's frightened of a cricket ball.

He reads indoors for hours and hours,
He knows the names of beastly flowers.

He says his French just like Mossoo –
A beastly stuck-up thing to do –
He won't keep cave, shirks his turn
And says he came to school to learn!

He won't play football, says it hurts;
He wouldn't fight with Paley Terts;
He couldn't whistle if he tried,
And when we laughed at him he cried!

Now, Wigsby Minor says that Parr
Is only like all new boys are.
I know when I first came to school
I wasn't such a jolly fool!

Jim could never understand how Mother could have been clever enough to do it. To the others it seemed nice, but natural. You see they had always been used to having a mother who could write verses just like the way people talk, even to the shocking expression at the end of the rhyme, which was Jim's very own.

Jim taught Peter to play chess and draughts and dominoes, and altogether it was a nice quiet time.

Only Jim's leg got better and better, and a general feeling began to spring up among Bobbie, Peter, and Phyllis that something ought to be done to amuse him; not just games, but something really handsome. But it was extraordinarily difficult to think of anything.

'It's no good,' said Peter, when all of them had thought and thought till their heads felt quite heavy and swollen; 'if we can't think of anything to amuse him, we just can't, and there's an end to it. Perhaps something will just happen of its own accord that he'll like.'

'Things *do* happen by themselves sometimes, without your making them,' said Phyllis, rather as though, usually, everything that happened in the world was her doing.

'I wish something would happen,' said Bobbie, dreamily, 'something wonderful.'

And something wonderful did happen exactly four days after she had said this. I wish I could say it was three days after, because in fairy tales it is always three days after that things happen. But this is not a fairy story, and besides, it really was four and not three, and I am nothing if not strictly truthful.

They seemed to be hardly Railway children at all in those days, and as the days went on each had an uneasy feeling about this which Phyllis expressed one day.

'I wonder if the Railway misses us,' she said, plaintively. 'We never go to see it now.'

'It seems ungrateful,' said Bobbie; 'we loved it so when we hadn't anyone to play with.'

'Perks is always coming up to ask after Jim,' said Peter, 'and the signalman's little boy is better. He told me so.'

'I didn't mean the people,' explained Phyllis; 'I meant the dear Railway itself.'

'The thing I don't like,' said Bobbie, on this fourth day, which was a Tuesday, 'is our having stopped waving to the 9.15 and sending our love to Father by it.'

'Let's begin again,' said Phyllis. And they did.

Somehow the change of everything that was made by having servants in the house and Mother not doing any writing, made the time seem extremely long since that strange morning at the beginning of things, when they had got up so early and burnt the bottom out of the kettle and had apple pie for breakfast and first seen the Railway.

It was September now, and the turf on the slope to the Railway was dry and crisp. Little long grass spikes stood up like bits of gold wire, frail blue harebells trembled on their tough, slender stalks. Gipsy roses opened wide and flat their lilac-coloured discs, and the golden stars of St John's Wort shone at the edges of the pool that lay halfway to the Railway. Bobbie gathered a generous handful of the flowers and thought how pretty they would look lying on the green-and-pink blanket of silk waste that now covered Jim's poor broken leg.

'Hurry up,' said Peter, 'or we shall miss the 9.15!'

'I can't hurry more than I am doing,' said Phyllis. 'Oh, bother it! My bootlace has come undone *again!*'

'When you're married,' said Peter, 'your bootlace will come undone going up the church aisle, and your man that you're going to get married to will tumble over it and smash his nose in on the ornamented pavement; and then you'll say you won't marry him, and you'll have to be an old maid.'

'I shan't,' said Phyllis. 'I'd much rather marry a man with his nose smashed in than not marry anybody.'

'It would be horrid to marry a man with a smashed nose all the same,' went on Bobbie. 'He wouldn't be able to smell the flowers at the wedding. Wouldn't that be awful!'

'Bother the flowers at the wedding!' cried Peter. 'Look! the signal's down. We must run!'

They ran. And once more they waved their handkerchiefs without at all minding whether the handkerchiefs were clean or not, to the 9.15.

'Take our love to Father!' cried Bobbie. And the others, too, shouted:

'Take our love to Father!'

The old gentleman waved from his first-class carriage window. Quite violently he waved. And there was nothing odd in that, for he always had waved. But what was really remarkable was that from every window handkerchiefs fluttered, newspapers signalled, hands waved wildly. The train swept by with a rustle and roar, the little pebbles jumped and danced under it as it passed, and the children were left looking at each other.

'Well!' said Peter.

'*Well!*' said Bobbie.

'WELL!' said Phyllis.

'Whatever on earth does that mean?' asked Peter, but he did not expect any answer.

'I *don't* know,' said Bobbie. 'Perhaps the old gentleman told the people at his station to look out for us and wave. He knew we should like it!'

Now, curiously enough, this was just what had happened. The old gentleman, who was very well known and respected at this particular station, had got there early this morning, and he had waited at the door where the young man stands holding the interesting machine that clips the tickets, and he had said something to every single passenger who passed through that door. And after nodding to what the old gentleman had said – and the nods expressed every shade of surprise, interest, doubt, cheerful pleasure, and grumpy

agreement – each passenger had gone on to the platform and read one certain part of his newspaper. And
when the passengers got into the train, they had told
the other passengers who were already there what the
old gentleman had said, and then the other passengers
had also looked at their newspapers and seemed very
astonished and, mostly, pleased. Then, when the train
passed the fence where the three children were, newspapers and hands and handkerchiefs were waved madly,
till all that side of the train was fluttery with white,
like pictures of the King's Coronation in the biography
at Maskelyne and Cook's. To the children it almost
seemed as though the train itself was alive, and was at
last responding to the love that they had given it so
freely and so long.

'It is most extraordinarily rum!' said Peter.

'Most stronery!' echoed Phyllis.

But Bobbie said, 'Don't you think the old gentleman's
waves seemed more significating than usual?'

'No,' said the others.

'I do,' said Bobbie. 'I thought he was trying to
explain something to us with his newspaper.'

'Explain what?' asked Peter, not unnaturally.

'*I* don't know,' Bobbie answered, 'but I do feel most
awfully funny. I feel just exactly as if something was
going to happen.'

'What is going to happen,' said Peter, 'is that Phyllis's
stocking is going to come down.'

This was but too true. The suspender had given way
in the agitation of the waves to the 9.15. Bobbie's
handkerchief served as first aid to the injured, and they
all went home.

Lessons were more than usually difficult to Bobbie

that day. Indeed, she disgraced herself so deeply over a quite simple sum about the division of 48 pounds of meat and 36 pounds of bread among 144 hungry children that Mother looked at her anxiously.

'Don't you feel quite well, dear?' she asked.

'I don't know,' was Bobbie's unexpected answer. 'I don't know how I feel. It isn't that I'm lazy. Mother, will you let me off lessons today? I feel as if I wanted to be quite alone by myself.'

'Yes, of course I'll let you off,' said Mother; 'but –'

Bobbie dropped her slate. It cracked just across the little green mark that is so useful for drawing patterns round, and it was never the same slate again. Without waiting to pick it up she bolted. Mother caught her in the hall feeling blindly among the waterproofs and umbrellas for her garden hat.

'What is it, my sweetheart?' said Mother. 'You don't feel ill, do you?'

'I *don't* know,' Bobbie answered, a little breathlessly, 'but I want to be by myself and see if my head really *is* all silly and my inside all squirmy-twisty.'

'Hadn't you better lie down?' Mother said, stroking her hair back from her forehead.

'I'd be more alive in the garden, I think,' said Bobbie.

But she could not stay in the garden. The hollyhocks and the asters and the late roses all seemed to be waiting for something to happen. It was one of those still, shiny autumn days, when everything does seem to be waiting.

Bobbie could not wait.

'I'll go down to the station,' she said, 'and talk to Perks and ask about the signalman's little boy.'

So she went down. On the way she passed the old

lady from the Post-office, who gave her a kiss and a hug, but rather to Bobbie's surprise, no words except:

'God bless you, love –' and, after a pause, 'run along – do.'

The draper's boy, who had sometimes been a little less than civil and a little more than contemptuous, now touched his cap, and uttered the remarkable words:

''Morning, Miss. I'm sure –'

The blacksmith, coming along with an open newspaper in his hand, was even more strange in his manner. He grinned broadly, though, as a rule, he was a man not given to smiles, and waved the newspaper long before he came up to her. And as he passed her, he said, in answer to her 'Good morning':

'Good morning to you, Missie, and many of them! I wish you joy, that I do!'

'Oh!' said Bobbie to herself, and her heart quickened its beats, 'something *is* going to happen! I know it is – everyone is so odd, like people are in dreams.'

The Station Master wrung her hand warmly. In fact he worked it up and down like a pump-handle. But he gave her no reason for this unusually enthusiastic greeting. He only said:

'The 11.54's a bit late, Miss – the extra luggage this holiday time,' and went away very quickly into that inner Temple of his into which even Bobbie dared not follow him.

Perks was not to be seen, and Bobbie shared the solitude of the platform with the Station Cat. This tortoise-shell lady, usually of a retiring disposition, came today to rub herself against the brown stockings of Bobbie with arched back, waving tail, and reverberating purrs.

'Dear me!' said Bobbie, stooping to stroke her, 'how very kind everybody is today – even you, pussy!'

Perks did not appear until the 11.54 was signalled, and then he, like everybody else that morning, had a newspaper in his hand.

'Hullo!' he said, ''ere you are. Well, if *this* is the train, it'll be smart work! Well, God bless you, my dear! I see it in the paper, and I don't think I was ever so glad of anything in all my born days!' He looked at Bobbie a moment, then said, 'One I must have, Miss, and no offence, I know, on a day like this 'ere!' and with that he kissed her, first on one cheek and then on the other.

'You ain't offended, are you?' he asked anxiously. 'I ain't took too great a liberty? On a day like this, you know –'

'No, no,' said Bobbie, 'of course it's not a liberty, dear Mr Perks; we love you quite as much as if you were an uncle of ours – but – on a day like *what*?'

'Like this 'ere!' said Perks. 'Don't I tell you I see it in the paper?'

'Saw *what* in the paper?' asked Bobbie, but already the 11.54 was steaming into the station and the Station Master was looking at all the places where Perks was not and ought to have been.

Bobbie was left standing alone, the Station Cat watching her from under the bench with friendly golden eyes.

Of course you know already exactly what was going to happen. Bobbie was not so clever. She had the vague, confused, expectant feeling that comes to one's heart in dreams. What her heart expected I can't tell – perhaps the very thing that you and I know was going to happen

– but her mind expected nothing; it was almost blank, and felt nothing but tiredness and stupidness and an empty feeling like your body has when you have been a long walk and it is very far indeed past your proper dinner-time.

Only three people got out of the 11.54. The first was a countrywoman with two baskety boxes full of live chickens who stuck their russet heads out anxiously through the wicker bars; the second was Miss Peckitt, the grocer's wife's cousin, with a tin box and three brown-paper parcels; and the third –

'Oh! my Daddy, my Daddy!' That scream went like a knife into the heart of everyone in the train, and people put their heads out of the windows to see a tall pale man with lips set in a thin close line, and a little girl clinging to him with arms and legs, while his arms went tightly round her.

~

'I knew something wonderful was going to happen,' said Bobbie, as they went up the road, 'but I didn't think it was going to be this. Oh, my Daddy, my Daddy!'

'Then didn't Mother get my letter?' Father asked.

'There weren't any letters this morning. Oh! Daddy! it *is* really you, isn't it?'

The clasp of a hand she had forgotten assured her that it was.

'You must go in by yourself, Bobbie, and tell Mother quite quietly that it's all right. They've caught the man who did it. Everyone knows now that it wasn't your Daddy.'

'*I* always knew it wasn't,' said Bobbie. 'Me and Mother and our old gentleman.'

'Yes,' he said, 'it's all his doing. Mother wrote and told me you had found out. And she told me what you'd been to her. My own little girl!' They stopped a minute then.

And now I see them crossing the field. Bobbie goes into the house, trying to keep her eyes from speaking before her lips have found the right words to 'tell Mother quite quietly' that the sorrow and the struggle and the parting are over and done, and that Father has come home.

I see Father walking in the garden, waiting – waiting. He is looking at the flowers, and each flower is a miracle to eyes that all these months of Spring and Summer have seen only flag-stones and gravel and a little grudging grass. But his eyes keep turning towards the house. And presently he leaves the garden and goes to stand outside the nearest door. It is the back door, and across the yard the swallows are circling. They are getting ready to fly away from cold winds and keen frost to the land where it is always summer. They are the same swallows that the children built the little clay nests for.

～

Now the door opens. Bobbie's voice calls:

'Come in, Daddy; come in!'

He goes in and the door is shut. I think we will not open the door to follow him. I think that just now we are not wanted there. I think it will be best for us to go quickly and quietly away. At the end of the field, among the thin gold spikes of grass and the harebells and Gipsy roses and St John's Wort, we may just take one last look, over our shoulders, at the white house where neither we nor anyone else is wanted now.

CLASSIC LITERATURE: WORDS AND PHRASES
adapted from the Collins English Dictionary

Accoucheur NOUN a male midwife or doctor ❏ *I think my sister must have had some general idea that I was a young offender whom an Accoucheur Policemen had taken up (on my birthday) and delivered over to her* (*Great Expectations* by Charles Dickens)

addled ADJ confused and unable to think properly ❏ *But she counted and counted till she got that addled* (*The Adventures of Huckleberry Finn* by Mark Twain)

admiration NOUN amazement or wonder ❏ *lifting up his hands and eyes by way of admiration* (*Gulliver's Travels* by Jonathan Swift)

afeard ADJ afeard means afraid ❏ *shake it – and don't be afeard* (*The Adventures of Huckleberry Finn* by Mark Twain)

affected VERB affected means followed ❏ *Hadst thou affected sweet divinity* (*Doctor Faustus 5.2* by Christopher Marlowe)

aground ADV when a boat runs aground, it touches the ground in a shallow part of the water and gets stuck ❏ *what kep' you? – boat get aground?* (*The Adventures of Huckleberry Finn* by Mark Twain)

ague NOUN a fever in which the patient has alternate hot and cold shivering fits ❏ *his exposure to the wet and cold had brought on fever and ague* (*Oliver Twist* by Charles Dickens)

alchemy ADJ false or worthless ❏ *all wealth alchemy* (*The Sun Rising* by John Donne)

all alike PHRASE the same all the time ❏ *Love, all alike* (*The Sun Rising* by John Donne)

alow and aloft PHRASE alow means in the lower part or bottom, and aloft means on the top, so alow and aloft means on the top and in the bottom or throughout ❏ *Someone's turned the chest out alow and aloft* (*Treasure Island* by Robert Louis Stevenson)

ambuscade NOUN ambuscade is not a proper word. Tom means an ambush, which is when a group of people attack their enemies, after hiding and waiting for them ❏ *and so we would lie in ambuscade, as he called it* (*The Adventures of Huckleberry Finn* by Mark Twain)

amiable ADJ likeable or pleasant ❏ *Such amiable qualities must speak for themselves* (*Pride and Prejudice* by Jane Austen)

amulet NOUN an amulet is a charm thought to drive away evil spirits. ❏ *uttered phrases at once occult and familiar, like the amulet worn on the heart* (*Silas Marner* by George Eliot)

amusement NOUN here amusement means a strange and disturbing puzzle ❏ *this was an amusement the other way* (*Robinson Crusoe* by Daniel Defoe)

ancient NOUN an ancient was the flag displayed on a ship to show which country it belongs to. It is also called the ensign ❏ *her ancient and pendants out* (*Robinson Crusoe* by Daniel Defoe)

antic ADJ here antic means horrible or grotesque ❏ *armed and dressed after a very antic manner* (*Gulliver's Travels* by Jonathan Swift)

antics NOUN antics is an old word meaning clowns, or people who do silly things to make other people laugh ❏ *And point like antics at his triple crown* (*Doctor Faustus 3.2* by Christopher Marlowe)

appanage NOUN an appanage is a living allowance ❑ *As if loveliness were not the special prerogative of woman – her legitimate appanage and heritage!* (*Jane Eyre* by Charlotte Brontë)

appended VERB appended means attached or added to ❑ *and these words appended* (*Treasure Island* by Robert Louis Stevenson)

approver NOUN an approver is someone who gives evidence against someone he used to work with ❑ *Mr. Noah Claypole: receiving a free pardon from the Crown in consequence of being admitted approver against Fagin* (*Oliver Twist* by Charles Dickens)

areas NOUN the areas is the space, below street level, in front of the basement of a house ❑ *The Dodger had a vicious propensity, too, of pulling the caps from the heads of small boys and tossing them down areas* (*Oliver Twist* by Charles Dickens)

argument NOUN theme or important idea or subject which runs through a piece of writing ❑ *Thrice needful to the argument which now* (*The Prelude* by William Wordsworth) .

artificially ADJ artfully or cleverly ❑ *and he with a sharp flint sharpened very artificially* (*Gulliver's Travels* by Jonathan Swift)

artist NOUN here artist means a skilled workman ❑ *This man was a most ingenious artist* (*Gulliver's Travels* by Jonathan Swift)

assizes NOUN assizes were regular court sessions which a visiting judge was in charge of ❑ *you shall hang at the next assizes* (*Treasure Island* by Robert Louis Stevenson)

attraction NOUN gravitation, or Newton's theory of gravitation ❑ *he predicted the same fate to attraction* (*Gulliver's Travels* by Jonathan Swift)

aver VERB to aver is to claim something strongly ❑ *for Jem Rodney, the mole catcher, averred that one evening as he was returning homeward* (*Silas Marner* by George Eliot)

baby NOUN here baby means doll, which is a child's toy that looks like a small person ❑ *and skilful dressing her baby* (*Gulliver's Travels* by Jonathan Swift)

bagatelle NOUN bagatelle is a game rather like billiards and pool ❑ *Breakfast had been ordered at a pleasant little tavern, a mile or so away upon the rising ground beyond the green; and there was a bagatelle board in the room, in case we should desire to unbend our minds after the solemnity.* (*Great Expectations* by Charles Dickens)

bah EXCLAM Bah is an exclamation of frustration or anger ❑ *"Bah," said Scrooge.* (*A Christmas Carol* by Charles Dickens)

bairn NOUN a northern word for child ❑ *Who has taught you those fine words, my bairn?* (*Wuthering Heights* by Emily Brontë)

bait VERB to bait means to stop on a journey to take refreshment ❑ *So, when they stopped to bait the horse, and ate and drank and enjoyed themselves, I could touch nothing that they touched, but kept my fast unbroken.* (*David Copperfield* by Charles Dickens)

balustrade NOUN a balustrade is a row of vertical columns that form railings ❑ *but I mean to say you might have got a hearse up that staircase, and taken it broadwise, with the splinter-bar towards the wall, and the door towards the balustrades: and done it easy* (*A Christmas Carol* by Charles Dickens)

bandbox NOUN a large lightweight box for carrying bonnets or hats ❑ *I am glad I bought my bonnet, if it is only for the fun of having another bandbox* (*Pride and Prejudice* by Jane Austen)

barren NOUN a barren here is a stretch or expanse of barren land ❑ *a line* *of upright stones, continued the length of the barren* (*Wuthering Heights* by Emily Brontë)

basin NOUN a basin was a cup without a handle ❑ *who is drinking his tea out of a basin* (*Wuthering Heights* by Emily Brontë)

battalia NOUN the order of battle ❑ *till I saw part of his army in battalia* (*Gulliver's Travels* by Jonathan Swift)

battery NOUN a Battery is a fort or a place where guns are positioned ❑ *You bring the lot to me, at that old Battery over yonder* (*Great Expectations* by Charles Dickens)

battledore and shuttlecock NOUN The game battledore and shuttlecock was an early version of the game now known as badminton. The aim of the early game was simply to keep the shuttlecock from hitting the ground. ❑ *Battledore and shuttlecock's a wery good game vhen you an't the shuttlecock and two lawyers the battledores, in which case it gets too excitin' to be pleasant* (*Pickwick Papers* by Charles Dickens)

beadle NOUN a beadle was a local official who had power over the poor ❑ *But these impertinences were speedily checked by the evidence of the surgeon, and the testimony of the beadle* (*Oliver Twist* by Charles Dickens)

bearings NOUN the bearings of a place are the measurements or directions that are used to find or locate it ❑ *the bearings of the island* (*Treasure Island* by Robert Louis Stevenson)

beaufet NOUN a beaufet was a sideboard ❑ *and sweet-cake from the beaufet* (*Emma* by Jane Austen)

beck NOUN a beck is a small stream ❑ *a beck which follows the bend of the glen* (*Wuthering Heights* by Emily Brontë)

bedight VERB decorated ❑ *and bedight with Christmas holly stuck into the top.* (*A Christmas Carol* by Charles Dickens)

Bedlam NOUN Bedlam was a lunatic asylum in London which had statues carved by Caius Gabriel Cibber at its entrance ❑ *Bedlam, and those carved maniacs at the gates* (*The Prelude* by William Wordsworth)

beeves NOUN oxen or castrated bulls which are animals used for pulling vehicles or carrying things ❑ *to deliver in every morning six beeves* (*Gulliver's Travels* by Jonathan Swift)

begot VERB created or caused ❑ *Begot in thee* (*On His Mistress* by John Donne)

behoof NOUN behoof means benefit ❑ *"Yes, young man," said he, releasing the handle of the article in question, retiring a step or two from my table, and speaking for the behoof of the landlord and waiter at the door* (*Great Expectations* by Charles Dickens)

berth NOUN a berth is a bed on a boat ❑ *this is the berth for me* (*Treasure Island* by Robert Louis Stevenson)

bevers NOUN a bever was a snack, or small portion of food, eaten between main meals ❑ *that buys me thirty meals a day and ten bevers* (*Doctor Faustus 2.1* by Christopher Marlowe)

bilge water NOUN the bilge is the widest part of a ship's bottom, and the bilge water is the dirty water that collects there ❑ *no gush of bilge-water had turned it to fetid puddle* (*Jane Eyre* by Charlotte Brontë)

bills NOUN bills is an old term meaning prescription. A prescription is the piece of paper on which your doctor writes an order for medicine and which you give to a chemist to get the medicine ❑ *Are not thy bills hung up as monuments* (*Doctor Faustus 1.1* by Christopher Marlowe)

black cap NOUN a judge wore a black cap when he was about to sentence a prisoner to death ❑ *The judge*

227

assumed the black cap, and the prisoner still stood with the same air and gesture. (*Oliver Twist* by Charles Dickens)

black gentleman NOUN this was another word for the devil ❏ *for she is as impatient as the black gentleman* (*Emma* by Jane Austen)

boot-jack NOUN a wooden device to help take boots off ❏ *The speaker appeared to throw a boot-jack, or some such article, at the person he addressed* (*Oliver Twist* by Charles Dickens)

booty NOUN booty means treasure or prizes ❏ *would be inclined to give up their booty in payment of the dead man's debts* (*Treasure Island* by Robert Louis Stevenson)

Bow Street runner PHRASE Bow Street runners were the first British police force, set up by the author Henry Fielding in the eighteenth century ❏ *as would have convinced a judge or a Bow Street runner* (*Treasure Island* by Robert Louis Stevenson)

brawn NOUN brawn is a dish of meat which is set in jelly ❏ *Heaped up upon the floor, to form a kind of throne, were turkeys, geese, game, poultry, brawn, great joints of meat, sucking-pigs* (*A Christmas Carol* by Charles Dickens)

bray VERB when a donkey brays, it makes a loud, harsh sound ❏ *and she doesn't bray like a jackass* (*The Adventures of Huckleberry Finn* by Mark Twain)

break VERB in order to train a horse you first have to break it ❏ "*If a high-mettled creature like this,*" *said he,* "*can't be broken by fair means, she will never be good for anything*" (*Black Beauty* by Anna Sewell)

bullyragging VERB bullyragging is an old word which means bullying. To bullyrag someone is to threaten or force someone to do something they don't want to do ❏ *and a lot of loafers bullyragging him for sport* (*The Adventures of Huckleberry Finn* by Mark Twain)

but PREP except for (this) ❏ *but this, all pleasures fancies be* (*The Good-Morrow* by John Donne)

by hand PHRASE by hand was a common expression of the time meaning that baby had been fed either using a spoon or a bottle rather than by breast-feeding ❏ *My sister, Mrs. Joe Gargery, was more than twenty years older than I, and had established a great reputation with herself . . . because she had bought me up 'by hand'* (*Great Expectations* by Charles Dickens)

bye-spots NOUN bye-spots are lonely places ❏ *and bye-spots of tales rich with indigenous produce* (*The Prelude* by William Wordsworth)

calico NOUN calico is plain white fabric made from cotton ❏ *There was two old dirty calico dresses* (*The Adventures of Huckleberry Finn* by Mark Twain)

camp-fever NOUN camp-fever was another word for the disease typhus ❏ *during a severe camp-fever* (*Emma* by Jane Austen)

cant NOUN cant is insincere or empty talk ❏ "*Man,*" *said the Ghost,* "*if man you be in heart, not adamant, forbear that wicked cant until you have discovered What the surplus is, and Where it is.*" (*A Christmas Carol* by Charles Dickens)

canty ADJ canty means lively, full of life ❏ *My mother lived til eighty, a canty dame to the last* (*Wuthering Heights* by Emily Brontë)

canvas VERB to canvas is to discuss ❏ *We think so very differently on this point Mr Knightley, that there can be no use in canvassing it* (*Emma* by Jane Austen)

capital ADJ capital means excellent or extremely good ❏ *for it's capital, so shady, light, and big* (*Little Women* by Louisa May Alcott)

capstan NOUN a capstan is a device used on a ship to lift sails and anchors ❏ *capstans going, ships going out to sea, and unintelligible sea creatures* roaring curses over the bulwarks at respondent lightermen (*Great Expectations* by Charles Dickens)

case-bottle NOUN a square bottle designed to fit with others into a case ❏ *The spirit being set before him in a huge case-bottle, which had originally come out of some ship's locker* (*The Old Curiosity Shop* by Charles Dickens)

casement NOUN casement is a word meaning window. The teacher in *Nicholas Nickleby* misspells window showing what a bad teacher he is ❏ *W-i-n, win, d-e-r, der, winder, a casement.'* (*Nicholas Nickleby* by Charles Dickens)

cataleptic ADJ a cataleptic fit is one in which the victim goes into a trance-like state and remains still for a long time ❏ *It was at this point in their history that Silas's cataleptic fit occurred during the prayer-meeting* (*Silas Marner* by George Eliot)

cauldron NOUN a cauldron is a large cooking pot made of metal ❏ *stirring a large cauldron which seemed to be full of soup* (*Alice's Adventures in Wonderland* by Lewis Carroll)

cephalic ADJ cephalic means to do with the head ❏ *with ink composed of a cephalic tincture* (*Gulliver's Travels* by Jonathan Swift)

chaise and four NOUN a closed four-wheel carriage pulled by four horses ❏ *he came down on Monday in a chaise and four to see the place* (*Pride and Prejudice* by Jane Austen)

chamberlain NOUN the main servant in a household ❏ *In those times a bed was always to be got there at any hour of the night, and the chamberlain, letting me in at his ready wicket, lighted the candle next in order on his shelf* (*Great Expectations* by Charles Dickens)

characters NOUN distinguishing marks ❏ *Impressed upon all forms the characters* (*The Prelude* by William Wordsworth)

chary ADJ cautious ❏ *I should have been chary of discussing my guardian too freely even with her* (*Great Expectations* by Charles Dickens)

cherishes VERB here cherishes means cheers or brightens ❏ *some philosophic song of Truth that cherishes our daily life* (*The Prelude* by William Wordsworth)

chickens' meat PHRASE chickens' meat is an old term which means chickens' feed or food ❏ *I had shook a bag of chickens' meat out in that place* (*Robinson Crusoe* by Daniel Defoe)

chimeras NOUN a chimera is an unrealistic idea or a wish which is unlikely to be fulfilled ❏ *with many other wild impossible chimeras* (*Gulliver's Travels* by Jonathan Swift)

chines NOUN chine is a cut of meat that includes part or all of the backbone of the animal ❏ *and they found hams and chines uncut* (*Silas Marner* by George Eliot)

chits NOUN chits is a slang word which means girls ❏ *I hate affected, niminy-piminy chits!* (*Little Women* by Louisa May Alcott)

chopped VERB chopped means come suddenly or accidentally ❏ *if I had chopped upon them* (*Robinson Crusoe* by Daniel Defoe)

chute NOUN a narrow channel ❏ *One morning about day-break, I found a canoe and crossed over a chute to the main shore* (*The Adventures of Huckleberry Finn* by Mark Twain)

circumspection NOUN careful observation of events and circumstances; caution ❏ *I honour your circumspection* (*Pride and Prejudice* by Jane Austen)

clambered VERB clambered means to climb somewhere with difficulty, usually using your hands and your feet ❏ *he clambered up and down stairs* (*Treasure Island* by Robert Louis Stevenson)

clime NOUN climate ❏ *no season knows nor clime* (*The Sun Rising* by John Donne)

clinched VERB clenched ❏ *the tops whereof I could but just reach with my fist clinched* (*Gulliver's Travels* by Jonathan Swift)

close chair NOUN a close chair is a sedan chair, which is an covered chair which has room for one person. The sedan chair is carried on two poles by two men, one in front and one behind ❏ *persuaded even the Empress herself to let me hold her in her close chair* (*Gulliver's Travels* by Jonathan Swift)

clown NOUN clown here means peasant or person who lives off the land ❏ *In ancient days by emperor and clown* (*Ode on a Nightingale* by John Keats)

coalheaver NOUN a coalheaver loaded coal onto ships using a spade ❏ *Good, strong, wholesome medicine, as was given with great success to two Irish labourers and a coalheaver* (*Oliver Twist* by Charles Dickens)

coal-whippers NOUN men who worked at docks using machines to load coal onto ships ❏ *here, were colliers by the score and score, with the coal-whippers plunging off stages on deck* (*Great Expectations* by Charles Dickens)

cobweb NOUN a cobweb is the net which a spider makes for catching insects ❏ *the walls and ceilings were all hung round with cobwebs* (*Gulliver's Travels* by Jonathan Swift)

coddling VERB coddling means to treat someone too kindly or protect them too much ❏ *and I've been coddling the fellow as if I'd been his grandmother* (*Little Women* by Louisa May Alcott)

coil NOUN coil means noise or fuss or disturbance ❏ *What a coil is there?* (*Doctor Faustus 4.7* by Christopher Marlowe)

collared VERB to collar something is a slang term which means to capture.

In this sentence, it means he stole it [the money] ❏ *he collared it* (*The Adventures of Huckleberry Finn* by Mark Twain)

colling VERB colling is an old word which means to embrace and kiss ❏ *and no clasping and colling at all* (*Tess of the D'Urbervilles* by Thomas Hardy)

colloquies NOUN colloquy is a formal conversation or dialogue ❏ *Such colloquies have occupied many a pair of pale-faced weavers* (*Silas Marner* by George Eliot)

comfit NOUN sugar-covered pieces of fruit or nut eaten as sweets ❏ *and pulled out a box of comfits* (*Alice's Adventures in Wonderland* by Lewis Carroll)

coming out VERB when a girl came out in society it meant she was of marriageable age. In order to 'come out' girls were expecting to attend balls and other parties during a season ❏ *The younger girls formed hopes of coming out a year or two sooner than they might otherwise have done* (*Pride and Prejudice* by Jane Austen)

commit VERB commit means arrest or stop ❏ *Commit the rascals* (*Doctor Faustus 4.7* by Christopher Marlowe)

commodious ADJ commodious means convenient ❏ *the most commodious and effectual ways* (*Gulliver's Travels* by Jonathan Swift)

commons NOUN commons is an old term meaning food shared with others ❏ *his pauper assistants ranged themselves behind him; the gruel was served out; and a long grace was said over the short commons.* (*Oliver Twist* by Charles Dickens)

complacency NOUN here complacency means a desire to please others. Today complacency means feeling pleased with oneself without good reason. ❏ *Twas thy power that raised the first complacency in me* (*The Prelude* by William Wordsworth)

complaisance NOUN complaisance was eagerness to please ❑ *we cannot wonder at his complaisance* (*Pride and Prejudice* by Jane Austen)

complaisant ADJ complaisant means polite ❑ *extremely cheerful and complaisant to their guest* (*Gulliver's Travels* by Jonathan Swift)

conning VERB conning means learning by heart ❑ *Or conning more* (*The Prelude* by William Wordsworth)

consequent NOUN consequence ❑ *as avarice is the necessary consequent of old age* (*Gulliver's Travels* by Jonathan Swift)

consorts NOUN concerts ❑ *The King, who delighted in music, had frequent consorts at Court* (*Gulliver's Travels* by Jonathan Swift)

conversible ADJ conversible meant easy to talk to, companionable ❑ *He can be a conversible companion* (*Pride and Prejudice* by Jane Austen)

copper NOUN a copper is a large pot that can be heated directly over a fire ❑ *He gazed in stupefied astonishment on the small rebel for some seconds, and then clung for support to the copper* (*Oliver Twist* by Charles Dickens)

copper-stick NOUN a copper-stick is the long piece of wood used to stir washing in the copper (or boiler) which was usually the biggest cooking pot in the house ❑ *It was Christmas Eve, and I had to stir the pudding for next day, with a copper-stick, from seven to eight by the Dutch clock* (*Great Expectations* by Charles Dickens)

counting-house NOUN a counting house is a place where accountants work ❑ *Once upon a time – of all the good days in the year, on Christmas Eve – old Scrooge sat busy in his countinghouse* (*A Christmas Carol* by Charles Dickens)

courtier NOUN a courtier is someone who attends the king or queen – a member of the court ❑ *next the ten courtiers;* (*Alice's Adventures in Wonderland* by Lewis Carroll)

covies NOUN covies were flocks of partridges ❑ *and will save all of the best covies for you* (*Pride and Prejudice* by Jane Austen)

cowed VERB cowed means frightened or intimidated ❑ *it cowed me more than the pain* (*Treasure Island* by Robert Louis Stevenson)

cozened VERB cozened means tricked or deceived ❑ *Do you remember, sir, how you cozened me* (*Doctor Faustus 4.7* by Christopher Marlowe)

cravats NOUN a cravat is a folded cloth that a man wears wrapped around his neck as a decorative item of clothing ❑ *we'd'a' slept in our cravats to-night* (*The Adventures of Huckleberry Finn* by Mark Twain)

crock and dirt PHRASE crock and dirt is an old expression meaning soot and dirt ❑ *and the mare catching cold at the door, and the boy grimed with crock and dirt* (*Great Expectations* by Charles Dickens)

crockery NOUN here crockery means pottery ❑ *By one of the parrots was a cat made of crockery* (*The Adventures of Huckleberry Finn* by Mark Twain)

crooked sixpence PHRASE it was considered unlucky to have a bent sixpence ❑ *You've got the beauty, you see, and I've got the luck, so you must keep me by you for your crooked sixpence* (*Silas Marner* by George Eliot)

croquet NOUN croquet is a traditional English summer game in which players try to hit wooden balls through hoops ❑ *and once she remembered trying to box her own ears for having cheated herself in a game of croquet* (*Alice's Adventures in Wonderland* by Lewis Carroll)

cross PREP across ❑ *The two great streets, which run cross and divide it into four quarters* (*Gulliver's Travels* by Jonathan Swift)

culpable ADJ if you are culpable for something it means you are to blame ❑ *deep are the sorrows that spring from false ideas for which no man is culpable.* (*Silas Marner* by George Eliot)

cultured ADJ cultivated ❑ *Nor less when spring had warmed the cultured Vale* (*The Prelude* by William Wordsworth)

cupidity NOUN cupidity is greed ❑ *These people hated me with the hatred of cupidity and disappointment.* (*Great Expectations* by Charles Dickens)

curricle NOUN an open two-wheeled carriage with one seat for the driver and space for a single passenger ❑ *and they saw a lady and a gentleman in a curricle* (*Pride and Prejudice* by Jane Austen)

cynosure NOUN a cynosure is something that strongly attracts attention or admiration ❑ *Then I thought of Eliza and Georgiana; I beheld one the cynosure of a ballroom, the other the inmate of a convent cell* (*Jane Eyre* by Charlotte Brontë)

dalliance NOUN someone's dalliance with something is a brief involvement with it ❑ *nor sporting in the dalliance of love* (*Doctor Faustus Chorus* by Christopher Marlowe)

darkling ADV darkling is an archaic way of saying in the dark ❑ *Darkling I listen* (*Ode on a Nightingale* by John Keats)

delf-case NOUN a sideboard for holding dishes and crockery ❑ *at the pewter dishes and delf-case* (*Wuthering Heights* by Emily Brontë)

determined ■ VERB here determined means ended ❑ *and be out of vogue when that was determined* (*Gulliver's Travels* by Jonathan Swift) ■ VERB determined can mean to have been learned or found especially by investigation or experience ❑ *All the sensitive feelings it wounded so cruelly, all the shame and misery it kept alive within my breast, became more poignant as I*

thought of this; and I determined that the life was unendurable (*David Copperfield* by Charles Dickens)

Deuce NOUN a slang term for the Devil ❑ *Ah, I dare say I did. Deuce take me, he added suddenly, I know I did. I find I am not quite unscrewed yet.* (*Great Expectations* by Charles Dickens)

diabolical ADJ diabolical means devilish or evil ❑ *and with a thousand diabolical expressions* (*Treasure Island* by Robert Louis Stevenson)

direction NOUN here direction means address ❑ *Elizabeth was not surprised at it, as Jane had written the direction remarkably ill* (*Pride and Prejudice* by Jane Austen)

discover VERB to make known or announce ❑ *the Emperor would discover the secret while I was out of his power* (*Gulliver's Travels* by Jonathan Swift)

dissemble VERB hide or conceal ❑ *Dissemble nothing* (*On His Mistress* by John Donne)

dissolve VERB dissolve here means to release from life, to die ❑ *Fade far away, dissolve, and quite forget* (*Ode on a Nightingale* by John Keats)

distrain VERB to distrain is to seize the property of someone who is in debt in compensation for the money owed ❑ *for he's threatening to distrain for it* (*Silas Marner* by George Eliot)

Divan NOUN a Divan was originally a Turkish council of state – the name was transferred to the couches they sat on and is used to mean this in English ❑ *Mr Brass applauded this picture very much, and the bed being soft and comfortable, Mr Quilp determined to use it, both as a sleeping place by night and as a kind of Divan by day.* (*The Old Curiosity Shop* by Charles Dickens)

divorcement NOUN separation ❑ *By all pains which want and* *divorcement hath* (*On His Mistress* by John Donne)

dog in the manger, PHRASE this phrase describes someone who prevents you from enjoying something that they themselves have no need for ❑ *You are a dog in the manger, Cathy, and desire no one to be loved but yourself* (*Wuthering Heights* by Emily Brontë)

dolorifuge NOUN dolorifuge is a word which Thomas Hardy invented. It means pain-killer or comfort ❑ *as a species of dolorifuge* (*Tess of the D'Urbervilles* by Thomas Hardy)

dome NOUN building ❑ *that river and that mouldering dome* (*The Prelude* by William Wordsworth)

domestic PHRASE here domestic means a person's management of the house ❑ *to give some account of my domestic* (*Gulliver's Travels* by Jonathan Swift)

dunce NOUN a dunce is another word for idiot ❑ *Do you take me for a dunce? Go on?* (*Alice's Adventures in Wonderland* by Lewis Carroll)

Ecod EXCLAM a slang exclamation meaning 'oh God!' ❑ *"Ecod,"* replied Wemmick, shaking his head, *"that's not my trade."* (*Great Expectations* by Charles Dickens)

egg-hot NOUN an egg-hot (see also 'flip' and 'negus') was a hot drink made from beer and eggs, sweetened with nutmeg ❑ *She fainted when she saw me return, and made a little jug of egg-hot afterwards to console us while we talked it over.* (*David Copperfield* by Charles Dickens)

encores NOUN an encore is a short extra performance at the end of a longer one, which the entertainer gives because the audience has enthusiastically asked for it ❑ *we want a little something to answer encores with, anyway* (*The Adventures of Huckleberry Finn* by Mark Twain)

equipage NOUN an elegant and impressive carriage ❑ *and besides, the equipage did not answer to any of*

their neighbours (*Pride and Prejudice* by Jane Austen)

exordium NOUN an exordium is the opening part of a speech ❑ *"Now, Handel,"* as if it were the grave beginning of a portentous business exordium, he had suddenly given up that tone (*Great Expectations* by Charles Dickens)

expect VERB here expect means to wait for ❑ *to expect his farther commands* (*Gulliver's Travels* by Jonathan Swift)

familiars NOUN familiars means spirits or devils who come to someone when they are called ❑ *I'll turn all the lice about thee into familiars* (*Doctor Faustus* 1.4 by Christopher Marlowe)

fantods NOUN a fantod is a person who fidgets or can't stop moving nervously ❑ *It most give me the fantods* (*The Adventures of Huckleberry Finn* by Mark Twain)

farthing NOUN a farthing is an old unit of British currency which was worth a quarter of a penny ❑ *Not a farthing less. A great many back-payments are included in it, I assure you.* (*A Christmas Carol* by Charles Dickens)

farthingale NOUN a hoop worn under a skirt to extend it ❑ *A bell with an old voice – which I dare say in its time had often said to the house, Here is the green farthingale* (*Great Expectations* by Charles Dickens)

favours NOUN here favours is an old word which means ribbons ❑ *A group of humble mourners entered the gate: wearing white favours* (*Oliver Twist* by Charles Dickens)

feigned VERB pretend or pretending ❑ *not my feigned page* (*On His Mistress* by John Donne)

fence ■ NOUN a fence is someone who receives and sells stolen goods ❑ *What are you up to? Ill-treating the boys, you covetous, avaricious, in-sa-ti-a-ble old fence?* (*Oliver Twist* by

Charles Dickens) ■ NOUN defence or protection ❏ *but honesty hath no fence against superior cunning* (*Gulliver's Travels* by Jonathan Swift)

fess ADJ fess is an old word which means pleased or proud ❏ *You'll be fess enough, my poppet* (*Tess of the D'Urbervilles* by Thomas Hardy)

fettered ADJ fettered means bound in chains or chained ❏ *"You are fettered," said Scrooge, trembling. "Tell me why?"* (*A Christmas Carol* by Charles Dickens)

fidges VERB fidges means fidgets, which is to keep moving your hands slightly because you are nervous or excited ❏ *Look, Jim, how my fingers fidges* (*Treasure Island* by Robert Louis Stevenson)

finger-post NOUN a finger-post is a sign-post showing the direction to different places ❏ *"The gallows," continued Fagin, "the gallows, my dear, is an ugly finger-post, which points out a very short and sharp turning that has stopped many a bold fellow's career on the broad highway."* (*Oliver Twist* by Charles Dickens)

fire-irons NOUN fire-irons are tools kept by the side of the fire to either cook with or look after the fire ❏ *the fire-irons came first* (*Alice's Adventures in Wonderland* by Lewis Carroll)

fire-plug NOUN a fire-plug is another word for a fire hydrant ❏ *The pony looked with great attention into a fire-plug, which was near him, and appeared to be quite absorbed in contemplating it* (*The Old Curiosity Shop* by Charles Dickens)

flank NOUN flank is the side of an animal ❏ *And all her silken flanks with garlands dressed* (*Ode on a Grecian Urn* by John Keats)

flip NOUN a flip is a drink made from warmed ale, sugar, spice and beaten egg ❏ *The events of the day, in combination with the twins, if not with the flip, had made Mrs. Micawber hysterical, and she shed tears as she replied* (*David Copperfield* by Charles Dickens)

flit VERB flit means to move quickly ❏ *and if he had meant to flit to Thrushcross Grange* (*Wuthering Heights* by Emily Brontë)

floorcloth NOUN a floorcloth was a hard-wearing piece of canvas used instead of carpet ❏ *This avenging phantom was ordered to be on duty at eight on Tuesday morning in the hall (it was two feet square, as charged for floorcloth)* (*Great Expectations* by Charles Dickens)

fly-driver NOUN a fly-driver is a carriage drawn by a single horse ❏ *The fly-drivers, among whom I inquired next, were equally jocose and equally disrespectful* (*David Copperfield* by Charles Dickens)

fob NOUN a small pocket in which a watch is kept ❏ *"Certain," replied the man, drawing a gold watch from his fob* (*Oliver Twist* by Charles Dickens)

folly NOUN folly means foolishness or stupidity ❏ *the folly of beginning a work* (*Robinson Crusoe* by Daniel Defoe)

fond ADJ fond means foolish ❏ *Fond worldling* (*Doctor Faustus 5.2* by Christopher Marlowe)

fondness NOUN silly or foolish affection ❏ *They have no fondness for their colts or foals* (*Gulliver's Travels* by Jonathan Swift)

for his fancy PHRASE for his fancy means for his liking or as he wanted ❏ *and as I did not obey quick enough for his fancy* (*Treasure Island* by Robert Louis Stevenson)

forlorn ADJ lost or very upset ❏ *you are from that day forlorn* (*Gulliver's Travels* by Jonathan Swift)

foster-sister NOUN a foster-sister was someone brought up by the same nurse or in the same household ❏ *I had been his foster-sister* (*Wuthering Heights* by Emily Brontë)

fox-fire NOUN fox-fire is a weak glow that is given off by decaying, rotten wood ❏ *what we must have was a lot of them rotten chunks* *that's called fox-fire* (*The Adventures of Huckleberry Finn* by Mark Twain)

frozen sea PHRASE the Arctic Ocean ❏ *into the frozen sea* (*Gulliver's Travels* by Jonathan Swift)

gainsay VERB to gainsay something is to say it isn't true or to deny it ❏ *"So she had," cried Scrooge. "You're right. I'll not gainsay it, Spirit. God forbid!"* (*A Christmas Carol* by Charles Dickens)

gaiters NOUN gaiters were leggings made of a cloth or piece of leather which covered the leg from the knee to the ankle ❏ *Mr Knightley was hard at work upon the lower buttons of his thick leather gaiters* (*Emma* by Jane Austen)

galluses NOUN galluses is an old spelling of gallows, and here means suspenders. Suspenders are straps worn over someone's shoulders and fastened to their trousers to prevent the trousers falling down ❏ *and home-knit galluses* (*The Adventures of Huckleberry Finn* by Mark Twain)

galoot NOUN a sailor but also a clumsy person ❏ *and maybe a galoot on it chopping* (*The Adventures of Huckleberry Finn* by Mark Twain)

gayest ADJ gayest means the most lively and bright or merry ❏ *Beth played her gayest march* (*Little Women* by Louisa May Alcott)

gem NOUN here gem means jewellery ❏ *the mountain shook off turf and flower, had only heath for raiment and crag for gem* (*Jane Eyre* by Charlotte Brontë)

giddy ADJ giddy means dizzy ❏ *and I wish you wouldn't keep appearing and vanishing so suddenly; you make one quite giddy.* (*Alice's Adventures in Wonderland* by Lewis Carroll)

gig NOUN a light two-wheeled carriage ❏ *when a gig drove up to the garden gate: out of which there jumped a fat gentleman* (*Oliver Twist* by Charles Dickens)

gladsome ADJ gladsome is an old word meaning glad or happy ❏ *Nobody ever stopped him in the street to say, with gladsome looks* (*A Christmas Carol* by Charles Dickens)

glen NOUN a glen is a small valley; the word is used commonly in Scotland ❏ *a beck which follows the bend of the glen* (*Wuthering Heights* by Emily Brontë)

gravelled VERB gravelled is an old term which means to baffle or defeat someone ❏ *Gravelled the pastors of the German Church* (*Doctor Faustus 1.1* by Christopher Marlowe)

grinder NOUN a grinder was a private tutor ❏ *but that when he had had the happiness of marrying Mrs Pocket very early in his life, he had impaired his prospects and taken up the calling of a Grinder* (*Great Expectations* by Charles Dickens)

gruel NOUN gruel is a thin, watery corn-meal or oatmeal soup ❏ *and the little saucepan of gruel (Scrooge had a cold in his head) upon the hob.* (*A Christmas Carol* by Charles Dickens)

guinea, half a NOUN a half guinea was ten shillings and sixpence ❏ *but lay out half a guinea at Ford's* (*Emma* by Jane Austen)

gull VERB gull is an old term which means to fool or deceive someone ❏ *Hush, I'll gull him supernaturally* (*Doctor Faustus 3.4* by Christopher Marlowe)

gunnel NOUN the gunnel, or gunwhale, is the upper edge of a boat's side ❏ *But he put his foot on the gunnel and rocked her* (*The Adventures of Huckleberry Finn* by Mark Twain)

gunwale NOUN the side of a ship ❏ *He dipped his hand in the water over the boat's gunwale* (*Great Expectations* by Charles Dickens)

Gytrash NOUN a Gytrash is an omen of misfortune to the superstitious, usually taking the form of a hound ❏ *I remembered certain of Bessie's tales, wherein figured a*

North-of-England spirit, called a 'Gytrash' (*Jane Eyre* by Charlotte Brontë)

hackney-cabriolet NOUN a two-wheeled carriage with four seats for hire and pulled by a horse ❑ *A hackney-cabriolet was in waiting; with the same vehemence which she had exhibited in addressing Oliver, the girl pulled him in with her, and drew the curtains close.* (*Oliver Twist* by Charles Dickens)

hackney-coach NOUN a four-wheeled horse-drawn vehicle for hire ❑ *The twilight was beginning to close in, when Mr. Brownlow alighted from a hackney-coach at his own door, and knocked softly.* (*Oliver Twist* by Charles Dickens)

haggler NOUN a haggler is someone who travels from place to place selling small goods and items ❑ *when I be plain Jack Durbeyfield, the haggler* (*Tess of the D'Urbervilles* by Thomas Hardy)

halter NOUN a halter is a rope or strap used to lead an animal or to tie it up ❑ *I had of course long been used to a halter and a headstall* (*Black Beauty* by Anna Sewell)

hamlet NOUN a hamlet is a small village or a group of houses in the countryside ❑ *down from the hamlet* (*Treasure Island* by Robert Louis Stevenson)

hand-barrow NOUN a hand-barrow is a device for carrying heavy objects. It is like a wheelbarrow except that it has handles, rather than wheels, for moving the barrow ❑ *his sea chest following behind him in a hand-barrow* (*Treasure Island* by Robert Louis Stevenson)

handspike NOUN a handspike was a stick which was used as a lever ❑ *a bit of stick like a handspike* (*Treasure Island* by Robert Louis Stevenson)

haply ADV haply means by chance or perhaps ❑ *And haply the Queen-Moon is on her throne* (*Ode on a Nightingale* by John Keats)

harem NOUN the harem was the part of the house where the women lived ❑ *mostly they hang round the harem* (*The Adventures of Huckleberry Finn* by Mark Twain)

hautboys NOUN hautboys are oboes ❑ *sausages and puddings resembling flutes and hautboys* (*Gulliver's Travels* by Jonathan Swift)

hawker NOUN a hawker is someone who sells goods to people as he travels rather than from a fixed place like a shop ❑ *to buy some stockings from a hawker* (*Treasure Island* by Robert Louis Stevenson)

hawser NOUN a hawser is a rope used to tie up or tow a ship or boat ❑ *Again among the tiers of shipping, in and out, avoiding rusty chain-cables, frayed hempen hawsers* (*Great Expectations* by Charles Dickens)

headstall NOUN the headstall is the part of the bridle or halter that goes around a horse's head ❑ *I had of course long been used to a halter and a headstall* (*Black Beauty* by Anna Sewell)

hearken VERB hearken means to listen ❑ *though we sometimes stopped to lay hold of each other and hearken* (*Treasure Island* by Robert Louis Stevenson)

heartless ADJ here heartless means without heart or dejected ❑ *I am not heartless* (*The Prelude* by William Wordsworth)

hebdomadal ADJ hebdomadal means weekly ❑ *It was the hebdomadal treat to which we all looked forward from Sabbath to Sabbath* (*Jane Eyre* by Charlotte Brontë)

highwaymen NOUN highwaymen were people who stopped travellers and robbed them ❑ *We are highwaymen* (*The Adventures of Huckleberry Finn* by Mark Twain)

hinds NOUN hinds means farm hands, or people who work on a farm ❑ *He called his hinds about him* (*Gulliver's Travels* by Jonathan Swift)

histrionic ADJ if you refer to someone's behaviour as histrionic, you are being critical of it because it is dramatic and exaggerated ❏ *But the histrionic muse is the darling* (*The Adventures of Huckleberry Finn* by Mark Twain)

hogs NOUN hogs is another word for pigs ❏ *Tom called the hogs 'ingots'* (*The Adventures of Huckleberry Finn* by Mark Twain)

horrors NOUN the horrors are a fit, called delirium tremens, which is caused by drinking too much alcohol ❏ *I'll have the horrors* (*Treasure Island* by Robert Louis Stevenson)

huffy ADJ huffy means to be obviously annoyed or offended about something ❏ *They will feel that more than angry speeches or huffy actions* (*Little Women* by Louisa May Alcott)

hulks NOUN hulks were prison-ships ❏ *The miserable companion of thieves and ruffians, the fallen outcast of low haunts, the associate of the scourings of the jails and hulks* (*Oliver Twist* by Charles Dickens)

humbug NOUN humbug means nonsense or rubbish ❏ *"Bah," said Scrooge. "Humbug!"* (*A Christmas Carol* by Charles Dickens)

humours NOUN it was believed that there were four fluids in the body called humours which decided the temperament of a person depending on how much of each fluid was present ❏ *other peccant humours* (*Gulliver's Travels* by Jonathan Swift)

husbandry NOUN husbandry is farming animals ❏ *bad husbandry were plentifully anointing their wheels* (*Silas Marner* by George Eliot)

huswife NOUN a huswife was a small sewing kit ❏ *but I had put my huswife on it* (*Emma* by Jane Austen)

ideal ADJ ideal in this context means imaginary ❏ *I discovered the yell was not ideal* (*Wuthering Heights* by Emily Brontë)

If our two PHRASE if both our ❏ *If our two loves be one* (*The Good-Morrow* by John Donne)

ignis-fatuus NOUN ignis-fatuus is the light given out by burning marsh gases, which lead careless travellers into danger ❏ *it is madness in all women to let a secret love kindle within them, which, if unreturned and unknown, must devour the life that feeds it; and, if discovered and responded to, must lead ignis-fatuus-like, into miry wilds whence there is no extrication.* (*Jane Eyre* by Charlotte Brontë)

imaginations NOUN here imaginations means schemes or plans ❏ *soon drove out those imaginations* (*Gulliver's Travels* by Jonathan Swift)

impressible ADJ impressible means open or impressionable ❏ *for Marner had one of those impressible, self-doubting natures* (*Silas Marner* by George Eliot)

in good intelligence PHRASE friendly with each other ❏ *that these two persons were in good intelligence with each other* (*Gulliver's Travels* by Jonathan Swift)

inanity NOUN inanity is silliness or dull stupidity ❏ *Do we not wile away moments of inanity* (*Silas Marner* by George Eliot)

incivility NOUN incivility means rudeness or impoliteness ❏ *if it's only for a piece of incivility like to-night's* (*Treasure Island* by Robert Louis Stevenson)

indigenae NOUN indigenae means natives or people from that area ❏ *an exotic that the surly indigenae will not recognise for kin* (*Wuthering Heights* by Emily Brontë)

indocible ADJ unteachable ❏ *so they were the most restive and indocible* (*Gulliver's Travels* by Jonathan Swift)

ingenuity NOUN inventiveness ❏ *entreated me to give him something as an encouragement to ingenuity*

(*Gulliver's Travels* by Jonathan Swift)

ingots NOUN an ingot is a lump of a valuable metal like gold, usually shaped like a brick ❑ *Tom called the hogs 'ingots'* (*The Adventures of Huckleberry Finn* by Mark Twain)

inkstand NOUN an inkstand is a pot which was put on a desk to contain either ink or pencils and pens ❑ *throwing an inkstand at the Lizard as she spoke* (*Alice's Adventures in Wonderland* by Lewis Carroll)

inordinate ADJ without order. Today inordinate means 'excessive'. ❑ *Though yet untutored and inordinate* (*The Prelude* by William Wordsworth)

intellectuals NOUN here intellectuals means the minds (of the workmen) ❑ *those instructions they give being too refined for the intellectuals of their workmen* (*Gulliver's Travels* by Jonathan Swift)

interview NOUN meeting ❑ *By our first strange and fatal interview* (*On His Mistress* by John Donne)

jacks NOUN jacks are rods for turning a spit over a fire ❑ *It was a small bit of pork suspended from the kettle hanger by a string passed through a large door key, in a way known to primitive housekeepers unpossessed of jacks* (*Silas Marner* by George Eliot)

jews-harp NOUN a jews-harp is a small, metal, musical instrument that is played by the mouth ❑ *A jews-harp's plenty good enough for a rat* (*The Adventures of Huckleberry Finn* by Mark Twain)

jorum NOUN a large bowl ❑ *while Miss Skiffins brewed such a jorum of tea, that the pig in the back premises became strongly excited* (*Great Expectations* by Charles Dickens)

jostled VERB jostled means bumped or pushed by someone or some people ❑ *being jostled himself into the kennel* (*Gulliver's Travels* by Jonathan Swift)

keepsake NOUN a keepsake is a gift which reminds someone of an event or of the person who gave it to them. ❑ *books and ornaments they had in their boudoirs at home: keepsakes that different relations had presented to them* (*Jane Eyre* by Charlotte Brontë)

kenned VERB kenned means knew ❑ *though little kenned the lamplighter that he had any company but Christmas!* (*A Christmas Carol* by Charles Dickens)

kennel NOUN kennel means gutter, which is the edge of a road next to the pavement, where rain water collects and flows away ❑ *being jostled himself into the kennel* (*Gulliver's Travels* by Jonathan Swift)

knock-knee ADJ knock-knee means slanted, at an angle. ❑ *LOT 1 was marked in whitewashed knock-knee letters on the brewhouse* (*Great Expectations* by Charles Dickens)

ladylike ADJ to be ladylike is to behave in a polite, dignified and graceful way ❑ *No, winking isn't ladylike* (*Little Women* by Louisa May Alcott)

lapse NOUN flow ❑ *Stealing with silent lapse to join the brook* (*The Prelude* by William Wordsworth)

larry NOUN larry is an old word which means commotion or noisy celebration ❑ *That was all a part of the larry!* (*Tess of the D'Urbervilles* by Thomas Hardy)

laths NOUN laths are strips of wood ❑ *The panels shrunk, the windows cracked; fragments of plaster fell out of the ceiling, and the naked laths were shown instead* (*A Christmas Carol* by Charles Dickens)

leer NOUN a leer is an unpleasant smile ❑ *with a kind of leer* (*Treasure Island* by Robert Louis Stevenson)

lenitives NOUN these are different kinds of drugs or medicines: lenitives and palliatives were pain relievers; aperitives were laxatives;

absorbsives caused vomiting; corrosives destroyed human tissue; restringents caused constipation; cephalalgics stopped headaches; icterics were used as medicine for jaundice; apophlegmatics were cough medicine, and acoustics were cures for the loss of hearing ❑ *lenitives, aperitives, abstersives, corrosives, restringents, palliatives, laxatives, cephalalgics, icterics, apophlegmatics, acoustics* (*Gulliver's Travels* by Jonathan Swift)

lest CONJ in case. If you do something lest something (usually) unpleasant happens you do it to try to prevent it happening ❑ *She went in without knocking, and hurried upstairs, in great fear lest she should meet the real Mary Ann* (*Alice's Adventures in Wonderland* by Lewis Carroll)

levee NOUN a levee is an old term for a meeting held in the morning, shortly after the person holding the meeting has got out of bed ❑ *I used to attend the King's levee once or twice a week* (*Gulliver's Travels* by Jonathan Swift)

life-preserver NOUN a club which had lead inside it to make it heavier and therefore more dangerous ❑ *and with no more suspicious articles displayed to view than two or three heavy bludgeons which stood in a corner, and a 'life-preserver' that hung over the chimney-piece.* (*Oliver Twist* by Charles Dickens)

lighterman NOUN a lighterman is another word for sailor ❑ *in and out, hammers going in ship-builders' yards, saws going at timber, clashing engines going at things unknown, pumps going in leaky ships, capstans going, ships going out to sea, and unintelligible sea creatures roaring curses over the bulwarks at respondent lightermen* (*Great Expectations* by Charles Dickens)

livery NOUN servants often wore a uniform known as a livery ❑ *suddenly a footman in livery came running out of the wood* (*Alice's Adventures in Wonderland* by Lewis Carroll)

livid ADJ livid means pale or ash coloured. Livid also means very angry ❑ *a dirty, livid white* (*Treasure Island* by Robert Louis Stevenson)

lottery-tickets NOUN a popular card game ❑ *and Mrs. Philips protested that they would have a nice comfortable noisy game of lottery tickets* (*Pride and Prejudice* by Jane Austen)

lower and upper world PHRASE the earth and the heavens are the lower and upper worlds ❑ *the changes in the lower and upper world* (*Gulliver's Travels* by Jonathan Swift)

lustres NOUN lustres are chandeliers. A chandelier is a large, decorative frame which holds light bulbs or candles and hangs from the ceiling ❑ *the lustres, lights, the carving and the guilding* (*The Prelude* by William Wordsworth)

lynched VERB killed without a criminal trial by a crowd of people ❑ *He'll never know how nigh he come to getting lynched* (*The Adventures of Huckleberry Finn* by Mark Twain)

malingering VERB if someone is malingering they are pretending to be ill to avoid working ❑ *And you stand there malingering* (*Treasure Island* by Robert Louis Stevenson)

managing PHRASE treating with consideration ❑ *to think the honour of my own kind not worth managing* (*Gulliver's Travels* by Jonathan Swift)

manhood PHRASE manhood means human nature ❑ *concerning the nature of manhood* (*Gulliver's Travels* by Jonathan Swift)

man-trap NOUN a man-trap is a set of steel jaws that snap shut when trodden on and trap a person's leg ❑ *"Don't go to him," I called out of the window, "he's an assassin! A* man-trap!" (*Oliver Twist* by Charles Dickens)

maps NOUN charts of the night sky ❑ *Let maps to others, worlds on worlds have shown* (*The Good-Morrow* by John Donne)

mark VERB look at or notice ❑ *Mark but this flea, and mark in this* (*The Flea* by John Donne)

maroons NOUN A maroon is someone who has been left in a place which it is difficult for them to escape from, like a small island ❑ *if schooners, islands, and maroons* (*Treasure Island* by Robert Louis Stevenson)

mast here mast means the fruit of forest trees ❑ *a quantity of acorns, dates, chestnuts, and other mast* (*Gulliver's Travels* by Jonathan Swift)

mate VERB defeat ❑ *Where Mars did mate the warlike Carthigens* (*Doctor Faustus Chorus* by Christopher Marlowe)

mealy ADJ Mealy when used to describe a face meant palid, pale or colourless ❑ *I only know two sorts of boys. Mealy boys, and beef-faced boys* (*Oliver Twist* by Charles Dickens)

middling ADJ fairly or moderately ❑ *she worked me middling hard for about an hour* (*The Adventures of Huckleberry Finn* by Mark Twain)

mill NOUN a mill, or treadmill, was a device for hard labour or punishment in prison ❑ *Was you never on the mill?* (*Oliver Twist* by Charles Dickens)

milliner's shop NOUN a milliner's sold fabrics, clothing, lace and accessories; as time went on they specialized more and more in hats ❑ *to pay their duty to their aunt and to a milliner's shop just over the way* (*Pride and Prejudice* by Jane Austen)

minching un' munching PHRASE how people in the north of England used to describe the way people from the south speak ❑ *Minching*

un' munching! (*Wuthering Heights* by Emily Brontë)

mine NOUN gold ❑ *Whether both th'Indias of spice and mine* (*The Sun Rising* by John Donne)

mire NOUN mud ❑ *Tis my fate to be always ground into the mire under the iron heel of oppression* (*The Adventures of Huckleberry Finn* by Mark Twain)

miscellany NOUN a miscellany is a collection of many different kinds of things ❑ *under that, the miscellany began* (*Treasure Island* by Robert Louis Stevenson)

mistarshers NOUN mistarshers means moustache, which is the hair that grows on a man's upper lip ❑ *when he put his hand up to his mistarshers* (*Tess of the D'Urbervilles* by Thomas Hardy)

morrow NOUN here good-morrow means tomorrow and a new and better life ❑ *And now good-morrow to our waking souls* (*The Good-Morrow* by John Donne)

mortification NOUN mortification is an old word for gangrene which is when part of the body decays or 'dies' because of disease ❑ *Yes, it was a mortification – that was it* (*The Adventures of Huckleberry Finn* by Mark Twain)

mought PARTICIPLE mought is an old spelling of might ❑ *what you mought call me? You mought call me captain* (*Treasure Island* by Robert Louis Stevenson)

move VERB move me not means do not make me angry ❑ *Move me not, Faustus* (*Doctor Faustus 2.1* by Christopher Marlowe)

muffin-cap NOUN a muffin cap is a flat cap made from wool ❑ *the old one, remained stationary in the muffin-cap and leathers* (*Oliver Twist* by Charles Dickens)

mulatter NOUN a mulatter was another word for mulatto, which is a person with parents who are from different races ❑ *a mulatter, most as white as* a white man (*The Adventures of Huckleberry Finn* by Mark Twain)

mummery NOUN mummery is an old word that meant meaningless (or pretentious) ceremony ❑ *When they were all gone, and when Trabb and his men – but not his boy: I looked for him – had crammed their mummery into bags, and were gone too, the house felt wholesomer.* (*Great Expectations* by Charles Dickens)

nap NOUN the nap is the woolly surface on a new item of clothing. Here the surface has been worn away so it looks bare ❑ *like an old hat with the nap rubbed off* (*The Adventures of Huckleberry Finn* by Mark Twain)

natural ◼ NOUN a natural is a person born with learning difficulties ❑ *though he had been left to his particular care by their deceased father, who thought him almost a natural.* (*David Copperfield* by Charles Dickens) ◼ ADJ natural meant illegitimate ❑ *Harriet Smith was the natural daughter of somebody* (*Emma* by Jane Austen)

navigator NOUN a navigator was originally someone employed to dig canals. It is the origin of the word 'navvy' meaning a labourer ❑ *She ascertained from me in a few words what it was all about, comforted Dora, and gradually convinced her that I was not a labourer – from my manner of stating the case I believe Dora concluded that I was a navigator, and went balancing myself up and down a plank all day with a wheelbarrow – and so brought us together in peace.* (*David Copperfield* by Charles Dickens)

necromancy NOUN necromancy means a kind of magic where the magician speaks to spirits or ghosts to find out what will happen in the future ❑ *He surfeits upon cursed necromancy* (*Doctor Faustus chorus* by Christopher Marlowe)

negus NOUN a negus is a hot drink made from sweetened wine and water ❑ *He sat placidly perusing the newspaper, with his little head on one side, and a glass of warm sherry negus at his elbow.* (*David Copperfield* by Charles Dickens)

nice ADJ discriminating. Able to make good judgements or choices ❑ *consequently a claim to be nice* (*Emma* by Jane Austen)

nigh ADV nigh means near ❑ *He'll never know how nigh he come to getting lynched* (*The Adventures of Huckleberry Finn* by Mark Twain)

nimbleness NOUN nimbleness means being able to move very quickly or skillfully ❑ *and with incredible accuracy and nimbleness* (*Treasure Island* by Robert Louis Stevenson)

noggin NOUN a noggin is a small mug or a wooden cup ❑ *you'll bring me one noggin of rum* (*Treasure Island* by Robert Louis Stevenson)

none ADJ neither ❑ *none can die* (*The Good-Morrow* by John Donne)

notices NOUN observations ❑ *Arch are his notices* (*The Prelude* by William Wordsworth)

occiput NOUN occiput means the back of the head ❑ *saw off the occiput of each couple* (*Gulliver's Travels* by Jonathan Swift)

officiously ADJ kindly ❑ *the governess who attended Glumdalclitch very officiously lifted me up* (*Gulliver's Travels* by Jonathan Swift)

old salt PHRASE old salt is a slang term for an experienced sailor ❑ *a 'true sea-dog', and a 'real old salt'* (*Treasure Island* by Robert Louis Stevenson)

or ere PHRASE before ❑ *or ere the Hall was built* (*The Prelude* by William Wordsworth)

ostler NOUN one who looks after horses at an inn ❑ *The bill paid, and the waiter remembered, and the ostler not forgotten, and the chambermaid taken into consideration* (*Great Expectations* by Charles Dickens)

ostry NOUN an ostry is an old word for a pub or hotel ❏ *lest I send you into the ostry with a vengeance* (*Doctor Faustus 2.2* by Christopher Marlowe)

outrunning the constable PHRASE outrunning the constable meant spending more than you earn ❏ *but I shall by this means be able to check your bills and to pull you up if I find you outrunning the constable.* (*Great Expectations* by Charles Dickens)

over ADJ across ❏ *It is in length six yards, and in the thickest part at least three yards over* (*Gulliver's Travels* by Jonathan Swift)

over the broomstick PHRASE this is a phrase meaning 'getting married without a formal ceremony' ❏ *They both led tramping lives, and this woman in Gerrard-street here, had been married very young, over the broomstick (as we say), to a tramping man, and was a perfect fury in point of jealousy.* (*Great Expectations* by Charles Dickens)

own VERB own means to admit or to acknowledge ❏ *It's my old girl that advises. She has the head. But I never own to it before her. Discipline must be maintained* (*Bleak House* by Charles Dickens)

page NOUN here page means a boy employed to run errands ❏ *not my feigned page* (*On His Mistress* by John Donne)

paid pretty dear PHRASE paid pretty dear means paid a high price or suffered quite a lot ❏ *I paid pretty dear for my monthly fourpenny piece* (*Treasure Island* by Robert Louis Stevenson)

pannikins NOUN pannikins were small tin cups ❏ *of lifting light glasses and cups to his lips, as if they were clumsy pannikins* (*Great Expectations* by Charles Dickens)

pards NOUN pards are leopards ❏ *Not charioted by Bacchus and his pards* (*Ode on a Nightingale* by John Keats)

parlour boarder NOUN a pupil who lived with the family ❏ *and somebody had lately raised her from the condition of scholar to parlour boarder* (*Emma* by Jane Austen)

particular, a London PHRASE London in Victorian times and up to the 1950s was famous for having very dense fog – which was a combination of real fog and the smog of pollution from factories ❏ *This is a London particular . . . A fog, miss'* (*Bleak House* by Charles Dickens)

patten NOUN pattens were wooden soles which were fixed to shoes by straps to protect the shoes in wet weather ❏ *carrying a basket like the Great Seal of England in plaited straw, a pair of pattens, a spare shawl, and an umbrella, though it was a fine bright day* (*Great Expectations* by Charles Dickens)

paviour NOUN a paviour was a labourer who worked on the street pavement ❏ *the paviour his pickaxe* (*Oliver Twist* by Charles Dickens)

peccant ADJ peccant means unhealthy ❏ *other peccant humours* (*Gulliver's Travels* by Jonathan Swift)

penetralium NOUN penetralium is a word used to describe the inner rooms of the house ❏ *and I had no desire to aggravate his impatience previous to inspecting the penetralium* (*Wuthering Heights* by Emily Brontë)

pensive ADV pensive means deep in thought or thinking seriously about something ❏ *and she was leaning pensive on a tomb-stone on her right elbow* (*The Adventures of Huckleberry Finn* by Mark Twain)

penury NOUN penury is the state of being extremely poor ❏ *Distress, if not penury, loomed in the distance* (*Tess of the D'Urbervilles* by Thomas Hardy)

perspective NOUN telescope ❏ *a pocket perspective* (*Gulliver's Travels* by Jonathan Swift)

phaeton NOUN a phaeton was an open carriage for four people ❏ *often* condescends to drive by my humble abode in her little phaeton and ponies (*Pride and Prejudice* by Jane Austen)

phantasm NOUN a phantasm is an illusion, something that is not real. It is sometimes used to mean ghost ❑ *Experience had bred no fancies in him that could raise the phantasm of appetite* (*Silas Marner* by George Eliot)

physic NOUN here physic means medicine ❑ *there I studied physic two years and seven months* (*Gulliver's Travels* by Jonathan Swift)

pinioned VERB to pinion is to hold both arms so that a person cannot move them ❑ *But the relentless Ghost pinioned him in both his arms, and forced him to observe what happened next.* (*A Christmas Carol* by Charles Dickens)

piquet NOUN piquet was a popular card game in the C18th ❑ *Mr Hurst and Mr Bingley were at piquet* (*Pride and Prejudice* by Jane Austen)

plaister NOUN a plaister is a piece of cloth on which an apothecary (or pharmacist) would spread ointment. The cloth is then applied to wounds or bruises to treat them ❑ *Then, she gave the knife a final smart wipe on the edge of the plaister, and then sawed a very thick round off the loaf: which she finally, before separating from the loaf, hewed into two halves, of which Joe got one, and I the other.* (*Great Expectations* by Charles Dickens)

plantations NOUN here plantations means colonies, which are countries controlled by a more powerful country ❑ *besides our plantations in America* (*Gulliver's Travels* by Jonathan Swift)

plastic ADV here plastic is an old term meaning shaping or a power that was forming ❑ *A plastic power abode with me* (*The Prelude* by William Wordsworth)

players NOUN actors ❑ *of players which*

upon the world's stage be (*On His Mistress* by John Donne)

plump ADV all at once, suddenly ❑ *But it took a bit of time to get it well round, the change come so uncommon plump, didn't it? (Great Expectations* by Charles Dickens)

plundered VERB to plunder is to rob or steal from ❑ *These crosses stand for the names of ships or towns that they sank or plundered* (*Treasure Island* by Robert Louis Stevenson)

pommel ■ VERB to pommel someone is to hit them repeatedly with your fists ❑ *hug him round the neck, pommel his back, and kick his legs in irrepressible affection!* (*A Christmas Carol* by Charles Dickens) ◪ NOUN a pommel is the part of a saddle that rises up at the front ❑ *He had his gun across his pommel* (*The Adventures of Huckleberry Finn* by Mark Twain)

poor's rates NOUN poor's rates were property taxes which were used to support the poor ❑ *"Oh!" replied the undertaker; "why, you know, Mr. Bumble, I pay a good deal towards the poor's rates." (Oliver Twist* by Charles Dickens)

popular ADJ popular means ruled by the people, or Republican, rather than ruled by a monarch ❑ *With those of Greece compared and popular Rome* (*The Prelude* by William Wordsworth)

porringer NOUN a porringer is a small bowl ❑ *Of this festive composition each boy had one porringer, and no more* (*Oliver Twist* by Charles Dickens)

postboy NOUN a postboy was the driver of a horse-drawn carriage ❑ *He spoke to a postboy who was dozing under the gateway* (*Oliver Twist* by Charles Dickens)

post-chaise NOUN a fast carriage for two or four passengers ❑ *Looking round, he saw that it was a post-chaise, driven at great speed* (*Oliver Twist* by Charles Dickens)

postern NOUN a small gate usually at the back of a building ❏ *The little servant happening to be entering the fortress with two hot rolls, I passed through the postern and crossed the drawbridge, in her company* (*Great Expectations* by Charles Dickens)

pottle NOUN a pottle was a small basket ❏ *He had a paper-bag under each arm and a pottle of strawberries in one hand . . .* (*Great Expectations* by Charles Dickens)

pounce NOUN pounce is a fine powder used to prevent ink spreading on untreated paper ❏ *in that grim atmosphere of pounce and parchment, red-tape, dusty wafers, inkjars, brief and draft paper, law reports, writs, declarations, and bills of costs* (*David Copperfield* by Charles Dickens)

pox NOUN pox means sexually transmitted diseases like syphilis ❏ *how the pox in all its consequences and denominations* (*Gulliver's Travels* by Jonathan Swift)

prelibation NOUN prelibation means a foretaste of or an example of something to come ❏ *A prelibation to the mower's scythe* (*The Prelude* by William Wordsworth)

prentice NOUN an apprentice ❏ *and Joe, sitting on an old gun, had told me that when I was 'prentice to him regularly bound, we would have such Larks there!* (*Great Expectations* by Charles Dickens)

presently ADV immediately ❏ *I presently knew what they meant* (*Gulliver's Travels* by Jonathan Swift)

pumpion NOUN pumpkin ❏ *for it was almost as large as a small pumpion* (*Gulliver's Travels* by Jonathan Swift)

punctual ADJ kept in one place ❏ *was not a punctual presence, but a spirit* (*The Prelude* by William Wordsworth)

quadrille ■ NOUN a quadrille is a dance invented in France which is usually performed by four couples ❏ *However, Mr Swiveller had Miss Sophy's hand for the first quadrille (country-dances being low, were utterly proscribed)* (*The Old Curiosity Shop* by Charles Dickens) ■ NOUN quadrille was a card game for four people ❏ *to make up her pool of quadrille in the evening* (*Pride and Prejudice* by Jane Austen)

quality NOUN gentry or upper-class people ❏ *if you are with the quality* (*The Adventures of Huckleberry Finn* by Mark Twain)

quick parts PHRASE quick-witted ❏ *Mr Bennet was so odd a mixture of quick parts* (*Pride and Prejudice* by Jane Austen)

quid NOUN a quid is something chewed or kept in the mouth, like a piece of tobacco ❏ *rolling his quid* (*Treasure Island* by Robert Louis Stevenson)

quit VERB quit means to avenge or to make even ❏ *But Faustus's death shall quit my infamy* (*Doctor Faustus 4.3* by Christopher Marlowe)

rags NOUN divisions ❏ *Nor hours, days, months, which are the rags of time* (*The Sun Rising* by John Donne)

raiment NOUN raiment means clothing ❏ *the mountain shook off turf and flower, had only heath for raiment and crag for gem* (*Jane Eyre* by Charlotte Brontë)

rain cats and dogs PHRASE an expression meaning rain heavily. The origin of the expression is unclear ❏ *But it'll perhaps rain cats and dogs to-morrow* (*Silas Marner* by George Eliot)

raised Cain PHRASE raised Cain means caused a lot of trouble. Cain is a character in the Bible who killed his brother Abel ❏ *and every time he got drunk he raised Cain around town* (*The Adventures of Huckleberry Finn* by Mark Twain)

rambling ADJ rambling means confused and not very clear ❏ *my* *head began to be filled very early with rambling thoughts* (*Robinson Crusoe* by Daniel Defoe)

raree-show NOUN a raree-show is an old term for a peep-show or a fairground entertainment ❏ *A raree-show is here, with children gathered round* (*The Prelude* by William Wordsworth)

recusants NOUN people who resisted authority ❏ *hardy recusants* (*The Prelude* by William Wordsworth)

redounding VERB eddying. An eddy is a movement in water or air which goes round and round instead of flowing in one direction ❏ *mists and steam-like fogs redounding everywhere* (*The Prelude* by William Wordsworth)

redundant ADJ here redundant means overflowing but Wordsworth also uses it to mean excessively large or too big ❏ *A tempest, a redundant energy* (*The Prelude* by William Wordsworth)

reflex NOUN reflex is a shortened version of reflexion, which is an alternative spelling of reflection ❏ *To cut across the reflex of a star* (*The Prelude* by William Wordsworth)

Reformatory NOUN a prison for young offenders/criminals ❏ *Even when I was taken to have a new suit of clothes, the tailor had orders to make them like a kind of Reformatory, and on no account to let me have the free use of my limbs.* (*Great Expectations* by Charles Dickens)

remorse NOUN pity or compassion ❏ *by that remorse* (*On His Mistress* by John Donne)

render VERB in this context render means give. ❏ *and Sarah could render no reason that would be sanctioned by the feeling of the community.* (*Silas Marner* by George Eliot)

repeater NOUN a repeater was a watch that chimed the last hour when a button was pressed – as a result it

was useful in the dark ❏ *And his watch is a gold repeater, and worth a hundred pound if it's worth a penny.* (*Great Expectations* by Charles Dickens)

repugnance NOUN repugnance means a strong dislike of something or someone ❏ *overcoming a strong repugnance* (*Treasure Island* by Robert Louis Stevenson)

reverence NOUN reverence means bow. When you bow to someone, you briefly bend your body towards them as a formal way of showing them respect ❏ *made my reverence* (*Gulliver's Travels* by Jonathan Swift)

reverie NOUN a reverie is a day dream ❏ *I can guess the subject of your reverie* (*Pride and Prejudice* by Jane Austen)

revival NOUN a religious meeting held in public ❏ *well I'd ben a-running' a little temperance revival thar' bout a week* (*The Adventures of Huckleberry Finn* by Mark Twain)

revolt VERB revolt means turn back or stop your present course of action and go back to what you were doing before ❏ *Revolt, or I'll in piecemeal tear thy flesh* (*Doctor Faustus 5.1* by Christopher Marlowe)

rheumatics/rheumatism NOUN rheumatics [rheumatism] is an illness that makes your joints or muscles stiff and painful ❏ *a new cure for the rheumatics* (*Treasure Island* by Robert Louis Stevenson)

riddance NOUN riddance is usually used in the form good riddance which you say when you are pleased that something has gone or been left behind ❏ *I'd better go into the house, and die and be a riddance* (*David Copperfield* by Charles Dickens)

rimy ADJ rimy is an ADJECTIVE which means covered in ice or frost ❏ *It was a rimy morning, and very damp* (*Great Expectations* by Charles Dickens)

riper ADJ riper means more mature or older ❑ *At riper years to Wittenberg he went* (*Doctor Faustus chorus* by Christopher Marlowe)

rubber NOUN a set of games in whist or backgammon ❑ *her father was sure of his rubber* (*Emma* by Jane Austen)

ruffian NOUN a ruffian is a person who behaves violently ❑ *and when the ruffian had told him* (*Treasure Island* by Robert Louis Stevenson)

sadness NOUN sadness is an old term meaning seriousness ❑ *But I prithee tell me, in good sadness* (*Doctor Faustus 2.2* by Christopher Marlowe)

sailed before the mast PHRASE this phrase meant someone who did not look like a sailor ❑ *he had none of the appearance of a man that sailed before the mast* (*Treasure Island* by Robert Louis Stevenson)

scabbard NOUN a scabbard is the covering for a sword or dagger ❑ *Girded round its middle was an antique scabbard; but no sword was in it, and the ancient sheath was eaten up with rust* (*A Christmas Carol* by Charles Dickens)

schooners NOUN A schooner is a fast, medium-sized sailing ship ❑ *if schooners, islands, and maroons* (*Treasure Island* by Robert Louis Stevenson)

science NOUN learning or knowledge ❑ *Even Science, too, at hand* (*The Prelude* by William Wordsworth)

scrouge VERB to scrouge means to squeeze or to crowd ❑ *to scrouge in and get a sight* (*The Adventures of Huckleberry Finn* by Mark Twain)

scrutore NOUN a scrutore, or escritoire, was a writing table ❑ *set me gently on my feet upon the scrutore* (*Gulliver's Travels* by Jonathan Swift)

scutcheon/escutcheon NOUN an escutcheon is a shield with a coat of arms, or the symbols of a family name, engraved on it ❑ *On the*

scutcheon we'll have a bend (*The Adventures of Huckleberry Finn* by Mark Twain)

sea-dog PHRASE sea-dog is a slang term for an experienced sailor or pirate ❑ *a 'true sea-dog', and a 'real old salt,'* (*Treasure Island* by Robert Louis Stevenson)

see the lions PHRASE to see the lions was to go and see the sights of London. Originally the phrase referred to the menagerie in the Tower of London and later in Regent's Park ❑ *We will go and see the lions for an hour or two – it's something to have a fresh fellow like you to show them to, Copperfield* (*David Copperfield* by Charles Dickens)

self-conceit NOUN self-conceit is an old term which means having too high an opinion of oneself, or deceiving yourself ❑ *Till swollen with cunning, of a self-conceit* (*Doctor Faustus chorus* by Christopher Marlowe)

seneschal NOUN a steward ❑ *where a grey-headed seneschal sings a funny chorus with a funnier body of vassals* (*Oliver Twist* by Charles Dickens)

sensible ADJ if you were sensible of something you are aware or conscious of something ❑ *If my children are silly I must hope to be always sensible of it* (*Pride and Prejudice* by Jane Austen)

sessions NOUN court cases were heard at specific times of the year called sessions ❑ *He lay in prison very ill, during the whole interval between his committal for trial, and the coming round of the Sessions.* (*Great Expectations* by Charles Dickens)

shabby ADJ shabby places look old and in bad condition ❑ *a little bit of a shabby village named Pikesville* (*The Adventures of Huckleberry Finn* by Mark Twain)

shay-cart NOUN a shay-cart was a small cart drawn by one horse ❑ *"I were at the Bargemen t'other night, Pip;"*

whenever he subsided into affection, he called me Pip, and whenever he relapsed into politeness he called me Sir; "when there come up in his shay-cart Pumblechook." (*Great Expectations* by Charles Dickens)

shilling NOUN a shilling is an old unit of currency. There were twenty shillings in every British pound ❑ *"Ten shillings too much," said the gentleman in the white waistcoat.* (*Oliver Twist* by Charles Dickens)

shines NOUN tricks or games ❑ *well, it would make a cow laugh to see the shines that old idiot cut* (*The Adventures of Huckleberry Finn* by Mark Twain)

shirking VERB shirking means not doing what you are meant to be doing, or evading your duties ❑ *some of you shirking lubbers* (*Treasure Island* by Robert Louis Stevenson)

shiver my timbers PHRASE shiver my timbers is an expression which was used by sailors and pirates to express surprise ❑ *why, shiver my timbers, if I hadn't forgotten my score!* (*Treasure Island* by Robert Louis Stevenson)

shoe-roses NOUN shoe-roses were roses made from ribbons which were stuck on to shoes as decoration ❑ *the very shoe-roses for Netherfield were got by proxy* (*Pride and Prejudice* by Jane Austen)

singular ADJ singular means very great and remarkable or strange ❑ *"Singular dream," he says* (*The Adventures of Huckleberry Finn* by Mark Twain)

sire NOUN sire is an old word which means lord or master or elder ❑ *She also defied her sire* (*Little Women* by Louisa May Alcott)

sixpence NOUN a sixpence was half of a shilling ❑ *if she had only a shilling in the world, she would be very lilkely to give away sixpence of it* (*Emma* by Jane Austen)

slavey NOUN the word slavey was used when there was only one servant in a house or boarding-house – so she had to perform all the duties of a larger staff ❑ *Two distinct knocks, sir, will produce the slavey at any time* (*The Old Curiosity Shop* by Charles Dickens)

slender ADJ weak ❑ *In slender accents of sweet verse* (*The Prelude* by William Wordsworth)

slop-shops NOUN slop-shops were shops where cheap ready-made clothes were sold. They mainly sold clothes to sailors ❑ *Accordingly, I took the jacket off, that I might learn to do without it; and carrying it under my arm, began a tour of inspection of the various slop-shops.* (*David Copperfield* by Charles Dickens)

sluggard NOUN a lazy person ❑ *"Stand up and repeat 'Tis the voice of the sluggard,'" said the Gryphon.* (*Alice's Adventures in Wonderland* by Lewis Carroll)

smallpox NOUN smallpox is a serious infectious disease ❑ *by telling the men we had smallpox aboard* (*The Adventures of Huckleberry Finn* by Mark Twain)

smalls NOUN smalls are short trousers ❑ *It is difficult for a large-headed, small-eyed youth, of lumbering make and heavy countenance, to look dignified under any circumstances; but it is more especially so, when superadded to these personal attractions are a red nose and yellow smalls* (*Oliver Twist* by Charles Dickens)

sneeze-box NOUN a box for snuff was called a sneeze-box because sniffing snuff makes the user sneeze ❑ *To think of Jack Dawkins — lummy Jack — the Dodger — the Artful Dodger — going abroad for a common twopenny-halfpenny sneeze-box!* (*Oliver Twist* by Charles Dickens)

snorted VERB slept ❑ *Or snorted we in the Seven Sleepers' den?* (*The Good-Morrow* by John Donne)

snuff NOUN snuff is tobacco in powder form which is taken by sniffing ❑

as he thrust his thumb and fore-finger into the proffered snuff-box of the undertaker: which was an ingenious little model of a patent coffin. (*Oliver Twist* by Charles Dickens)

soliloquized VERB to soliloquize is when an actor in a play speaks to himself or herself rather than to another actor ❑ *"A new servitude! There is something in that," I soliloquized (mentally, be it understood; I did not talk aloud) (Jane Eyre* by Charlotte Brontë)

sough NOUN a sough is a drain or a ditch ❑ *as you may have noticed the sough that runs from the marshes* (*Wuthering Heights* by Emily Brontë)

spirits NOUN a spirit is the nonphysical part of a person which is believed to remain alive after their death ❑ *that I might raise up spirits when I please* (*Doctor Faustus* 1.5 by Christopher Marlowe)

spleen ◼ NOUN here spleen means a type of sadness or depression which was thought to only affect the wealthy ❑ *yet here I could plainly discover the true seeds of spleen* (*Gulliver's Travels* by Jonathan Swift) ◼ NOUN irritability and low spirits ❑ *Adieu to disappointment and spleen* (*Pride and Prejudice* by Jane Austen)

spondulicks NOUN spondulicks is a slang word which means money ❑ *not for all his spondulicks and as much more on top of it* (*The Adventures of Huckleberry Finn* by Mark Twain)

stalled of VERB to be stalled of something is to be bored with it ❑ *I'm stalled of doing naught* (*Wuthering Heights* by Emily Brontë)

stanchion NOUN a stanchion is a pole or bar that stands upright and is used as a buidling support ❑ *and slid down a stanchion* (*The Adventures of Huckleberry Finn* by Mark Twain)

stang NOUN stang is another word for pole which was an old measurement ❑ *These fields were intermingled*

with woods of half a stang (*Gulliver's Travels* by Jonathan Swift)

starlings NOUN a starling is a wall built around the pillars that support a bridge to protect the pillars ❑ *There were states of the tide when, having been down the river, I could not get back through the eddy-chafed arches and starlings of old London Bridge* (*Great Expectations* by Charles Dickens)

startings NOUN twitching or night-time movements of the body ❑ *with midnight's startings* (*On His Mistress* by John Donne)

stomacher NOUN a panel at the front of a dress ❑ *but send her aunt the pattern of a stomacher* (*Emma* by Jane Austen)

stoop VERB swoop ❑ *Once a kite hovering over the garden made a swoop at me* (*Gulliver's Travels* by Jonathan Swift)

succedaneum NOUN a succedaneum is a substitute ❑ *But as a succedaneum* (*The Prelude* by William Wordsworth)

suet NOUN a hard animal fat used in cooking ❑ *and your jaws are too weak For anything tougher than suet* (*Alice's Adventures in Wonderland* by Lewis Carroll)

sultry ADJ sultry weather is hot and damp. Here sultry means unpleasant or risky ❑ *for it was getting pretty sultry for us* (*The Adventures of Huckleberry Finn* by Mark Twain)

summerset NOUN summerset is an old spelling of somersault. If someone does a somersault, they turn over completely in the air ❑ *I have seen him do the summerset* (*Gulliver's Travels* by Jonathan Swift)

supper NOUN supper was a light meal taken late in the evening. The main meal was dinner which was eaten at four or five in the afternoon ❑ *and the supper table was all set out* (*Emma* by Jane Austen)

surfeits VERB to surfeit in something is to have far too much of it, or to overindulge in it to an unhealthy degree ❑ *He surfeits upon cursed necromancy* (*Doctor Faustus chorus* by Christopher Marlowe)

surtout NOUN a surtout is a long close-fitting overcoat ❑ *He wore a long black surtout reaching nearly to his ankles* (*The Old Curiosity Shop* by Charles Dickens)

swath NOUN swath is the width of corn cut by a scythe ❑ *while thy hook Spares the next swath* (*Ode to Autumn* by John Keats)

sylvan ADJ sylvan means belonging to the woods ❑ *Sylvan historian* (*Ode on a Grecian Urn* by John Keats)

taction NOUN taction means touch. This means that the people had to be touched on the mouth or the ears to get their attention ❑ *without being roused by some external taction upon the organs of speech and hearing* (*Gulliver's Travels* by Jonathan Swift)

Tag and Rag and Bobtail PHRASE the riff-raff, or lower classes. Used in an insulting way ❑ *"No," said he; "not till it got about that there was no protection on the premises, and it come to be considered dangerous, with convicts and Tag and Rag and Bobtail going up and down."* (*Great Expectations* by Charles Dickens)

tallow NOUN tallow is hard animal fat that is used to make candles and soap ❑ *and a lot of tallow candles* (*The Adventures of Huckleberry Finn* by Mark Twain)

tan VERB to tan means to beat or whip ❑ *and if I catch you about that school I'll tan you good* (*The Adventures of Huckleberry Finn* by Mark Twain)

tanyard NOUN the tanyard is part of a tannery, which is a place where leather is made from animal skins ❑ *hid in the old tanyard* (*The Adventures of Huckleberry Finn* by Mark Twain)

tarry ADJ tarry means the colour of tar or black ❑ *his tarry pig-tail* (*Treasure Island* by Robert Louis Stevenson)

thereof PHRASE from there ❑ *By all desires which thereof did ensue* (*On His Mistress* by John Donne)

thick with, be PHRASE if you are 'thick with someone' you are very close, sharing secrets – it is often used to describe people who are planning something secret ❑ *Hasn't he been thick with Mr Heathcliff lately?* (*Wuthering Heights* by Emily Brontë)

thimble NOUN a thimble is a small cover used to protect the finger while sewing ❑ *The paper had been sealed in several places by a thimble* (*Treasure Island* by Robert Louis Stevenson)

thirtover ADJ thirtover is an old word which means obstinate or that someone is very determined to do want they want and can not be persuaded to do something in another way ❑ *I have been living on in a thirtover, lackadaisical way* (*Tess of the D'Urbervilles* by Thomas Hardy)

timbrel NOUN timbrel is a tambourine ❑ *What pipes and timbrels?* (*Ode on a Grecian Urn* by John Keats)

tin NOUN tin is slang for money/cash ❑ *Then the plain question is, an't it a pity that this state of things should continue, and how much better would it be for the old gentleman to hand over a reasonable amount of tin, and make it all right and comfortable* (*The Old Curiosity Shop* by Charles Dickens)

tincture NOUN a tincture is a medicine made with alcohol and a small amount of a drug ❑ *with ink composed of a cephalic tincture* (*Gulliver's Travels* by Jonathan Swift)

tithe NOUN a tithe is a tax paid to the church and held farms which, speaking from a spiritual point of view, paid highly-desirable tithes (*Silas Marner* by George Eliot)

towardly ADJ a towardly child is dutiful or obedient ❑ *and a towardly child* (Gulliver's Travels by Jonathan Swift)

toys NOUN trifles are things which are considered to have little importance, value, or significance ❑ *purchase my life from them by some bracelets, glass rings, and other toys* (Gulliver's Travels by Jonathan Swift)

tract NOUN a tract is a religious pamphlet or leaflet ❑ *and Joe Harper got a hymn-book and a tract* (The Adventures of Huckleberry Finn by Mark Twain)

train-oil NOUN train-oil is oil from whale blubber ❑ *The train-oil and gunpowder were shoved out of sight in a minute* (Wuthering Heights by Emily Brontë)

tribulation NOUN tribulation means the suffering or difficulty you experience in a particular situation ❑ *Amy was learning this distinction through much tribulation* (Little Women by Louisa May Alcott)

trivet NOUN a trivet is a three-legged stand for resting a pot or kettle ❑ *a pocket-knife in his right; and a pewter pot on the trivet* (Oliver Twist by Charles Dickens)

trot line NOUN a trot line is a fishing line to which a row of smaller fishing lines are attached ❑ *when he got along I was hard at it taking up a trot line* (The Adventures of Huckleberry Finn by Mark Twain)

troth NOUN oath or pledge ❑ *I wonder, by my troth* (The Good-Morrow by John Donne)

truckle NOUN a truckle bedstead is a bed that is on wheels and can be slid under another bed to save space ❑ *It rose under my hand, and the door yielded. Looking in, I saw a lighted candle on a table, a bench, and a mattress on a truckle bedstead.* (Great Expectations by Charles Dickens)

trump NOUN a trump is a good, reliable person wo can be trusted ❑ *This lad Hawkins is a trump, I*

perceive (Treasure Island by Robert Louis Stevenson)

tucker NOUN a tucker is a frilly lace collar which is worn around the neck ❑ *Whereat Scrooge's niece's sister the plump one with the lace tucker: not the one with the roses blushed.* (A Christmas Carol by Charles Dickens)

tureen NOUN a large bowl with a lid from which soup or vegetables are served ❑ *Waiting in a hot tureen!* (Alice's Adventures in Wonderland by Lewis Carroll)

turnkey NOUN a prison officer; jailer ❑ *As we came out of the prison through the lodge, I found that the great importance of my guardian was appreciated by the turnkeys, no less than by those whom they held in charge.* (Great Expectations by Charles Dickens)

turnpike NOUN the upkeep of many roads of the time was paid for by tolls (fees) collected at posts along the road. There was a gate to prevent people travelling further along the road until the toll had been paid. ❑ *Traddles, whom I have taken up by appointment at the turnpike, presents a dazzling combination of cream colour and light blue; and both he and Mr. Dick have a general effect about them of being all gloves.* (David Copperfield by Charles Dickens)

twas PHRASE it was ❑ *twas but a dream of thee* (The Good-Morrow by John Donne)

tyrannized VERB tyrannized means bullied or forced to do things against their will ❑ *for people would soon cease coming there to be tyrannized over and put down* (Treasure Island by Robert Louis Stevenson)

'un NOUN 'un is a slang term for one – usually used to refer to a person ❑ *She's been thinking the old 'un* (David Copperfield by Charles Dickens)

undistinguished ADJ undiscriminating or incapable of making a distinction between good and bad things ❏ *their undistinguished appetite to devour everything* (*Gulliver's Travels* by Jonathan Swift)

use NOUN habit ❏ *Though use make you apt to kill me* (*The Flea* by John Donne)

vacant ADJ vacant usually means empty, but here Wordsworth uses it to mean carefree ❏ *To vacant musing, unreproved neglect* (*The Prelude* by William Wordsworth)

valetudinarian NOUN one too concerned with his or her own health. ❏ *for having been a valetudinarian all his life* (*Emma* by Jane Austen)

vamp VERB vamp means to walk or tramp to somewhere ❏ *Well, vamp on to Marlott, will 'ee* (*Tess of the D'Urbervilles* by Thomas Hardy)

vapours NOUN the vapours is an old term which means unpleasant and strange thoughts, which make the person feel nervous and unhappy ❏ *and my head was full of vapours* (*Robinson Crusoe* by Daniel Defoe)

vegetables NOUN here vegetables means plants ❏ *the other vegetables are in the same proportion* (*Gulliver's Travels* by Jonathan Swift)

venturesome ADJ if you are venturesome you are willing to take risks ❏ *he must be either hopelessly stupid or a venturesome fool* (*Wuthering Heights* by Emily Brontë)

verily ADJ verily means really or truly ❏ *though I believe verily* (*Robinson Crusoe* by Daniel Defoe)

vicinage NOUN vicinage is an area or the residents of an area ❏ *and to his thought the whole vicinage was haunted by her.* (*Silas Marner* by George Eliot)

victuals NOUN victuals means food ❏ *grumble a little over the victuals* (*The Adventures of Huckleberry Finn* by Mark Twain)

vintage NOUN vintage in this context means wine ❏ *Oh, for a draught of*

vintage! (*Ode on a Nightingale* by John Keats)

virtual ADJ here virtual means powerful or strong ❏ *had virtual faith* (*The Prelude* by William Wordsworth)

vittles NOUN vittles is a slang word which means food ❏ *There never was such a woman for givin' away vittles and drink* (*Little Women* by Louisa May Alcott)

voided straight PHRASE voided straight is an old expression which means emptied immediately ❏ *see the rooms be voided straight* (*Doctor Faustus 4.1* by Christopher Marlowe)

wainscot NOUN wainscot is wood panel lining in a room so wainscoted means a room lined with wooden panels ❏ *in the dark wainscoted parlor* (*Silas Marner* by George Eliot)

walking the plank PHRASE walking the plank was a punishment in which a prisoner would be made to walk along a plank on the side of the ship and fall into the sea, where they would be abandoned ❏ *about hanging, and walking the plank* (*Treasure Island* by Robert Louis Stevenson)

want VERB want means to be lacking or short of ❏ *The next thing wanted was to get the picture framed* (*Emma* by Jane Austen)

wanting ADJ wanting means lacking or missing ❏ *wanting two fingers of the left hand* (*Treasure Island* by Robert Louis Stevenson)

wanting, I was not PHRASE I was not wanting means I did not fail ❏ *I was not wanting to lay a foundation of religious knowledge in his mind* (*Robinson Crusoe* by Daniel Defoe)

ward NOUN a ward is, usually, a child who has been put under the protection of the court or a guardian for his or her protection ❏ *I call the Wards in Jarndcye. The* are caged up with all the others. (*Bleak House* by Charles Dickens)

waylay VERB to waylay someone is to lie in wait for them or to intercept them ❑ *I must go up the road and waylay him* (*The Adventures of Huckleberry Finn* by Mark Twain)

weazen NOUN weazen is a slang word for throat. It actually means shrivelled ❑ *You with a uncle too! Why, I knowed you at Gargery's when you was so small a wolf that I could have took your weazen betwixt this finger and thumb and chucked you away dead* (*Great Expectations* by Charles Dickens)

wery ■ ADV very ❑ *Be wery careful o' vidders all your life* (*Pickwick Papers* by Charles Dickens) ■ *See* wibrated

wherry NOUN wherry is a small swift rowing boat for one person ❑ *It was flood tide when Daniel Quilp sat himself down in the wherry to cross to the opposite shore.* (*The Old Curiosity Shop* by Charles Dickens)

whether PREP whether means which of the two in this example ❑ *we came in full view of a great island or continent (for we knew not whether)* (*Gulliver's Travels* by Jonathan Swift)

whetstone NOUN a whetstone is a stone used to sharpen knives and other tools ❑ *I dropped pap's whetstone there too* (*The Adventures of Huckleberry Finn* by Mark Twain)

wibrated VERB in Dickens's use of the English language 'w' often replaces 'v' when he is reporting speech. So here 'wibrated' means 'vibrated'. In Pickwick Papers a judge asks Sam Weller (who constantly confuses the two letters) 'Do you spell is with a 'v' or a 'w'?' to which Weller replies 'That depends upon the taste and fancy of the speller, my Lord' ❑ *There are strings . . . in the human heart that had better not be wibrated'* (*Barnaby Rudge* by Charles Dickens)

wicket NOUN a wicket is a little door in a larger entrance ❑ *Having rested here, for a minute or so, to collect a*

good burst of sobs and an imposing show of tears and terror, he knocked loudly at the wicket; (*Oliver Twist* by Charles Dickens)

without CONJ without means unless ❑ *You don't know about me, without you have read a book by the name of The Adventures of Tom Sawyer* (*The Adventures of Huckleberry Finn* by Mark Twain)

wittles ■ NOUN vittles is a slang word which means food ❑ *I live on broken wittles – and I sleep on the coals* (*David Copperfield* by Charles Dickens) ■ *See* wibrated

woo VERB courts or forms a proper relationship with ❑ *before it woo* (*The Flea* by John Donne)

words, to have PHRASE if you have words with someone you have a disagreement or an argument ❑ *I do not want to have words with a young thing like you.* (*Black Beauty* by Anna Sewell)

workhouse NOUN workhouses were places where the homeless were given food and a place to live in return for doing very hard work ❑ *And the Union workhouses? demanded Scrooge. Are they still in operation?* (*A Christmas Carol* by Charles Dickens)

yawl NOUN a yawl is a small boat kept on a bigger boat for short trips. Yawl is also the name for a small fishing boat ❑ *She sent out her yawl, and we went aboard* (*The Adventures of Huckleberry Finn* by Mark Twain)

yeomanry NOUN the yeomanry was a collective term for the middle classes involved in agriculture ❑ *The yeomanry are precisely the order of people with whom I feel I can have nothing to do* (*Emma* by Jane Austen)

yonder ADV yonder means over there ❑ *all in the same second we seem to hear low voices in yonder!* (*The Adventures of Huckleberry Finn* by Mark Twain)